ABOVE THE FOLD

CARNIVALESQUE
BOOK 1

TAMARA GIRARDI

WISE WOLF
BOOKS

WISE WOLF BOOKS
An Imprint of Wolfpack Publishing
wisewolfbooks.com
9850 S. Maryland Parkway, Suite A-5 #323, Las Vegas, Nevada 89183

Cover design by Wise Wolf Books

Paperback ISBN 978-1-953944-85-6
Hardcover ISBN 978-1-953944-86-3
eBook ISBN 978-1-953944-36-8

To everyone who enters the world of Carnivalesque,
Best of luck in finding your true self.

ABOVE THE FOLD

ONE

I FLICKED open the crisp pages of *The Muse* and searched for my byline—Mackenzie Davis, Staff Writer. My editor, Lola St. James, had promised at least page three. None of my stories had bested page nine all year. I couldn't wait to show my dad. Maybe my article would be above the fold, finally. Giddiness tickled my stomach at the thought.

Instead, on page three I found a spotlight about a sophomore guitar prodigy, an article detailing the history of our rivalry with the basketball team's upcoming opponent, and an interview with someone from the cafeteria staff.

"Unreal," I muttered when my name was nowhere to be seen on page five. With each flip of the noisy sheets, my stomach clenched tighter.

Page seven? Not even. Page nine? Nope. My story about the school's new marble planters ran on page eleven. *Beneath* the fold.

I could see the headline of my life now:

JUNIOR REPORTER FALLS SHORT OF EVERY EXPECTATION IN
SENSATIONAL FASHION.

I tossed the newspaper aside onto my desk. Nearly four months of writing for Lola, and first-years regularly scored better assignments. I peeked at the cover and saw one of their names. Dallas Cleveland. A kid named after two cities. Lola had joked at the beginning of the school year that he had a classic reporter's name. As if that mattered.

"Lola, can I talk to you a sec?" I asked.

"Sure." She crossed her arms and watched me expectantly.

"Right, well, the thing is that you said my story about the planters would run on page three."

"I did."

I waited, thinking she might realize her own mistake. Maybe apologize. Maybe explain. She stared at me.

"Okay…" I said, wanting to scream but miraculously keeping my tone even and professional. "You buried it on page eleven."

"I know."

I took pride in the smile I was able to paste on my face. "Why?"

She sat on the stool next to the whiteboard. "Mac, I gave you an assignment, not a promise. Your story was stale."

"Stale?"

"At best."

I held still. Mostly so I wouldn't launch myself at Lola. "It was a story about the new planters in front of the school. Not the kind of material that's going to win anyone a Pulitzer."

Dallas Cleveland had scored an assignment to cover a major city-wide march planned by students at our school to protest gun violence. His story had been picked up by other high school newspapers across the country. A few major markets, too.

And I'd been assigned marble planters.

"They were donated by the widow of one of this school's most beloved teachers," Lola argued.

"Who taught here, like, twenty years ago. Nobody cares about that."

"Really?" She crossed her arms. "What about Mrs. Graham?"

Mrs. Graham was our Journalism teacher. Everyone loved and respected her. Most especially me. "What about her?"

"She was a student at Homer when Mr. Sandoval taught here."

Did not know that.

"So were, like, four other current teachers. Did you even think of interviewing them to get the personal side of Mr. Sandoval's life? Or Mrs. Sandoval's loss?"

No.

"No," Lola said, echoing the pitiful voice in my head. She laughed like nothing was funny. "That's the thing. It's like you're waiting for this perfect story idea to come along. That doesn't exist."

I disagreed. Some stories wrote themselves. They had intrigue, excitement, and the perfect blend of sources. Their words transformed into action on the page. People read them and shared them and loved them.

Other stories were about marble planters.

"But my assignments could be a little better, don't you think?"

"I think that you, as a writer, need to make the best story out of every assignment you get."

"I do!"

Her raised eyebrow reflected my own skepticism. The truth was I'd hated the assignment and rushed through the story as quickly as I could. It could have been better. Maybe. Probably.

Lola checked her watch and packed up her books. "You want better stories, but you haven't shown me you're worthy of them."

"I'm a junior, Lola. I've been on this staff for more than two years." I'd also been considered alongside her for the editor position. She'd gotten the job, and I hadn't—her being a senior and me, a junior—which gave her license to stomp on me, her pitiful minion.

"That doesn't make you my strongest writer."

Stomp. Stomp.

"I won Best Story of the Year as a sophomore!"

"On a story you co-wrote with your boyfriend, who was a senior and the editor at the time." She cringed when she said the word *boyfriend*, which told me she'd heard the news that he was no longer my boyfriend, not since he'd published an opinion piece in his college newspaper a few days earlier publicly dumping me. It was impressive, really. He'd been able to humiliate me, elevate his own career, and taint my love for print journalism in fewer than five hundred words.

I forced my attention back to Lola. "What does that have to do with anything? My byline on that article was no accident."

Winning the Best Story of the Year as a co-writer had taught me to never collaborate with someone on a big story. My contribution was incessantly questioned, like Colin had written every word and I'd sat next to him batting my eyelashes while he'd done it.

Lola sighed. "Look. If you want better assignments and better placement in *The Muse*, you're going to have to earn it. Like everyone else."

The bell rang, signaling the start of our next class. Lola

offered a half smile. "I have to get to class. Write a better story next time."

I sucked in a breath at the harshness of her words and nearly choked on it when she turned around in the doorway and added, "Oh, and sorry to hear about Colin."

TWO

"DO YOU *BELIEVE* HER?" I forced my books one by one into my locker for effect. My best friend and fellow journalist extraordinaire, Dinah Zimmerman, gently stacked the books from her afternoon classes in her locker and closed it a lot easier than I'd slammed mine. With stacks of newspapers in our hands to replenish a few distribution points before leaving for the day, we headed for the cafeteria.

"Well…did you give the article your best?"

I stopped and stared at her. "What did we agree on when I'm using my exasperated voice?"

"Is that what you're doing?"

"Did you miss the breathiness?" I dropped a stack of papers into the rack outside the cafeteria. "All I'm saying is we can leave the unbiased reporting lectures out of this conversation."

"I'm…sorry?"

"Very convincing." I dropped twenty-five copies of the paper into the rack outside the principal's office. Dallas Cleveland's front-page, above-the-fold byline gazed back at me. It was the punctuation mark on my second-rate work.

"How much of this is frustration with Lola?" Dinah asked, interrupting my wishful thinking. "And how much is it you worrying what your dad is going to say?"

Ugh. My dad. I glanced at my watch. "I'm meeting him at The Climb in thirty minutes. Maybe I could say I forgot the paper at school."

"Don't you think he'll see right through that?"

Probably. He'd likely already read it online anyway. I'd get "the talk" about how I was too young to be so singularly focused. How I should try something different, find a new passion, and while I was at it a new boyfriend. I hadn't managed to tell him he could strike that last item off his list.

Speaking of boyfriends, Dinah's swooped behind her and kissed her neck way too suggestively for the hallway. Or anywhere, really. Dinah squirmed but tried to play off her discomfort with a giggle. "Todd!"

Best-case scenario: he mistook her response as a playful tease to continue.

Likely scenario: he was a jerk who didn't care about boundaries. His friends passed, hooting at him. He gave them a nod and pulled Dinah closer.

My dislike for Todd Wilkinson was sparked by many things—his insistence on touching Dinah constantly, for instance. Or the way he expected to spend every Friday and Saturday night with her, as if nobody else cared for her company. The way he'd managed to evolve—at least in my best friend's mind—from annoying boy next door who had launched water balloons from his bedroom at her and her unsuspecting friends to attractive (*yuck!*) boyfriend material. How he'd broken up with every other girlfriend he'd ever had three months into their relationships—give or take a week—which meant Dinah's time had basically expired. How he openly mocked the reporting done by *The Muse* staff. And I could go on.

"Didn't know the new issue of *The Snooze* came out today," he said, laughing to himself.

If only I could breathe fire. "Todd," I said. "Good to see you as always. Could you give us a sec to finish up here?"

He glanced at Dinah, who nodded confirmation. He kissed her on the lips this time. She tugged him by the shirt the slightest bit and then pushed him away. "Give us five minutes to finish delivering these, and then I'll be out."

"Sure thing, babe. Oh, and Mac?"

"Yeah?"

"Sorry to hear about Colin." He slithered away with a smirk on his face.

"Why does he do that?"

"He liked Colin. I really think he's sorry," Dinah said. "How are you holding up, by the way?"

"I didn't mean that." How long would it take for people to stop talking about Colin? Even three senior girls I'd never spoken to in my life had gushed their condolences that morning in the bathroom. Why? They didn't know him. They didn't even know me. All they knew was what they'd read in the very public breakup piece that had circulated the school like some viral video. Privacy was long dead.

"You sure you're okay," Dinah said, resting her hand on my forearm.

I refocused on her love life instead of mine. "Todd knows you don't like PDA."

She shrugged. "It was just a kiss."

I sighed and swallowed my words before I choked on them. When it came to my best friend, Todd could do no wrong. If you asked me, he could do no right. But she didn't ask me. Ever.

"You should go," she said. "You'll be late to meet your dad. I'll finish this up."

"You sure?"

"Definitely. Go."

I hugged her and sent a telepathic message for her to dump Todd and find someone worthy of her amazingness.

A few minutes later, I slid into the driver's seat of my late grandmother's sedan and turned over the engine. Dad and I climbed a couple times a week, and I usually loved it. But lately, the conversation had turned to journalism too often—and with my subpar stories being buried in each weekly issue of *The Muse*, the chats had come more frequently.

I'd definitely get one today.

I couldn't blame him. My father had worked nights at the same bar for years. He'd started there to put himself through college, where he'd been an English major. His work schedule had prevented him from seriously writing for the college newspaper. He'd never completed an internship. By the time he'd graduated and could have searched for a job, he'd met my mom. Who'd *thought* she'd wanted a child.

And then had left us when I'd been three and she'd realized she hadn't known what she'd wanted. My dad had gotten stuck with me and a combination of his bartending job and freelance work to make ends meet. Now a big time executive at some art company in London, my mom offered to send us money that my dad and I refused if we had any choice. Accepting her money felt like a dangerous segue into accepting the offers she'd repeatedly made for me to come to London and live with her, so we could "get to know each other better."

If you had to arrange to get to know a parent when you were already seventeen years old, you lived in the land of red flags.

For me, it was my dad all the way. When I thought of everything he'd done for me, I felt pride, not embarrassment, but I didn't think he saw that. He saw me marching—no, sprinting—down a path he knew too well. Journalism jobs were hard to come by. I could hear his voice in my mind: print news had been declining for decades, yada yada. I wanted to believe it was the industry, not me, that he didn't have faith in.

His lack of confidence was always a whisper in my mind. I'd have to be the best. Competitive. A writer who saw her print above the fold. Better yet, on page one. It was all part of the plan: Big stories. *The Herald*'s summer program. Acceptance to Northwestern. Job of my writerly dreams. All I needed was a killer clip to set the plan in motion.

After the day I'd had, rock climbing would be the perfect escape. The Climb offered a workout that rescued my and my dad's mental health. Rough day? Go to The Climb. Serious talk about life? The Climb it was. Random Tuesday? It worked for that, too.

Usually my stress melted away with the ding of the door and the welcoming seasonal scent of the diffuser, spitting into the air from the manager's desk. Since it was December, the lobby smelled of peppermint.

"Mackenzie!" Barb came out from behind the counter and hugged me. Her blond hair was twisted into a clip that looked like she'd spent about forty-five minutes perfecting every strand. Her hair always looked like that, even after climbing, which, as the manager, she did every morning. She wore a bulky sweatshirt over her tight yoga pants, reminding me more of someone in their early twenties than their early forties. "Your dad's already here."

"Thanks."

She looked around as if a juicy secret dangled on the tip of her tongue. "Watch out for the newbs."

I leaned against the counter for support. Newbs were

notorious for ignoring climbing etiquette—probably because they didn't know it existed.

"College boys who think they know…"

"Everything?" I offered.

Barb sighed in a way that meant *So much yes*. She patted my shoulder. "Show them how it's done, sweetie."

"Will do." I only hoped I could follow through with climbing better than I could with writing.

THREE

IN THE MAIN GYM, Dad moved along the colorful hand and foot holds on the otherwise gray wall. While Barb always looked put together, Dad could have just rolled out of bed. Rumpled shirt. Old shorts. Wild hair. He showed off his strength when he climbed though. Barb stood in the doorway watching him. She flirted with him every chance she got. Not that he noticed, which kind of blew me away. He was a writer and a bartender. His skills of observation and communication should have been stellar, but I guess when my mom had left, he'd sort of shut off that part of himself. No dating. No flirting. No relationships.

Just him and me.

"Hey, Dad."

He adjusted his footing and lifted an arm to wave.

I finessed my strawberry-blond spirals into a ponytail. "I'm gonna get started."

He nodded and reached for a red hold, the toughest on Barb's walls.

After some stretching, I headed for the emptiest part of the wall, away from the newbs who sprawled out over the mats to take a break and howled in laughter at who knew what. *Only red today,* I thought to myself. I reached for the first hold—not an easy task at my height, but with some teetering on another foothold, I managed it. I reached, tugged, and climbed until my muscles screamed and burned. And then I reached some more. One section had an obstacle that forced me to climb horizontally across the underside of the rock. The staff had placed a major stack of mats beneath to cushion a fall, but I didn't need them. I pressed my toes into holds, pulled with all my arm strength, and squeezed every muscle in my core as I inched my way through the obstacle. Sweat flooded the crevices in my body and every one of my muscles burned when I finally reached the perch at the highest point of the climb—the prize for managing the obstacle. I slumped against the wall and wished my water bottle wasn't so far down.

That was when I realized the eerie quiet in the gym. Barb and my dad stood next to each other, hands on hips. The newbs stared, mouths gaping. Everyone in the place was watching me. I gave a shy wave.

"Will you marry me?" one of the newbs shouted. I couldn't help but laugh.

Barb's face beamed with pride, and my dad even looked a little shocked. With an audience, I opted to take a quicker, less intensive route down.

Barb tossed me a towel, and when I passed the boys, one of them said, "No, seriously. Marry me."

"That was impressive," one of his friends declared. "I'm kind of intimidated."

"You're always intimidated," another said, and they all laughed.

"Thanks, guys." I made my way to my dad, who handed me my water bottle.

"I'm a little intimidated, too," he said.

"Shut up, Dad."

We laughed and collapsed against a mat. I let my body sink into it, one by one each muscle thanking me for the respite. That had been one of Barb's more challenging routes, and I'd conquered it on the first try. The more I climbed, the better I got at judging my physical strength and developing my mental strength. I had hoped writing would be like that this year—a challenge I could figure out on the first try. Or even the tenth.

But I still hadn't.

"I checked *The Muse* website today," my dad said, breaking the silence.

I hid my face against my knee in an obnoxiously long stretch.

"Macky?"

I took a deep breath. "What did you think?"

"Honestly?"

I held the stretch a little longer.

"You can do better."

A dull pain simmered in my chest and expanded outward. He tilted his head to the side in that knowing way of his, but I couldn't back down. Not when my future was at stake.

"I need a better assignment."

"The rule is if you pitch it, it's your story, right?" Dad said.

"Yes."

"How many ideas have you pitched this year?"

I took a swig from my bottle. The cold water did little to numb the shot of pain in my chest. I'd had ideas. First, a feature on a local nonprofit that had raised fifty thousand dollars for clean-water projects in Niger. The founder was an alum of our school *and* the university where Colin studied. He'd scooped the story and then apologized incessantly, saying he'd thought we were brainstorming that story idea for him, not me. My mistake. When I'd brainstormed a story idea with him about social networks' influence on teen anxiety, depression, and suicide, I'd made it clear the story was for me.

He'd made it clear he didn't care when he'd run a similar story.

I'd pitched mine to Lola after she'd read his. She'd rolled her eyes and told me to find something original and stop biting off my boyfriend's stories.

I'd stopped taking his calls, thinking I'd finally show him. I'd create boundaries. He'd honor them. Instead, he'd published the opinion about what to do when high school relationships went bad—which was great because I'd really needed that advice, personally speaking.

"Do *you* have an idea?" I asked, turning the question around on my dad, doing my best to squash my anger.

"I don't, sweetie."

"You always say ideas are the easy part," I said, "that you have too many to write. What kind of writer am I if I don't have any fresh ideas?" Or when I did have them, I was scooped by someone I trusted.

"You know, if you're having a…slump, you can always try something else for a while."

There it was.

I stood and took another sip, ready to escape the conversation.

"It's my job to tell you the truth about life," Dad said. "The truth is that putting all your faith in one path at your age, well…" He shrugged, probably not wanting to admit that I'd be a failure someday, before going on with his life philosophy. "Sometimes—actually a lot of times—the path isn't clear. Like the pictures from that mini Polaroid camera you loved as a kid, you have to give it time to develop."

Or you had to make the path clear yourself. I stood, no longer focused on climbing.

"Where are you going?"

I called over my shoulder, "I have a story to find."

On my way out, Barb stopped me. "You said you'd show those newbs, and you did."

"It was a good workout."

"But not a challenge," she said.

I shrugged, and she laughed.

"I'll have to come up with a more challenging route just for you."

"Thanks, Barb."

I turned to leave as the newbs entered the lobby from the gym.

"Oh, and sweetie," Barb called. "I was sorry to hear about Colin."

I spun to face her. How had she...?

"Who's Colin?" one of the guys asked.

"Nobody," I said quickly.

"Good," he said, a grin spreading across his admittedly adorable face. He tilted his head to the side and twinkled his eyes at me. I almost laughed at the obviousness. His black hair was shaved close to his head. He had dark skin and dark eyes.

"Leave the girl alone," one of his friends said.

"I'm being friendly," he insisted and held out his hand. "I'm Darius."

I shook it, noticing a cross tattoo on the inside of his wrist but not quite ready to give him my name.

"Run now!" a few of his friends shouted on their way out, and I couldn't help but laugh.

"Your friends don't have a lot of confidence in you," I said.

He smirked. "I'll have to prove them wrong." He pulled

a flier out of his bag and laid it on the desk in front of Barb. The paper was so light it could have blown away with the slightest exhale. The words appeared three-dimensional in golden lettering. *Carnivalesque. It's what you've been looking for and didn't even know it.*

An image swirled in so many directions, I could barely recognize what it was—up close. When I took a step back, I swore I saw a pair of eyes in the middle of the swirls. No web address. No social media profiles.

Teen Journalist May Have Found Big Lead

"What is this?" Barb asked.

"It's a new hangout. Kind of amusement park meets Mardi Gras meets escape room." Darius pointed over his shoulder. "I was hoping you'd hang it on your bulletin board."

Barb glanced at me.

"Where is this…*Carnivalesque*?" I asked.

He crossed his arms. "That's a secret."

"How's anyone supposed to go if it's a secret?" Barb said.

"That's the fun part," Darius said with a wicked smile.

My skin tingled, my journalistic instincts on high alert. A story whispered to me from behind the curtain. *There's something here,* it said. *Keep digging.*

"Wanna go?" Darius asked me.

"With you?"

He threw his head back in laughter, and I got the distinct impression he enjoyed a good time. "The guys will be even more impressed than I hoped, you asking me out and all."

I rolled my eyes, and he handed me an envelope.

"When you get there," he winked, "come find me."

He headed for the door. "Oh, and one more thing."

"Yeah?"

"Sorry about Colin." His eyes did that twinkling thing again.

"Something tells me you're not."

He adjusted his backpack on his shoulder. "Yeah. You're right. See you at the carnival."

After he left, Barb whispered, "Should I post it?"

I ran my fingers over the letters. "I'm going to look into it."

"Will you tell me what you find?"

I planned to tell everyone what I found, and to do it above the fold.

FOUR

MY FATHER HAD ALWAYS TAUGHT me that to find stories, writers had to pay attention to the world around them. I could have easily left The Climb, tossed that envelope onto the passenger seat of my car, and forgotten about it. But if I wanted to be a better journalist, I needed to question everything.

After showering and indulging in a smorgasbord of leftovers from the fridge, I climbed into bed with my green notebook and my laptop, eager to research the carnival. I searched carnivalesque and found a few articles and books about a philosophical concept by the same name but no *amusement part meets Mardi Gras meets escape room.* I added my hometown, Pittsburgh, to the search.

My stomach fell to the carpet. In a PDF of *The West Penn Gazette*, the college newspaper Colin wrote for, the swirly logo caught my attention *on page one! Above* the fold! My eyes shot to the byline, but it wasn't Colin's story. Someone named Sandra Evans had authored it. How had she gotten the scoop? I opened another window and searched her name. Pages of *The West Penn Gazette* articles with her byline populated, dating back to the year before, making it likely she was a sophomore, not a first-year like Colin.

Irritation swirled in my stomach. Not jealousy. Colin might've known Sandra or Sandy or whatever she called herself. I closed my eyes and sighed, wishing I wasn't going to do it but knowing I was. I opened another window and typed *Sandra Evans* into every social media search I could find. A relatively common name, there were several accounts, even several in Pittsburgh.

I tapped a couple and scrolled. When I found a shot of a girl kissing Colin on the cheek, I knew I had her.

They knew each other. Like, *knew* each other.

I fell back against my pillows, daggers teasing their sharp points against my heart.

Where had I gone wrong with Colin? Trusting him, I guessed. Thinking that we'd been anything more than two journalists who loved talking about stories.

My dad had been so right about him.

In one of Sandra's recent posts, she'd shared a link to the article and said it was worth it to break this story, even though she'd been banned from attending. Not that I wanted her to get what she wanted, but I didn't make the connection between writing about the carnival and getting locked out of it. Darius had said the location was a secret. The flier didn't include much information either. Did they honestly expect that in the world today, they could maintain privacy?

I dug a little more through social media and found several mentions of her violating people's privacy by writing about the carnival, so I guessed the answer to that question was yes. Like Darius had said, Carnivalesque prized secrecy. But wasn't that taking the secrecy a little far?

Lesson learned. I'd keep my plans to write about the carnival on a need-to-know basis.

The article, which was nearly a month old, also talked about a committee of high school and college students in the region that had supervised the planning and worked in the carnival, open on Friday and Saturday nights. People could enter by invitation only, and everyone had to dress up and wear masks a la Mardi Gras. The article stopped there, though, leaving so many questions unanswered: What would everyone do there? Was it a traditional carnival, the type with rides and funnel cake? Where would it be held? Outside…in western Pennsylvanian winter? Wouldn't invitation-only policies limit their attendees and their profit? And why be secretive? Starting a new business was tough. Businesses usually begged newspapers for publicity, but Carnivalesque officials hadn't respond to requests for comment in Sandra's article. All in the name of privacy? Something else had to be going on.

Among all the uncertainty, I had no doubt about one thing. Sandra's lack of access—and answers—meant there was still a space in the news cycle for my article. And this time, I wouldn't let Colin scoop me.

The owners might not have promoted via social media, but people had been there the week before, which meant content about the place had to be online somewhere.

I typed #carnivalesque into each of the social networks I could think of and found some chatter—mostly praise about the intrigue and secrecy of the carnival. People wrote about how sexy the carnival-goers were with their masks and cocktail dresses. Others begged friends and even strangers for an invitation. None of the pictures showed carnival rides or food. They were all taken in people's cars, bedrooms, or outside. After some more digging, I learned why. The place was cell-phone free.

Details about the carnival seemed to stop there. All the other search results focused more on the cultural aspects of Carnivalesque. Historically, the event had been called the Feast of Fools, Mardi Gras, or Carnivale depending on the culture. Carnivals in my world meant overpriced rides, cheap game prizes, and delicious funnel cakes, but centuries before my birth, people had used carnivals to explore desires polite society had deemed problematic, like kings dressing as peasants and one lucky destitute woman wearing the fine garments and jewels that made her queen for a day.

The historical research went even deeper, revealing a debate about whether the carnival was a spectacle for entertainment's sake or a legitimate opportunity to subvert societal norms and liberate oppressed people. The philosophers' arguments fascinated me. Whoever had created our local Carnivalesque had likely chosen the name carefully. Why not Carnivale? Or Feast of Fools? Or even Mardi Gras? What did the name Carnivalesque mean for my generation? What were we being liberated from?

The philosopher Mikhail Bakhtin kept popping up in the information I read. I found his work on carnivalesque and took it line by line until my eyes watered. Curled up in bed, I turned the envelope Darius had given me over in my hands. The black envelope with the golden Carnivalesque logo in the center sent a rush of energy through me, thinking about the carnival and all the potential a story about it held for my future. The black card inside read, *You're invited.* A printed web address and a number—*141620*—was on the back of the card. That was all.

I tapped the address into a web browser. A black screen appeared, shortly after which the word *Welcome* materialized in the trademark gold lettering. Then a box. *Please enter your invitation number.*

I did. Another box appeared.

Please enter your email address. A place as secretive as Carnivalesque wouldn't like a reporter snooping around. In a different browser, I created a new email account with my paternal grandmother's first name and maternal grandmother's last name—Jackie Goerman—and typed that into the Carnivalesque web form. Given the secrecy of the place, an undercover name seemed appropriate.

Thank you. You will receive an email with further instructions.

That was it?

Seconds later, an email arrived from one of those "no reply" addresses. The subject read, *You're invited!* The sender? Carnivalesque: Be Your True Self. My fingers shook so much that when I tried to click on the link I accidentally closed the window instead. Thankfully, when I tapped back to my inbox, it hadn't disappeared.

You are cordially invited to attend the carnival extravaganza of the year. Carnivalesque provides the rare opportunity to mask your outer identity and share your true self with the world. Attendees relish the liberating experience of anonymity and laughter—but only, of course, if you can find us. We wish you well in that endeavor.

Please join us by solving the riddle below:

*If intrigue and laughter are what you're
     after,
Be prepared to search deep.
You can only see me through these
And only if secrets, you keep.*

Sincerely,
The World of Carnivalesque

VIP Bonuses Apply

VIP bonuses? I tried to click the line, but it hadn't been hyperlinked. I read the riddle four times. I was *so* not good at riddles.

At the bottom of the invitation were GPS coordinates. I punched them into my phone but only saw woods. Didn't matter. I'd find it somehow.

My heart thumped. I'd score the biggest article of the year for *The Muse*. I'd impress the hell out of *The Herald* and earn a spot at their summer program.

I could practically feel my Northwestern University press pass around my neck.

FIVE

DAYS LATER, I wasn't any closer to solving the riddle. I hoped the GPS coordinates were enough to get me to the carnival that Friday night and inside without the answer—alone apparently. Dinah had refused to be my plus one. She had plans with Todd. As usual. With my only other option being my father—and not even, if I was being honest, since he had to work—I drove to the location on the invitation alone.

Snow had fallen most of the day, leaving the world coated in a sparkle of white. At least it was something nice to look at while I swirled the riddle around in my mind. What did it mean about searching deep? I hoped I didn't have to literally dig. Maybe it meant snow removal? Not much of a carnival activity.

MACKENZIE DAVIS HOPELESS AT SOLVING RIDDLES

MACKENZIE DAVIS MUST SOLVE RIDDLE TO SECURE HER FUTURE

MACKENZIE DAVIS—TOTALLY SCREWED

I had a guess for the line *You can only see me through these*. Everyone had to be masked to enter, so that meant I had to wear a mask. Misplaced confidence stroked my ego. One line out of three wouldn't win me any awards.

————

Soon after I turned off the highway, I found myself on back roads surrounded by trees. When the GPS advised me to turn onto a dirt driveway, a flash from a horror movie struck me and I slammed the brakes.

A few seconds later three cars from the opposite direction turned down the driveway. With a deep breath, I followed. The driveway widened. The GPS showed several roads branching off, but the coordinates for my destination were straight ahead. The cars in front of me took the other turns, but I continued in the darkness until I found a gravel parking lot overflowing with cars. Carnival music sounded through the trees.

I hadn't even gone inside yet, and in a way, I got it—all the intrigue and curiosity. Carnivalesque had *made* me want to go, to come inside, to spend my money, to explore.

I checked my backpack, locked my car, and followed the crowds toward the music. All at once, a line of carnival booths with twinkle lights appeared through the trees. People in gold jackets and various-colored masks passed out plain black masks to everyone.

"Secure it before you go any farther, please."

With some effort, I tied the mask over the puffy curls of my hair. It fell too loose. I tied it again, my hair getting twisted in the silk ribbons. Securing the mask was easier said than done.

"Need some help?" one of the girls in a gold jacket and a stunning, sparkling blue mask asked.

"I think I do."

She handed the guy next to her the masks she'd been passing out and came behind me. "I learned it's best to go under half your hair." She parted my hair horizontally and then clipped the top portion to my head. "Last week I didn't have a clip. This week, I came prepared. You tie the mask tightly here, and then let your hair fall over. Your hair is gorgeous, by the way. I love the color."

"Thank you."

"This way the mask fits, and you still look good." She stepped back, assessing me. "Perfect. Have fun."

Disoriented, I took a few steps. Not being able to see any direction other than straight ahead triggered a survival instinct in me. *This is for the story,* I told myself. *I'm going to dig deep, and I can't do that without experiencing this world.*

Lights and voices filtered through the thick trees. My boots crunched in the snow as I followed the path, lit by paper lanterns. Around the bend, the forest carnival exploded into view. I stood at the edge of a clearing with rows of booths on either side and people packed in tight. My breath caught at the sight of them in their everyday winter coats, a totally normal occurrence, but then colorful masks on their faces—so not normal.

I strolled through the center of the booths, turning awkwardly to dodge the crowd and to see each activity through the holes of my mask. There was a basketball shot, fish bowl toss, balloon darts, poster darts, spinning wheel, ring toss, and even a duck pond. Instead of boasting kid-friendly colors, the booths had an elegance to them. Painted black with gold embellishments, the lights enhanced the sparkle. Where most carnivals gave stuffed animals and cheap kids toys as prizes, this carnival listed prizes like riding on a parade float or free masks, beignets, or milk-shakes. The grand prize—free entry to Carnivalesque—told me this was not the main carnival but an appetizer.

A girl bumped into me and quickly apologized. Her mask wasn't black and plain like mine but stylish swirls of emerald green and sparkling.

"Hey, wait," I said. "Where did you get that mask?"

She called on her friends to go ahead, and she'd catch up. "I bought mine there." She pointed to a booth at the far end of the carnival, close to a door to the only building in sight. "But you can win one at any of the games. If you want, you can play here all night."

"Is the parade here?"

"No. That's inside."

"I don't want to miss it."

"Take your invitation to that booth"—she pointed to a booth with a long line—"solve your riddle, and go inside."

"Solve my riddle?"

"Yeah. It's usually not as bad as you think," she said.

"You've been here before?"

"Every weekend since it opened. I help with some of the designs. It's fun."

MACKENZIE DAVIS FINDS HER FIRST CARNIVALESQUE SOURCE

"Mind if I hang with you a few minutes? I'm new, and my friend wasn't able to make it tonight."

She introduced herself as Kay and waved me on, chat-ting the whole way back to her friends who passed us cups of hot chocolate and introduced themselves, too. I gave her my grandmother's name, Jackie, thinking it best to use the name I'd signed up with. She told me her team had worked on the designs for the carnival over the summer in an internship but it had taken most of the fall for carpenter teams at high schools across the region to build the booths. Her focus had been exterior design, but she hoped to join the committee and design an exhibit for inside.

"It's going to look incredible on my resume," she said, grinning.

I could appreciate that, from one career-minded woman to another.

We passed a dart-throwing game. A green mask edged with white glitter caught my attention. "I have to have that mask."

Kay stopped and waved down the guy running the game. "Three darts, please. My treat," she said to me.

"You don't have to."

"I want to." She held open her delicate hand, the darts in her palm. "You can do this."

The first dart went wide. The second one hit the poster. I cheered.

"Not how it works," the game guy said. "You have to hit the mask."

"C'mon, Z. This is my friend, Jackie."

He crossed his arms. I glared at him as much as a person could glare from behind a mask and threw my last dart. It hit the green mask on the tip of the nose. Kay and her friends cheered.

I held up the top half of my hair while she tightened the new mask in place.

"You look amazing. Green is your color."

"Thanks. Are you heading inside now?"

"Nah. The girls like to play games until parade time. You should though. There's a lot to see."

I forced a smile, urging my brain to figure out some way

to stay with her and ask more questions without drawing attention.

JOURNALIST LOSES BIG LEAD DUE TO COWARDICE

Oh, shut up, headlines.

I'd have to find another source.

I side-stepped through the crowd toward the line to enter the carnival. I tapped my invitation against my hand, waiting.

The line moved quickly, and within minutes, I was under intense scrutiny by the blond at the door.

"Do I know you?" she challenged.

I crossed my arms at her tone. "Isn't it some kind of violation of privacy to ask that?"

She scowled. "You have a VIP invitation. I know everyone who has VIP access, but I don't know you."

"I don't know you either," I said, not willing to give anything about myself away and land in the kind of trouble Sandra had.

The girl returned the invitation to me. "You don't have to solve a riddle for entrance."

What? I slumped against the booth in relief. So that was one of the VIP bonuses? *Thank you, Darius!* If not everyone had access to VIP invitations, that meant Darius had status at the carnival. *I might have to find him after all.*

She waved toward the building behind her. "Pass through the building, and take the shuttle on the other side."

Inside, more twinkle lights swayed overhead. Around me, masked people smiled, laughed, chatted with their friends. I couldn't see their faces, couldn't know their intentions.

Then I realized they didn't know me either.

That philosopher, Bakhtin, had been right: it felt liberating.

————

The shuttle stopped in front of a massive red-brick building with a facade like I'd never seen before. It could have easily covered a city block—if we'd been in the city. Instead, it sat tall and wide, a dominant force in the middle of the wooded night. I'd have to look at satellite pictures again when I got home. Somehow the roof blended in with the trees. Now that I knew where the building was, I'd be able to find it again. Ideally.

Masked people lined the sidewalk in both directions, while more masked people holding tablets directed the flow. While I waited, I counted roughly one hundred and fifty people also waiting to get inside, yet the process seemed efficient, and the lines moved quickly. Five more shuttles arrived. The numbers were adding up.

When I reached the front of the line, the girl with the tablet smiled with bright white, perfectly straight teeth below her black-and-white checkered mask. "Welcome to Carnivalesque!"

"Thank you."

"Can I have your email address, please?"

I spelled it out for her, oddly aware that the people around me could potentially hear. Good thing I'd created a fake one for the carnival.

"Excellent. I have you right here." She tapped at the screen a few more times. "I see it's your first visit with us and you're VIP. How wonderful!"

"Thanks," I said automatically.

She handed me a black rubber wristband that reminded me of the one Dinah had worn for months after her family's trip to Disney World—this one without the iconic Mickey logo, of course. Part of me was surprised they didn't have the gold mask logo. "Please wear this at all times. Through the entrance and to the right you'll find the Welcome Shop. VIP entitles you to a free dress and mask if you want one. Best of luck in finding your true self."

SIX

I STEPPED inside the building into a massive hallway that led in both directions as far as I could see. Straight ahead was a store with a glowing sign that read *Welcome Shop*. The *o* in *Shop* wore a Mardi Gras mask. The store smelled of citrus. Pop music played, and masked carnival-goers slid hangers back and forth along round racks of dresses and costumes. Masks lined the walls.

Someone wearing a black Carnivalesque tee pointed to the invitation in my hands. "You have a VIP invitation. Come this way."

She led me through a back hallway into a private changing room. She pressed a button on the wall, and an announcement boomed. "Welcome to Carnivalesque! Please select clothes that show your true self."

"Please feel free to pick a dress and mask," the salesperson said.

"Thank you."

"Would you like something to drink while you shop?"

Something to drink? Like a fancy boutique or something?

"No, thank you," I said.

She smiled and gently closed the door behind her.

So, this was VIP.

I pulled my notebook from my bag and scribbled every detail of the carnival in the woods: the games, the prizes, the riddles, the transportation, the building. It was sloppy, but I hoped that getting it down would keep me from forgetting. Not to mention I couldn't ignore the gorgeous closet in front of me any longer. It reminded me of a vending machine but with clothes, shoes, and accessories instead of snacks. It was like my childhood dreams of a Barbie closet magically growing to my size.

Despite the number of masks adorning every spare surface of the closet, I didn't want to change mine. I peeked in the mirror. My dark hair contrasted against the mask in a stunning effect, giving me an idea. Mentally thanking Darius for my VIP status, I searched the closet for anything white and found a short cocktail dress with a tight white-and-silver bedazzled bodice and a white tulle skirt. It would match the mask—and my shoes—perfectly. I laughed out loud. About to play dress-up, I felt five years old again, which didn't for a second stop me from retrieving the dress and transforming myself from cold, wet winter clothes into a masked party-goer.

The girl who had led me into the room had been waiting for me outside. "All set?"

"Maybe. Is there a place I can leave my things?"

"We have a bank of lockers right outside the shop. You may enter the carnival with only your wristband, which can be linked to your credit card for purchases and/or serve as your tab that can be paid with cash when you reclaim your belongings. Cameras, phones, tablets, or electronic devices are strictly prohibited inside Carnivalesque."

I'd read that on social before tonight, but it was hard to

believe everyone listened. I didn't have a choice though. I couldn't let anyone in the carnival know what I was up to, and holding on to my phone would call unnecessary attention to myself.

"Great. Just one second." I closed the door again and stuffed all of my things into my bag with a sigh. A journalist without her notebook and pen was like Wonder Woman without her lasso and shield. Opening the door again, I smiled at my personal attendee. "All set."

"If I may say so," she offered, "you are gorgeous tonight."

I thanked her and let her guide me down a hallway to the lockers.

"Is this your first time here?"

"Yes."

"You'll want to select a Carnivalesque name, then."

"A new name?"

"Anonymity liberates us," she said, holding up a tablet. "Scan your band, and type whatever name you like. It will be associated with this band moving forward."

I stepped closer to the touch screen. I had selected a new name—Jackie Goerman—but the carnival didn't know that identity was already a mask. I could choose something Mardi Gras–related. What did I know about Fat Tuesday? There was a lot of eating. It happened in New Orleans. Ooh! The Big Easy. I choked a little at the thought of introducing myself to masked strangers, *Hi. I'm the Big Easy.*

Worst. Idea. Ever.

Mackenzie meant born of fire. Fire? Pyre? No.

S-P-A-R-K. I typed in the letters carefully and tilted my head to the side to study them on the screen. I was on to something, but... I deleted the last letter and typed an *X* instead. Then hit *Enter*.

"Thank you, Sparx." She helped me program a code for my locker and led me farther down the hall.

Ahead, a cement block wall had been transformed into a masterpiece. Color burst across the surface from floor to ceiling. Painted bricks outlined the mural. A golden ribbon curved around the highlights—a café under the stars, a milkshake, parade floats, a maze.

"It's a mural honoring the original exhibits of the carnival," my makeshift tour guide said. "To the right, you'll find more detailed maps of every floor. There are symbols for food and drink and explorations. You'll find other painted maps throughout the carnival in case you get lost."

"Get lost?" I asked.

"It happens." She smiled. "The carnival is a big place."

"Thanks," I said when she took a call through her earpiece and told me she had to get back to the shop. I ran my fingers over the mural. It must have taken weeks to paint. Even the maps, which were smaller, boasted beauty in their details.

I memorized the way to the Starlight Café. Sounded like magic to me.

People crowded the twinkle light–adorned hallways that had been mostly empty before I'd gone into the shop. They stopped to whisper to each other, laugh, hug, and generally block my way. I worked around them and missed a turn. Maybe. My first clue was when I pushed through another door into a hallway without twinkle lights or people. The door slammed and locked behind me.

Not good.

My stomach urged me to follow the scent of something fried and delicious. Around a corner, I tugged an old, wooden screen door open, thinking it might be the way back to the carnival. Massive ovens warmed the room inside.

Workers covered in flour, wearing white aprons and colorful masks, kneaded, rolled, and cut little square dough shapes. Across the room, a trio of masked people fried them, and closest to us, one worker scrambled to shake powdered sugar over the fried squares and bag them quickly enough to keep the line moving, which by the looks of it didn't seem to end.

Without a doubt, I should not have been there.

"Get a move on back there," shouted a round-around-the-middle woman with gray strands peeking out from behind her mask. Her name badge read *Sweet Cheeks*.

"I'm trying my best," the guy closest to me shouted. "You come back here and see how well you can do." To punctuate his words, he swung the shaker, and the lid flew off.

White powder exploded into a cloud that rained down on me like a sudden storm impossible to escape. I closed my eyes. The substance settled coolly over my skin.

"Smooth!" one of the guys at the fryer shouted and laughed.

The sweetness seeped between my lips to my tongue.

"I did *not* mean to do that," a voice said.

Comforting.

There was scuffling around me, but I stood with my eyes closed. Someone put a towel into my hands, and I reached for my mask to slide it off and wipe away the sugar.

"Wait!" Sweet Cheeks—I could tell by her voice— grabbed my wrist and told me to walk. "Never take your mask off in front of another person here."

"Right. I forgot. The sugar, and…"

"I'm so sorry about that. I'm gonna close you into a Welcome Room. Once you hear the door shut, you can take off your mask and get cleaned up."

"Thank you."

"It's the least I can do, but it's probably a good idea you don't wander back into my kitchen any time soon."

I couldn't agree more.

SEVEN

THE DOOR SLAMMED SHUT. I stood still, afraid to open my eyes. *I am an important journalist,* I told myself. *This is an important story.*

The social media posts about the carnival had read like movie reviews —*The best time I've had in a while, Intriguing, Fun and attractive.*

I did not feel attractive.

I felt like a pastry.

I reached forward until my fingers found a sink. I splashed water in my face, sweetness dripping into my mouth. I dug powdered sugar out of my everything for a good fifteen minutes, managing to wipe the front of the dress and mask I'd loved so much clean—although I totally smelled like a sugar cookie.

I looked in the mirror, at the occasional white streak in my hair, prominent against my red locks, and my face completely devoid of makeup. "You are a professional," I told myself. "You can do this."

Colin's face flashed in my mind, looking unimpressed. Next was Lola and—I hated to admit it—my dad. While some people had a cheering section of supporters, I had the people closest to me questioning everything I thought I could accomplish.

My dad's heart would break if he knew I felt that way.

I studied the mural map in the hallway, searching for places marked with their *Food and Drink* symbol. My eyes locked on a drink icon that read "Milkshake Ballroom." I groaned at the thought of a milkshake. I appreciated milkshakes as much as I appreciated a front-page, must-read, award-winning story. My stomach rumbled, and I memorized the way, paying much better attention to the directions this time around. A group of laughing carnival-goers nodded to me and moved in the opposite direction. A tiny voice suggested I go follow them, interview them, find the story behind the story, but a milkshake called to me. I recited the directions in my head: down the hall, then right, then right at another hall, up an elevator to the third floor.

Other than the twinkle lights in the hallway, the walls were plain. The paint was fresh, but otherwise, the whole effect wasn't nearly as extravagant as I expected given the logo and the fancy clothes.

I bounced on my toes in the elevator, eager for a carnival experience that didn't involve freezing in the snow or looking like I'd survived a snowstorm courtesy of an oversized helping of powdered sugar.

The doors parted, and Carnivalesque appeared before me in all its masked glory. From atop a set of golden—*legit* golden—carpeted stairs, I gaped at the most gorgeous display of color, light, and motion. Opulent hues of gold accentuated the light fixtures, railings, floors, and ceilings. Candelabras and chandeliers reflected the brilliance. And the people! They were packed in, wearing cocktail dresses, gowns, tuxedos, and even peasant clothes. I would have given anything to have my camera.

Instead, I made mental notes of every detail: the band across the room wearing strategically torn tuxedo jackets over bare, glitter-covered chests. The couples tucked into corners whispering in ears and nuzzling necks. Groups of friends laughing and talking at the tables. Sparkling snow falling from the ceiling.

"Pretty cool, huh?" asked a tall guy wearing a red velvet jacket over a white button-down shirt. His mask matched his outfit with tiger-like stripes of black, gold, and red. His dark brown hair was thick above his mask, with a wild swoop to the side, and when he smiled, a scar appeared along his bottom lip. I wouldn't have recognized him at all if it weren't for the streak of white in his hair that happened to match mine.

"Yes," I agreed, crossing my arms. "Hi."

"First time?"

"Yep, and it hasn't been my night." At least I could have a little fun with the guy that'd covered me in sugar.

"You look familiar," he said. "Have we met here?"

"I'm surprised you recognized me without powdered sugar all over my face."

He dropped the wet rag he'd been using to wipe down the tables nearby. "That was you?"

I nodded.

"I'm so sorry. Seriously. I feel awful."

"I smell like a cookie," I said as straight-faced as possible.

"Cookies are amazing, but I get how that probably wasn't what you were going for."

"Not exactly."

"If it makes you feel any better, I got fired from Little NOLA—where they make the beignets, and that job came with a lot of benefits."

"Really?"

"Only one benefit actually, but it was a delicious benefit."

"And now you're relegated to the Milkshake Ballroom with its opulence, live music, and milkshakes," I said.

"It's a definite hardship," he played along with the joke. "For real though, fate totally brought us together so I could apologize to you." His lip twitched in the cutest way, so I decided to let him grovel a bit more.

I crossed my arms and leaned against a table.

"We were so busy, and someone called off. And then the powdered-sugar shaker got clogged. Well, you know the rest."

"I do."

"The worst thing is that I filled it up like two seconds before that happened."

"I can believe it," I said. "I still have sugar chunks in my hair."

The horror on his face, even with half of it hidden by a mask, was so genuine, I lost it. We both laughed so hard that we held our stomachs and hunched forward.

"C'mon," he said. "I owe you a milkshake at the very least."

"You make milkshakes, too?"

"I'm a sort of jack of all trades at the carnival, so yes. I have many talents."

If his goal had been to spark my interest in his talents, he'd succeeded. I followed him to the bar, taking in the swagger of the ballroom along the way. "I didn't expect the employees to wear masks." The statement came out like a question.

"Oh yeah," he slid behind the bar, wiping it down as he walked toward me. "Everyone's masked. It's the utmost rule. So…chocolate or vanilla?"

"Excuse me?"

"Milkshakes are our thing. First one's on me. I promise you'll be addicted after that and come back for more every visit."

I considered myself a milkshake connoisseur. But every visit? I doubted that. "If milkshakes are your thing, then why do you only have two flavors?"

He pulled a menu from under the counter and slapped it in front of me. "We have a ton of flavors, but I pegged you as more of a chocolate-or-vanilla girl."

I made random milkshake recipes all the time. My palate was more sophisticated than chocolate or vanilla. I scanned the list of flavors. Cocoa Pebbles. How did you drink that without the pebbles getting stuck in the straw? Pass. Chocolate avocado? Did I just vomit in my mouth?

The man behind the counter stepped away to wait on another customer while I pretended to consider drinking maple bacon, strawberry basil, and morning mint. Like toothpaste? After finishing the list, which included an array of coffee-flavored specialties spoiled by my stringent aversion to anything mocha-latte-frappe-espresso-cappuccino, I politely pushed the menu away and swallowed my pride. Better than swallowing any of those concoctions. Either I was a milkshake amateur—hard to believe—or Carnivalesque was too ambitious.

He leaned against the marble bar top. "You decide?"

"The options are a bit…"

"Strange?" he offered.

"That'll do."

Someone from across the bar called out to him, and he raised his index finger in the universal *wait a sec* gesture. "I didn't make them up. I only serve them."

"Have you tried any of them?" I asked.

"Um…"

"Chocolate it is," I said.

He earned points for not laughing in my face, although a slight smirk made an appearance. I could imagine girls falling for his charm, flirting with him over milkshakes.

I took a deep breath and closed my eyes. The pounding rock music washed over me, the bass thumping from the speakers. Voices as indistinct as the faces around me chattered. One by one, I'd listen to those voices. I'd find the story within the story.

EIGHT

"SO, WHAT FLAVORS WOULD YOU SUGGEST?" the milkshake man called while he collected his ingredients behind the bar.

"Strawberry cheesecake," I said.

He nodded.

"Chocolate peanut butter. M&M. Oreo. Mint Oreo. Snickers."

"Now that sounds good," he said. "Maybe next time."

While he scooped vanilla ice cream into the blender and dumped in a soup ladle of chocolate, I observed the room. The majority of guests laughed and smiled. They leaned toward each other, chatting.

Without cell phones, the scene differed from the usual view in clubs and restaurants of teens sitting beside each other, all tapping and smiling at their screens. Couples twirled on the dance floor, holding each other close and occasionally kissing right there in the open, masks rubbing against each other, feathers becoming entangled.

"Everyone seems to be having a good time," I called to the milkshake man.

"That's what it's all about." He smiled again, and I wondered if his appeal would exist without his mask. It could be like when a guy looked good in a baseball cap but then he took it off and suddenly his head didn't fit his face.

"You've been working here long?"

"Since before it opened."

I gestured to the room. "Are all the rooms like this?"

"No!" he shouted over the blender. "Every icon on the map leads you someplace different. This place is huge. You could get lost easily. It's part of the fun." He poured my shake into the tallest glass I'd ever seen. It bore the Carnivalesque logo. The whipped cream doubled the drink's size, and the cherry fell into the pillow of white so deeply that it was in danger of never being seen again. He punched a straw through the cream and slid the glass to me.

"This. Looks. Amazing." I sipped the milkshake and moaned.

He laughed.

"You're a milkshake genius."

"My only skill, really."

A commotion on the dance floor caught our attention. I sipped and observed as a team of three guards, also masked, dragged a man from the crowd toward an exit sign. One of the guards held a cell phone out of the guy's reach.

"People just don't get it," the milkshake man said.

"What?"

"The rules. Privacy is a thing of the past. Do you have any idea how many pictures and videos there could be of you online that you don't even know about? You and your family behind somebody taking a selfie on vacation, at the park, restaurants, the mall. We're filmed and photographed all the time."

"If we're filmed all the time, what's the big deal?"

He stared at me as if he were measuring ingredients for

one of his milkshakes. "People love escaping that in here. They can have fun with their friends or complete strangers without having to perform for a camera every three seconds."

I sipped, waiting for him to tell me more.

"I know you're new to Carnivalesque, so take it from me —the rules are absolute. People like their privacy here. They laugh, have fun, explore a side of themselves they might keep hidden in the outside world."

In other words, they wouldn't take kindly to a writer like me sneaking inside with the intention of revealing their secret safe space. I imagined the laughing, milkshake-guzzling teens around me transformed into a clan of brutal and cunning adversaries like in the royal, medieval courts Carnivalesque had been modeled after.

"You make it sound like Carnivalesque is some kind of epic destination."

"It could be. People change here."

Change wasn't always for the better. Colin had changed.

"So, what's your name?" the milkshake man asked.

"Sparx."

He nodded and extended his hand. "I'm Kierk."

A few girls across the bar called Kierk over for coffee-flavored shakes. While he moved around, bending and reaching for glasses and ingredients, the girls blatantly stared.

"You should get out there and dance," he shouted over the sound of the blender. The girls gave me the masked version of the stink eye.

"And find my true love?"

He laughed. "You know, when you talk about this place, you sound a little judgmental."

"And you sound like you're about to lead a pack of masked teens to drink a mysterious Kool-Aid."

He leaned across the bar and whispered, "I put it in the milkshakes, actually."

I rolled my eyes. "Very funny."

With a smile, he poured the girls' drinks into glasses, piled on the whipped cream and cherries, and delivered them. They touched his arm. They laughed. They conspired about the best places to see that night. I focused on the places on the map in front of me, wishing I had my notebook to copy them into. King's Court. The maze. The roof. It seemed the carnival had so many places to escape to. How could anyone find their friends? What did they do in all these rooms? Why were so many different places necessary? I had a lot to learn and thought Kierk could be just the person to teach me…if the girls would ever let him escape. He inched away from them, reaching for a rag to wipe the bar.

"Are you coming to the parade tonight?" one of them asked.

"Not tonight." He gestured to other customers waiting as if that were explanation enough. Eventually the girls went away, and he went back to making milkshakes.

"You're popular."

He grinned like he knew it.

"Carnivalesque's about being in the moment, right?"

"It is," he said.

"But you can't slip away with a hot girl even for a few minutes?"

He studied me as if I'd said something puzzling. Or maybe he didn't want to share his dating philosophies with a stranger. "I'm not the *love 'em and leave 'em* type."

"And that's what people are here for?" The question sparked a potential angle for my story behind the story.

"Sometimes," he admitted. When he looked at me, I swore there was a bit of a simmer. Like a sizzle. Or something. As if that ever happened. I'd been with Colin for a year. If glances had the power to sizzle, I'd know it.

I cleared my throat, urging my brain back to the task at hand. "You want something more?"

"Something like that." He delivered the drinks across the bar, and a bell sounded at the same time my wristband vibrated. A flurry of activity surrounded me. People guzzled their drinks and hustled to the exits.

"What's going on?"

He wiped down the milkshake machines in a few swift motions. "Time for the parade."

"Can you point me in the general direction?"

"Follow the crowds."

I stood and adjusted my dress, hesitant to leave such a good source behind, and not because of the way his lip curled when he smirked. Or how he moved around with ease and confidence. None of that mattered more than going to the parade. Everyone who had posted on social about the carnival had insisted—don't miss the parade!

"You sure I can't pay you for the shake?" I asked.

"Like I said, first one's on me." Kierk stopped cleaning and looked my way. I gave a little wave, and as I walked, I got the sense he was studying me. Or contemplating something.

"You know what?" He slapped a *We're Closed!* sign onto the bar. Then he locked the cash register and said, "My clumsiness nearly ruined your night. I know just the thing to turn things around. Let's go."

NINE

KIERK TOOK my hand and tugged me through the crowd. We ducked into doorways and behind decorations so he could tap his wristband to open doors I hadn't even realized were there. The hallways we traveled weren't adorned with twinkle lights, and while the main areas of the carnival that we darted through were packed with people, these halls were practically empty. Except for another guy in a dark blue, somewhat brooding mask with a lanky blonde draped over his arm. The couple bolted through a door that almost smacked me in the face.

"Sorry," the guy said, and I recognized his voice immediately. Fortunately, the girl next to him spoke, covering my gasp.

"Hey, Kierky," she called in a singsong voice.

I caught his eye and mouthed, *Kierk-y?*

He shook his head as if warning me from ever repeating the nickname. "Sparx, this is Harvey. Harvey, Sparx."

Harvey shook my hand, giving me the perfect opportunity to confirm my suspicions. He had a cross tattoo on the inside of his wrist. Harvey was Darius. I'd found him after all. Though I wanted to, my instincts told me not to reveal myself.

Harvey pointed to his friend. "This is DJ."

Kierk snapped his fingers. "That's right. Was on the tip of my tongue."

I was pretty sure it wasn't, but DJ smiled anyway.

"Kierk, you in the parade tonight?" Harvey asked.

"Not tonight. Taking Sparx to watch."

"From the lift?"

"Where else?" Kierk's grip tightened on my hand. We said a quick goodbye, and Kierk pulled me through another doorway. The cheers in the distance intensified. We must have been getting closer to the parade route, but it felt like we'd been running forever. As big as the building had looked from the outside, it felt even larger from the inside.

We pushed through one more door, and the chill of an outdoor café bit my skin. I looked up to see the sparkling night sky.

"The Starlight Café?" I said.

"Yep," Kierk said. "Do you like it?"

Trendy couches surrounded fire pits. High-top tables with umbrellas intermixed with lower tables—round, square, and rectangle. The mishmash of it all was oddly cohesive.

"I love it."

A few people waved and called greetings to Kierk.

"How do they recognize you?"

"Most everyone who works here sticks to two or three masks. Makes it easier to do our jobs."

"Most…?"

"Harvey might have a few more," he said with a smile.

"And his girlfriend? Does she work here?"

"She's not his girlfriend." Kierk scrunched his face in thought. "Not officially."

As opposed to an *unofficial* girlfriend? Had Kierk forgotten the girl's name because Harvey spent time with too many girls to track? Even having known Darius for a whole three minutes I couldn't say I was surprised. I wondered if Kierk had developed his philosophy for wanting something more than a random hookup from watching his friend doing the exact opposite.

The scent of fried dough and sugar blazed so strongly through the hall that I could taste it on my lips.

"Oh no!" I laughed. "You're not taking me to the scene of the crime, are you?"

He grinned over his shoulder. "I promise not to touch the sugar. This way."

"Sweet Cheeks said never to come back."

"You're with me." He pushed a screen door open to reveal the bakery. "You're good."

The gorgeous smell of dough blinded me. Good thing I hadn't finished my milkshake. Next to us, a series of fryers bubbled. Rows of fried squares lined the center island, and Sweet Cheeks sprinkled them with sugar. The white deliciousness fell like snow over the dough, far from my face.

When she noticed Kierk and me by the door, she pinched his cheeks as if he were five years old and handed him a brown paper bag with grease on the edges.

"Am I fired for good?" Kierk joked.

"You covered a girl in sugar."

Kierk laughed in that easy way of his and hugged Sweet Cheeks. He touched everyone with ease. He'd taken my hand when I'd barely known him, yet it had felt natural.

"Speaking of which," Kierk said, "this is Sparx, the girl I covered in powdered sugar."

"Aren't you a sweet thing giving him another chance." She winked at me. Kierk kissed her cheek and pulled me back into the hallway.

"That smells amazing, but I'm not sure I can hang with that much sugar, especially after the milkshake."

He laughed. "Trust me. You won't want to miss these."

Boisterous cheering greeted us when he opened a door revealing an incomparably huge open space. The arched ceiling was practically beyond view. It would make for an amazing climb. The architectural details gave away its age, as did the peeling paint, worn beams, and rusted walls. We climbed a set of steel stairs that rattled beneath our weight.

"Is this safe?"

"Hope so," he said.

From the top of the stairs, we boarded a steel platform that boasted the perfect view of the parade. At the far end of the massive building, the floats were poised to move toward us, down a lane created by hordes of people on both sides. The excess of sequins caught the light, and as the bodies turned, laughed, and stretched on tiptoes to get a glimpse of the budding parade, the crowd reflected like the movement of the ocean with the sun shining down on its waves.

"This place is stunning," I said.

"I know," Kierk said. "I love that it forces you to appreciate beauty. All the time."

I turned to catch him watching me and felt warmth creep up my neck. I coughed to clear my throat. "There are so many people."

They continued pouring from all directions.

"How many come here each night?"

"Usually about three thousand."

Three! Thousand!

"How do you even accommodate that?"

He gestured to the massive expanse of the room. "The facility is huge, and there are several buildings."

"But there were only a handful of people in my van. How do you transport so many people?"

"You ask a lot of questions."

"I do."

"All right, then. But if we don't get moving, we're going to miss it." He hit a lever, and the platform jerked into motion, taking my balance with it.

TEN

KIERK WRAPPED his arm around my waist, pulling me to the center of the platform. "Hold on."

I grabbed the pole as the platform jerked again. I yelped, gripping tighter, and Kierk hugged me to him. "You all right?"

"Fine," I lied. The platform continued to climb. And sway. And jingle. "I thought our view was pretty great before."

"Don't worry. This lift has been in use since the old factory days."

So, it was ancient. Excellent. He stopped the momentum with another shift and then sat down, dangling his feet over the edge.

"Where's the guard rail?"

"Have faith, Sparx."

My Carnivalesque name sounded so good on his lips that I knew it had been the right choice. Still, I had no intention of dangling my feet anywhere.

"You can watch from there, but it's more comfortable over here."

I doubted that, but not wanting to stand the entire parade, I carefully slid to the floor, my hand steady on the pole. I stayed in the center of the platform.

After a few minutes, Kierk scooted backward to join me. "Hungry?"

"I'm dangling from an aging steel pole far above safety. I'm not sure my stomach can take food."

"I'm sorry. I should have asked before bringing you up here. I'm so used to it. I didn't even think."

"I'm not afraid of heights," I said, thinking of Dinah and how she refused to climb with me. It didn't make sense to her to put yourself in the position of falling from several feet in the air. In my defense, I never fell. "My best friend would totally ride me on this because heights are her number one fear and I'm always teasing her."

"Do you want to go back down?"

I wasn't exactly at Carnivalesque for adventure, not like everyone else, but I wanted people like Kierk to believe I was. And I'd climbed higher without safety equipment before. I refused to think about the fact the ground beneath us was hard and unyielding instead of covered in cushy mats.

"I want to stay."

His grin was every ounce worth the risk.

"These you have to try." He opened the bag and pulled out a stash of napkins. He laid them down on the platform as if making a picnic for us. Then he pulled four dough squares covered in powdered sugar from the bag.

They looked even better than they had in the bakery. "What are these?"

"Heaven." Kierk laughed. "But some people call them beignets."

When I picked one up, the sugar immediately transferred to my fingers. "They're still warm."

"Gotta eat them fresh," Kierk said and shoved a huge bite into his mouth. He groaned.

I couldn't help but do the same. The warm dough. The sweet sugar. Melting on my tongue in such deliciousness. "This is how the powdered-sugar experience is supposed to go."

He threatened to throw a pinch of sugar in my direction.

"I've faced worse," I said.

The ground lights along the parade route lit as we finished our beignets in silence and licked our fingers clean. "Do you usually eat four?"

His cheeks reddened.

"I'm sorry. I didn't mean to offend you."

"No. You didn't." He was quiet for a few moments, so I studied the growing crowd and the parade floats in the distance to give him at least a semblance of privacy. "Sweet Cheeks has been like a mother to me. Every time she sees me, she asks about my nonexistent love life and gives me enough beignets to share—hoping I'll have someone to share them with."

Before I could help myself, a sound escaped my throat. "Awww!"

He laughed. "Stop. It's so embarrassing."

"No, seriously. That is the cutest thing. I want a Sweet Cheeks in my life."

"I don't think that was the outcome she intended, but..."

As we laughed, it struck me how easily laughter came to him. Or maybe it was this place. What had the entrance clue said? *If intrigue and laughter are what you're after.* They might have been on to something there.

Kierk turned his attention to the hustle below, watching with the same critical eye my father used to scan the bar at work. Dad checked on every person to make sure they were content in their conversations. If they weren't, he asked if they needed anything. If they needed to talk, he chatted with them himself. He found the voids, and he filled them.

I had a sense that was what Kierk was doing. He'd started out working in the bakery because they were busy. He shifted to the Milkshake Ballroom, blending specialties with ease. Now he watched the parade route as if running through a checklist in his mind. It was clear that he was a very important person at Carnivalesque.

"Thanks for the backstage look at the carnival. And the parade," I said.

"Anytime."

As if anticipating that the parade was about to begin, the raucousness of the crowd intensified.

Kierk leaned close and shouted in my ear. "Welcome to the best seats in the house."

An extravagant gingerbread house eased toward us. People dressed as lollipops, candy canes, and other treats danced on the platforms while snow shot from the chimney and fell onto the crowd below.

"Is that real snow?"

Kierk nodded. "Pretty cool, huh?"

A pristine white Pegasus led the next float. It appeared to soar through the air, pulling a chariot with two lovers inside. The couple waved to the crowd and threw treats while never letting each other go.

"Are they really together, or is it for show?"

"Everything's for show, but sometimes the people who volunteer for the parades are together. Sometimes people use it as an excuse to get together when they're too shy to do so otherwise."

"What's there to be shy about when you're wearing a mask?"

He shrugged. "No idea. I'm not the shy type."

The floats continued. Dancers on a flatbed decorated

like an ice castle. A little Pittsburgh pride with the Three Sisters, golden side-by-side bridges named after three prominent "yinzers"—baseball phenom Roberto Clemente, pop artist Andy Warhol, and a woman who wasn't afraid to challenge the science of the world, Rachel Carson. The float featured carnival-goers wearing Steelers, Pirates, and Penguins clothing.

Kierk leaned toward me again. "We had to include something pro-Pittsburgh. It's a proud city. The perfect place for Carnivalesque."

He turned back to the parade but didn't move away. It was as if with every declaration about the parade, he inched closer to me. Definitely not the shy type. I watched the pride in his vibrant eyes and upturned lips and replayed his words —we *had to include*.

Maybe he wasn't just on the committee. Maybe he was, like, a leader of it.

"Next week marks the start of summer," he said.

I pretended my head wasn't exploding. "It's not even Christmas!"

"Exactly. Carnivalesque delivers what people want most, and since winter has been particularly snowy already, that's summer."

"So, people just get whatever they want in the carnival?"

"It's possible."

Looking for the story behind the story, I dug deeper, "So what are relationships like in the carnival?"

"Like they are anywhere else."

I must have rolled my eyes.

"What's that about? You don't believe me?"

"People come here for an unrealistic fantasy experience—"

Kierk interrupted me. "Not at all. The carnival is meant to create opportunities for people to reveal their true selves."

Like the welcome attendant had said when I'd arrived. "What does that even mean?"

"Think about those people who like someone but can't bring themselves to admit it. What if they could be masked? What if the pressure of rejection wasn't as intense and they could be open about what they wanted?"

"What if they shouldn't be pressured in the first place?"

"Now you're talking about a systemic issue," Kierk said, and I loved that he could spar with me without breaking a sweat or raising his voice.

"Fine. Let's stick to the carnival, then. Do you really think that a relationship that begins in the carnival—when two people wear mysterious masks, dress up, and attend extravagant parades or dance in ballrooms—do you really think that relationship could survive in the relative dullness of reality?"

Kierk paused to think about it.

"With that, then," I continued, "the carnival creates even more pressure than realistic environments because the lines of reality are blurred." An angle for my story. I wished I had a pen to write it down.

"You've really thought this through, but there's one problem."

I crossed my arms. "What's that?"

"You're wrong."

ELEVEN

KIERK'S audacious statement came with a smirk—the kind that might make you choke on your drink. I was pretty sure that was the only kind of look he had, but I reminded myself of my very own point: everything in the carnival was an illusion.

"I'll prove it," Kierk said.

"You'll prove I'm wrong? About a philosophical belief?"

"Yes."

"Kierk!" Harvey yelled from the ground below, making a weird motion with his hands.

"I'm sorry, but we have to go." Kierk tugged on the array of pulleys and then pressed a button, and down we went.

"Is everything okay?"

"I hope so."

Harvey reached for my hand and helped me off the lift.

"What room?" Kierk asked.

"King's Court."

With a grim expression, Kierk turned and kissed my

hand, making me feel like we were in a king's court ourselves. "I'm sorry to cut out on you here, but this is the reality of the carnival."

"Ha-ha."

He tried to smile, but whatever had happened in the King's Court prevented him from committing to it.

Kierk pulled a device from his pocket and used it to scan my band. Then he tapped a few buttons on the screen. "When you leave the carnival, you'll get an invitation to come back. Find me when you're here again, and I'll live up to my end of the bargain."

"Proving me wrong?"

"No." His smile was real this time. "Proving me right."

He left me in the thick crowd, alive with streams of masked people moving this way or that. As the parade ended and the crowds thinned, I explored the massive space. Markings on the ground outlined where machines and equipment had once been installed. Along either side of the parade route were a few sets of bleachers, and beyond them, the aged walls were lined with doors. Some of the doors were modernized with new hardware and the Carnivalesque logo. But a few huge metal doors from the factory remained. Sea green paint peeled away from the industrial latches and the *Danger. High Volts. No Admittance* signs. Between them and the occasional metal staircase leading to a labyrinth of walkways above, the carnival maintained an authenticity of the place it had once been. Yet the massive center aisle appeared to have been built for the parade floats. It was as if the building was meant to have two lives, and the second had only begun.

I asked for directions to King's Court, curious what Kierk had run off to, but someone in a gold jacket told me it was closed for the night and to try the club across the hall. I did, and it was exactly as you'd expect a club to be—loud music, close dancing, and flashing lights. Not my style.

I explored a while longer but couldn't find any references to the name or location of the factory. A map painted on another wall caught my attention. What had all the other icons represented? Too many unanswered questions to even begin an article! In the next week, I'd do some research on the carnival concept, sketch out the places I'd been, and detail every thought or observation I could remember. Then I'd come back, and my article would come together.

———

Saturday, my dad surprised me with dinner on the grill despite the winter chill. Something was up.

He'd left his computer open on the kitchen table. I glanced at the screen, wondering if he'd been struggling writing a story. A headshot of Colin next to a headline about high school relationships going bad stared back at me.

Oh. No.

In the kitchen, Dad sprinkled salt and pepper over two Delmonico steaks and tossed asparagus in a bowl with olive oil.

"I read Colin's article." He pressed the salt and pepper into the meat. "I never liked that kid."

"I know."

He sighed. "I'm sorry, sweetie."

"It's okay. Really. I agreed with him."

He gave me the side-eye.

"I just didn't realize it at the time."

"Oh, honey." He hugged me and kissed the top of my head. "I bought a mishmash of milkshake ingredients. Make whatever you want while I throw this stuff on the grill. Afterward, I thought we'd do some climbing."

Milkshakes and rock climbing: Dad knew how to heal my soul. Maybe Kierk—who had popped into my head at the mention of a milkshake—did, too. I found myself smiling.

Dad hip-checked the door and disappeared onto the back porch while I raided the fridge. Some people drank milkshakes as dessert or even with their meal. In our house, milkshakes were appetizers.

I diced a slice of cheesecake and found strawberry syrup in the fridge. After whipping up a milkshake in the blender, I poured two glasses, piled them with whipped cream, and tossed a few pieces of diced cheesecake on top. I wondered what Kierk would think about it.

"I love your milkshakes," Dad said when he washed his hands. "What's this one?"

"Strawberry cheesecake."

"That sounds amazing."

"I've also mastered peach cobbler and key lime pie."

"That bring your list of potential flavors to four-thousand-seventy-two?"

I laughed. "Something like that."

"You should host a pop-up milkshake bar in your dorm and make a pot of spending money at college."

"That's the master plan," I said. Or to convince Kierk to add a few more palatable shakes to the Carnivalesque menu.

"You'll need to add some coffee-flavored concoctions for your customer base."

"Do you want me to vomit?"

I relished everything about my father's laugh, especially when it was accompanied by a twinkle in his eyes that he reserved only for me. We sat on the couch and slurped our milkshakes.

"You want to talk about Colin?" Dad asked.

Any time I allowed thoughts of Colin or our breakup

into my mind, they brought with them an awkward mix of confidence and confusion. Deep down, I had the sense that breaking up had been the right choice. Instead of assuaging the humiliation, sadness, and even a little anger, though, that only intensified those emotions. If Colin and I hadn't belonged together and I'd known that, why hadn't I had the strength to break up with him months ago? What did that say about me?

I shook my head.

"Okay." Dad took a sip of his milkshake. "Can *I* talk about it?"

Despite our disagreements about my career aspirations, my dad was sweeter than the treat in my glass, so I knew whatever he had to say would undoubtedly make me cry. "Sure." I braced myself for the onslaught of tears.

"He's an asshole."

I spit pink milkshake all over the front of my dad's shirt.

"Hear me out," he said, dabbing the offensive splotches. "He recognized your talent last year and used it to advance his position as editor. Your stories shined on those pages, and since the two of you brainstormed and collaborated, everyone thought he was the reason. But it was you all along."

"Careful, Dad. It sounds like you have confidence in my writing."

"Oh, honey." He scooped me into a hug. "I've always had confidence in you. It's the system that destroys people. This is a perfect example. Colin was like the worst editors in positions of power: terrified their incompetence will be discovered and eager to cover it with the strengths of the people beneath them, metaphorically speaking."

"He made me a better writer, Dad."

"*You* made yourself a better writer. He was just there when it happened."

TWELVE

I GOT to school early on Monday morning to meet Lola in the journalism lab. I handed her my official pitch letter for the Carnivalesque story, claiming it for myself.

"I've heard of this. You've actually been there?"

"This weekend," I said.

"Isn't it invitation-only? How'd you get in?"

"It is. I have a source."

Lola analyzed me with her squinted eyes. "How much time do you need?"

"For the feature I'm envisioning," I said, "probably a few weeks."

"A few weeks is a long time."

"I'm trying to do as you said and take my stories seriously. I want to be thorough."

"Will you be taking on other stories in the meantime?"

"Something small if you need it, but I expect this to be a major feature." Major features counted more toward our journalism class grades than shorter stories. If I could pull off Carnivalesque as a major feature, I could secure my grade for the grading period. If I couldn't and I didn't take on other stories, I'd be in trouble.

She huffed. "Fine. The story is yours."

My shoulders sagged with relief.

Minutes later, I found Dinah at her locker—alone, thankfully. "Wow! You look bright and shiny."

"I just pitched Carnivalesque to Lola."

We headed for chemistry class.

"How did it go?"

"The story's mine."

"Good for you, Mac." Dinah's pace slowed for a moment. "And you're over the Colin stuff?"

"Definitely."

"Because of the guy you met at the carnival?"

"No," I said before really giving it any thought. Sure, Kierk oozed appeal, but he was a source. That was all he could be right now. "Colin and I were just done."

We claimed our lab table and unpacked for class.

"How's the story coming along?" Dinah asked.

"I need to get back into the carnival—do more interviews, but it will get there. I'm heading for the library during my free period." I mixed a pink liquid with a blue liquid in a beaker, but nothing happened. "How are your stories coming?"

She picked at invisible fuzz on her sweater. "Okay, I guess."

I'd known Dinah long enough to read her reaction. There was something she didn't want to tell me. I'd have to make her.

"I don't remember you taking a new assignment at our last meeting."

"Yeah…"

"Are you working on something else?"

Dinah huffed and closed her eyes. "You're not going to quit until you get an answer, are you?"

"It's kind of my style."

She put down her pen and notebook. "I'm thinking of quitting the paper, okay?"

Her words hit me harder than Colin's article had ever had the power to do. "You're not serious."

Her silence confirmed she was.

She spent so much time outside of school with Todd that we barely saw each other. And in school, we had the paper. Now we were losing that, too?

"What about going to Northwestern together? What about writing for the same major newspaper and taking lunch breaks to eat heaping nachos and greasy burgers at dive bars together?" We'd planned our lives together. Around journalism. Around writing.

"Do you know how unlikely it is for us both get into the same journalism school and work for the same major newspaper?"

"Doesn't mean we shouldn't try." I debated the value of asking my next question but didn't have the kind of self-control required to stop myself. "Is this because of Todd? He hates the paper."

"No." Dinah folded her hands in her lap and lowered her voice. "Don't you think I can make my own decisions?"

"I do," I said. But not when the boyfriend she fawned over for no transparent reason constantly belittled her intended career. I couldn't let her quit something she loved for a guy. Especially one like Todd.

"You always do this."

I threw my hands up. "What? Care about you? Tell you that Todd is a jerk?"

"Give me no credit to make decisions for myself."

The problem was I didn't believe she was making the

decision for herself. Too many of her decisions revolved around Todd and what he wanted.

"While you think about that," she said, cheeks red from anger, "I'm gonna go. And don't bother talking to me until you're ready to treat me like I have a brain of my own." She piled her books with a succession of thumps and left me to finish the chemistry lab myself.

I pressed my fingertips against my temples. "Dinah, of course you have a brain of your own."

A few of the other kids in class watched us with raised eyebrows, but Dinah was out of the room before I could think of anything to say to stop her.

THIRTEEN

DINAH IGNORED MY TEXTS, my messages, my everything for days. If I could manage to send her an owl, she'd probably ignore that, too.

Without my best friend to talk to, the week dragged on. By Friday, I'd invented two new milkshake concoctions—caramel apple and butterscotch banana, to be exact; climbed every day; and searched map and satellite images to locate the carnival. Surprisingly, the wooded area near the coordinates we'd received housed several massive buildings, but none of them showed two buildings side by side, which had me a little stumped.

I studied the map sketch I'd made after my first visit. Once I went back, I'd fill in the details. Maybe the map could become a graphic for the article.

I spent every moment of journalism lab—far from my colleagues' prying eyes—researching carnival tradition and philosophy at the corner computer in the library. I specifically looked for nuggets of information I could use to connect with Kierk.

If he had social media, I couldn't find it.

But I *did* discover Søren Kierkegaard, a Danish philosopher, and wondered if he'd inspired Kierk's carnival name. The possible connection made me read Kierkegaard's philosophy—over all of the others I'd come across—more closely.

One of his quotes spoke to me louder than if he'd been in the same room: *Life can only be understood backwards; but it must be lived forwards.* Looking back on my relationship with Colin, I realized it had been designed out of convenience rather than passion. While I'd lived that relationship forward, as Kierkegaard would've said, I never would have realized that. Looking back, I understood it implicitly.

Twenty minutes into my reading, Dinah slipped into the chair next to me.

I stopped typing and sat back in my chair, holding my breath as if an exhale might scare her off. I looked sideways at her picking her fingernails, her nervous tell.

"How's the research going?" she asked.

"Okay," I said carefully. "How's…" *Your decision to quit journalism going?* Probably not the way to preserve the peace.

After a few more seconds of silence, she seemed to build herself up enough to offer, "If you want to talk about what you found, I could listen. Be a sounding board."

I lowered my head and whispered, "That's one of the things I've loved about us writing together."

"Me quitting journalism doesn't mean we have to stop talking about your stories."

Dinah quitting the newspaper seemed to be one of those things I had to accept, like my dad working long hours, my mom leaving us, Lola getting the editor position over me, struggling to get my byline above the fold. To my epic disappointment, everything in life didn't go the way I wanted it to.

"What will you do instead?" I asked.

"Art!" Her smile lit the room, and I knew I'd been defeated. "I'm taking Drawing and Painting next semester, and I'm applying to summer art programs. As long as I include graphic design or something in college, my parents said they are good with it."

"Art?"

She nodded.

"Congrats."

"Thanks, Mac. That means a lot to me. I'm sorry I lost my temper," she said.

"I'm sorry, too."

She nudged me with her shoulder. "So tell me what you found."

I did, leaving out how much I missed the carnival. The smells. The laughter. I even missed the mask despite how awkward it had felt to wear it at first.

"You look wistful," Dinah teased. "Feeling nostalgic already?"

"It's a fascinating place. Perfect for a story."

"Is that guy Kierk perfect, too?" She raised an eyebrow at me. "What does he look like?"

Admittedly? Gorgeous. And he smelled like sugar and chocolate. I shook the thoughts away and instead simply said, "Like someone whose face is hidden by a mask."

"But he's hot, right?"

"You're incorrigible." I clicked on an article about Mikhail Bakhtin and pretended to read.

"Bonus points for using a vocabulary word. I want you to be happy. Like me and Todd. I know he's not your favorite person, but I'm happy."

I bit my tongue. Dinah, happy? I wasn't convinced.

Happy he'd finally asked her out after years of her pining for the boy next door. Happy at the possibility of what could be between them if he wasn't such a player. But legitimately happy?

Not a chance.

"Thank you," I finally said. "You know you could come and meet him yourself. Help me with the story a little."

"You know my parents would never let me."

Her parents *and* Todd. I wondered if he was the one who'd told her parents it was a lecherous place to visit. If Dinah's parents respected anyone's opinion, it was Todd's. The "why" took me back to sizzling summer evenings in Dinah's backyard. As kids, we'd dipped in the cool water of her swimming pool while Todd had shot us with Nerf guns from his bedroom window next door. Or cannonballed while we'd played cards by the pool. Basically, anything to annoy us, and when Dinah had gotten angry, her parents had always given Todd Wilkinson the benefit of the doubt. He'd apologize, make it right. They'd smile.

I'd roll my eyes.

Somewhere along the way, Dinah had begun to find Todd more endearing than annoying. Her parents and I had reacted very differently to that outcome. I didn't want to wish away my best friend's relationship, but I didn't have to like it either.

"You okay?" she asked.

"I just miss you."

"Me, too. I'll do better about getting together. Promise."

I squeezed her. "Thanks. Maybe you can even illustrate the map I'm sketching of the carnival. It could be your first published piece." Inspiration struck, and I gasped. "Ooh! Maybe you can work in the graphic department of the same newspaper as me!"

"Mac…"

"Fine." I blew her a kiss.

"So," she said, poking me in the side. "Let's get back to how hot this Kierk guy is."

———

At the end of the period, we headed for the journalism lab. I looped my arm in my best friend's, knowing that our days of working together on the paper were numbered to the end of the semester. Lola sat at her desk, scissors in hand, clipping something from *The Herald*. Probably for our portfolio project of articles we admired. I hadn't started mine, yet Lola's binder could barely close.

"Mackenzie!" She was pleasant. *Too* pleasant.

I smiled back, playing the high school game. "Hi, Lola."

"Did you see *The Herald* yesterday?"

I'd scanned the features, hoping nobody had stolen my Carnivalesque idea. It was sadly only a matter of time—a realization that always twisted my stomach into an anxious knot. I hadn't seen any articles worth clipping. "Anything in particular?"

She handed me the clip, WHY SUMMER INTERNSHIPS MATTER FOR TEENS. Interesting idea. Surprising to see it picked up now considering Christmas was only days away. A few lines into the story, though, I saw why. The writer had suggested that now was the time to start searching for summer internships. I glanced at the byline.

"You published an article in *The Herald*?"

"I know! Isn't it great? Liz—she's the editor—and I even talked about the summer program!"

Liz? Lola St. James was on a first-name basis with an editor from *The Herald*?

"Mackenzie," Mrs. Graham said from behind us, "are you reading Lola's piece in *The Herald*? Great topic."

"Yes," I said. "Definitely. Excellent topic."

"As you know, the editor's a friend of mine, and I have some big news." She clapped her hands loudly to get everyone's attention. "Grab a seat!"

We pushed and pulled desks and chairs in a cacophony of scraping and screeching. Once we were all settled, Mrs. Graham continued, "My friend Liz Valentine is an editor at *The Herald*, as you all know. Lola worked with her these past few weeks, and you probably saw her wonderful article in yesterday's issue." She clapped, and the rest of the class politely joined in. "This afternoon, Miss Valentine will be here to speak about her work at *The Herald* and journalism overall."

Gasps spread through the room like a winter cold.

"Today?" I repeated.

"I know it's short notice, but she had some time and was in the area for a story, so I cleared it with the principal. You are all free to come back here after lunch to hear her speak, and—here's the best part—she will take one-on-one meetings with any staff member interested. In the meeting, you can pitch her a story idea for *The Herald*."

The ensuing commotion of my fellow staffers felt as distant as a permanent staff position writing for the Associated Press. My Carnivalesque story was as the perfect pitch for Liz Valentine.

Remembering Mrs. Graham's lecture about what made a story newsworthy, I ticked off the qualities on my fingers, mentally practicing my pitch. It was timely—the place had opened less than a month ago and people were talking about it. It was in the Pittsburgh area, so proximity applied. There was novelty. I couldn't find a carnival experience like it anywhere online, let alone locally.

This was my shot. And I didn't intend on wasting it.

FOURTEEN

LIZ VALENTINE FLOATED into the journalism lab with a Bluetooth earpiece, a fancy red suit jacket, and sunlight framing her face. She and Mrs. Graham embraced, and then she spoke.

I might have missed the first few sentences out of sheer awe.

"Editors must fill newspapers," she was saying. "We need content, yes, but that content must be engaging and newsworthy. I know your teacher has taught you what fits the bill." She glanced at Mrs. Graham with a smile, and hands shot up around the newsroom. Liz called on Dallas, who recited the basics. A news story must be timely and relevant to the publication's target audience. In other words, it should matter locally.

"Absolutely. But the piece must be well researched and well written."

Liz moved around the room as she spoke, making eye contact with the staff and offering encouraging smiles.

"The concept, or in other words the pitch," she continued, "gets your foot in the door. But to build a relationship with an editor, writers must continually deliver stories that are complete, comprehensive, and readable. Nothing hard about that, right?" Her joke lightened the mood in the room, but only slightly. "If that's not enough, stories must matter. We want writing that touches our readers. That keeps them coming back because they feel something. Learn something. Believe something."

Lola gave me a pointed look.

"I want to hear your pitches today. Good ones. Think of the newsworthy attributes we discussed, and develop a catchy pitch for *The Herald*'s readers." She held up a stack of handouts. "These worksheets will help you with that."

The worksheet gave a formula for the perfect pitch complete with pitch ideas, online resources, and email subject line examples to catch an editor's eye. I thought about Carnivalesque. It was timely, intriguing, and local, but how could I make the story complete and comprehensive?

I wrote a few words on my worksheet. I crossed them out. I wrote a few more. The process continued until I'd moved from the unreadable worksheet to my notebook. I underlined the best words and rewrote them on a clean sheet in my notebook. I closed the notebook, knowing if I looked again, I'd find something to change. I'd question myself.

I didn't want to do that.

"Okay, everyone," Mrs. Graham called. "Two more minutes to finish up. Liz is taking pitches in my office." She looked pointedly at me. "Head in there whenever you're ready."

Dinah nodded to me, patted my back, and practically had to drag me out of my seat.

"I can't do this."

"Shut up, and do this," my best friend said as she slapped my notebook into my stomach.

I teetered into Mrs. Graham's office and shook Liz Valentine's hand, introducing myself.

"Mackenzie, Mrs. Graham has told me a lot about you."

Mrs. Graham had talked me up. I took a deep breath, not sure if I appreciated that or if it set me up to be a bigger disappointment.

"What do you have for me?" Liz asked.

I fumbled with my notebook, unable to find the right page. "Just a second." *Crap, crap, crap.* Every page had words crossed out. No perfect pitch to be found.

"You know," Liz said, "sometimes I find it best to just talk about an idea. Generally. Without the pressure of the perfect words."

Right. Talk about it. Catchy. Relevant to the publication's readers. And...go!

"Have you heard of Carnivalesque?"

She sat forward, grinning. "I have."

"Teens in your coverage area are attending by the thousands, and thousands of others scrounge for invitations, just for the chance to get inside."

"Go on."

"Parents want to know what the place is all about, too. To know what their kids are getting in to."

She nodded.

"I've spent time in the carnival and have access that most people never get."

"Are you on the committee?"

"No, but I know someone who is."

"I see. And what's your angle?"

My angle? The story behind the story. "I have a few options but haven't yet committed to one. I go back tonight. I'm hopeful that another evening immersed in the experience will help me nail down the story behind the story."

Liz smiled. "I definitely see the potential."

EDITOR OF THE HERALD SEES THE POTENTIAL IN MAC'S
PITCH. MAC DIES.

Mrs. Graham knocked at the door. "Time's up."

"I'll send you some of my recent clips and my award-winning story from last year, so you can get a sense of my writing style, too."

Liz stood and shook my hand. "Thanks, Mackenzie. I'll share this story idea with the other editors and look over your clips. If all goes well, I really think this could be something we pick up."

Something they pick up! It took everything not to squeal right there in the office.

In my best professional voice, I thanked her and left the office with a smile on my face—until I heard Kierk's voice in my head and felt the rumble of his laugh in my chest. A dangerous guilt followed. He'd been kind to me, and I liked him—enough to stumble with uncertainty.

The truth was I was using Kierk. And it didn't feel good.

FIFTEEN

AFTER SCHOOL, I climbed alone, my thoughts trickling to my mother. She'd known she'd wanted to live abroad, working at a museum or some fancy manor house, curating art. Then she'd met my dad, and her confidence had faltered. They'd married and had me, which had been when she'd realized we were nothing more than a momentary tangent. She'd moved to London and built a life for herself. Now that I was practically an adult, she wanted to get to know me, to be my friend, I guess, since being a mother wasn't exactly something she excelled at.

After living through that family mess, my dad wondered why I refused to deviate from the path I'd chosen for myself.

Getting off track led to disaster.

At The Climb, Barb had planned a more difficult route to challenge me. As she stood back, arms crossed and a smile on her face, I swung and pulled myself, conquering it on the second attempt.

She shook her head. "Come back Sunday. I'll have something else for you."

"I look forward to it," I called on my way out the door. After a quick trip home to shower, I packed my bag, insistent on experiencing everything Carnivalesque had to offer that night and recording it all for the moment Liz would undoubtedly call and say my story was a go.

In *The Herald*.

The Herald!

My dad had only written a handful of articles for the paper over the years, mostly because he'd had a falling out with a different editor, but he'd still be proud of me. When Liz said yes, of course.

I mulled through my plan for the evening as the van bounced over the western Pennsylvania roads. I'd packed a tiny notebook and pencil in the pocket of my dress I'd chosen just for this reason. I'd experience part of the carnival, head back to a Welcome Room, and write down every detail I could. Then I'd venture back out into the carnival to do it again. One night with a tiny notebook, I hoped, would be enough to record everything I needed to finally write this story.

The carnival-goers hopped out of the van, and I rushed toward the growing entrance line. This time, it took forever to get inside—so long that by the time I left my things in a locker, the bell sounded for the parade. Kierk could be anywhere—the parade, the café, the ballroom. How was I supposed to find him without a phone? The hallway was full of people flooding toward the parade. It made sense to check there first, but the beignets from Little NOLA called to me. Maybe Sweet Cheeks could help me find Kierk. I found her taking orders at the beignet booth.

"Can I help you?" she asked when I worked my way to the front of the line.

"Hi. Sweet Cheeks, right?" I never thought in my life I'd

be calling someone by that name, let alone a woman three times my age.

"That's right."

"I was here with Kierk last week. He sprayed me in the face with—"

"Powdered sugar. I remember."

Excellent. "Is he here, by chance?"

She grinned the way older people did when they thought they knew things you really didn't want them to know. "Not here, love."

I sighed but didn't say anything else. Or leave.

"But I might know where he is," she said with a grin.

"You do? Thank you!"

"First…" She grabbed a paper bag of beignets from under the warmer. "A pretty girl like you better not hurt that boy."

Guilt swelled in my chest. The deception of lying to Kierk to get a story most definitely qualified as potentially hurting him.

"Second." She handed me the bag. "You share these with him."

"Deal."

———

I pushed through the crowd along the parade route, studying my surroundings, trying to get my bearings. Kierk was here somewhere—Sweet Cheeks had said so. I suppressed a nagging thought that he might be on the lift again but this week with a girl other than me. I'd have to eat the warm treats alone in misery.

It didn't matter. Even if I couldn't shake Dinah's teasing voice in my head, Kierk wasn't my date.

He'd been right about the view for sure. The perspective

from the floor of the parade route couldn't compare to that on the lift. In the distance, I saw it, empty. No other girls, but no Kierk either. I pushed and swiveled my way toward it, mumbling apologies as I bumped people along the way. I ducked under the rope separating the masses from the parade route and hustled across. I didn't stop moving until I reached the top of the rickety steel stairs and stepped onto the lift. I pressed the button and climbed to a height that Kierk couldn't miss no matter where he was in the room. If I couldn't find him, then I'd need him to find me.

My dress was different, but I'd chosen a mask with green again. I held up the greasy bag of beignets in a spot that had been ours. If he saw, he'd know it was me. He'd have to.

The smell of the warm treats tempted me, but I searched the crowd, willing him to appear before I gave into temptation.

I couldn't find him.

"Excuse me!" someone yelled from below. The voice wasn't Kierk's, so I ignored it.

"I can see up your dress, gorgeous," he said, and I instinctively stepped to the side and tucked my skirt close to my body.

He laughed and cupped his hands around his mouth. "I knew you could hear me. You can't be up there. Please come down."

Dammit.

"I'm waiting for someone," I called back.

"Come down, or I will need to climb up and bring you down."

That didn't seem possible, but I also didn't want to be ejected like that guy with the cell phone had been the week before. "I'm coming!"

Pressing the button to lower the lift, I searched the

parade crowd once more to no avail. When the lift jerked into place, a hand reached for my mine. It was Darius—I mean, Harvey.

"Come with me, please." His tone was formal now. Official. It filled my sneaky journalistic heart with dread.

"I didn't do anything wrong."

He smiled. "I know a place with a much better view."

I followed him. "Do you happen to know where Kierk is? Sweet Cheeks said he'd be at the parade."

"Sure," was all he said. Either that or the crowd was too loud for me to hear anything else. He reached backward for my hand. I held his tightly against the stream of people threatening to separate us. He tapped his band on a nondescript door I hadn't even seen. They seemed to be everywhere.

He glanced at my shoes—"Can you run in those?"

They were flats. "Yes."

"Good." We jogged through a hallway clearly marked for employees.

"Where are we going?"

"VIP access. Very VIP."

The parade bell rang again. At the end of the hallway, Harvey threw open another door. The parade floats sat before us in beautiful glory. An awkward contrast to the winter chill creeping in through the massive doors, they boasted fictitious beach scenes against a backdrop of very real snowy fields and trees carefully outlined in winter white. The smell in the air was a mixture of winter chill and pine from the surrounding woods and popcorn and boiled peanuts from the festive red carts strategically placed along the parade route.

"The summer parade," I said.

"Exactly." Harvey smirked. "And it just so happens we need a summer princess tonight."

As if on cue, a girl wearing a deep blue mask with pointed edges appeared, holding a blush-pink slip dress and a bridal gown. "The changing room's behind you."

I turned to Harvey. "Are you serious…?" I'd never been in a parade before. I didn't do theater at school. I was a writer, used to being behind the scenes, not in the spotlight. There was no way I could be the summer princess.

Harvey crossed his arms and smirked. "View's even better up there."

"I thought you were taking me to Kierk."

"I will."

The first parade float rolled by. I'd come back to experience the carnival. What could be a more authentic experience than riding in the parade?

"It's now or never, Sparx."

I grabbed the slip and ducked into the changing room. The wedding dress would apparently wait for a quick change on the actual float. When I was ready, another girl led me up the spiral stairs of the last float in line to where my tall—presumably—prince waited.

He wore a white mask outlined in black to match the tuxedo jacket hanging next to my bridal dress.

"The summer prince, I presume?" I asked, hoping my voice didn't give away my nerves.

He nodded without really looking my way. Super romantic. I hoped I wouldn't be expected to kiss him.

"After the white confetti, you disappear behind this curtain and slip your wedding dress over this one," the girl escorting me advised.

"While the float's moving?"

"It's a parade," she quipped. "Floats don't stop."

The float in front of us moved forward, and for the first time since I'd been outside of the building, my adrenaline wasn't enough to protect me from the cold. The float lurched to motion, and I grabbed the railing that surrounded our small platform. The summer prince chivalrously wrapped his arm around my waist to steady me. He bought himself a few recovery points there.

"Thanks."

It was only then that I looked at him closely, recognizing the scar over his bottom lip.

He leaned closer to whisper in my ear. "Any time, Sparx."

SIXTEEN

I GAPED at the white-masked prince beside me. "Kierk?"

He laughed and squeezed me tighter.

"I've—" I stopped myself before saying I'd been looking for him everywhere. No matter how you sliced it, that would come across as needy.

"Been looking for me?"

My cheeks warmed. Masks were beautiful things.

"I saw you on the lift with the beignets, so I sent Harvey to get you. I needed a princess for the parade."

"Oh no. I left them in the changing room," I said.

He shrugged. "We'll get more later. Now, we parade."

My mind rushed with the satisfaction that my plan had worked, even better than I'd realized. Carnivalesque might just be a puzzle I was beginning to figure out. *You picked me to be your princess* dangled on the edge of my tongue, but I stopped myself from uttering the words. They felt too much like flirting, and I wasn't at Carnivalesque to flirt.

Parade-goers shouted to us to throw them something. I picked up a string of beads from the bowl in front of us and raised an eyebrow at Kierk.

"Let me guess," he said. "You're going to ask about women and what they do to get beads."

"That crossed my mind."

Without moving his gaze from mine, he tossed a handful of beads into the crowd. "What we throw is meant to be a gift as part of the celebration. Expecting anything in return taints the purpose of carnival."

I filed this away for my article, then threw handfuls of beads in every direction I could. Hands with widespread fingers shot into the air. People dove over each other to score the cheap necklaces.

"Wow. Intense."

Kierk held up a few of the necklaces and pointed out the paper stapled to them. "Some of them have coupons for free beignets, free entrance to the carnival, free food...basically anything free."

"Clever," I said. "Keeps people coming to the parades."

"Marketing genius." Kierk threw another handful. Masked people clapped and waved. They snuggled and kissed. They looped their arms with their friends and danced. It was a good party down there. Maybe even more fun than being up in the float, until Kierk and I created mini competitions for who could throw the beads the farthest, how many we could throw at once, and if we could hit specific targets.

"Tall guy with the medieval knight armor," Kierk said.

I found him in the crowd, the lights reflecting on his suit, and took a moment to measure the distance between us. I launched, and...*clink!*

"Yes!" One of the many skills learned from a single dad.

"Not bad, Sparx."

The float in front of us had papier-mâché wild horses on the back. "Give one of those horses a necklace."

With confusion written all over his face, he followed where I pointed. "We can't throw at other floats."

"Why not?"

He struggled for a reason. "It's just not what we do."

"You admit defeat, then?"

He closed his eyes and lowered his head. "You're gonna get me into a world of trouble, Sparx."

"I wouldn't dream of it," I teased. In one motion, I flung a string of beads and it caught on the horse's ear. "Hell yeah!"

"That doesn't count! You said a necklace. That's an earring."

I brought my hands to my hips. "Can you do better, Your Highness?"

He offered a sideways glare, but the grin on his lips gave his true feelings away. He threw a glimmering green strand, and it soared wide. I laughed at the deliciousness of my obvious superiority. His next attempt bounced off the horse's side.

"Getting closer," I said. "How many strands do you have left?"

"Remind me to never compete against you again."

"Oh, is competing what you're doing?"

He laughed and shook his head. "You're brutal."

Before he could throw again, white confetti shot into the air. It was go time. Kierk ushered me behind the curtain. I retrieved the white dress from the hanger and pulled it down over the slip. The float lurched forward, and I fell flat against Kierk. My hands brushed bare skin. I turned to see him shirtless yet still masked.

"Sorry," I mumbled, turning away. But the beautiful image clung. He could eat all the beignets he wanted. Oh. My. Damn.

"It's fine, Sparx. You ready?" He secured a lacy veil on

the back of my head. "The people want to see their summer bride."

I nodded, and he moved aside so I could step out first. The crowd erupted. I waved and smiled. They threw confetti and rice. Kierk stood so close I could feel the warmth of his body and thought about what it had looked like shirtless. I smiled and waved even more to bring my thoughts back to this moment, to why I was here: to write an exposé about moments like these, the fireworks my peers felt at their cores when they'd had a fantasy experience at the carnival.

A clinking sound started quietly in the crowd, but it grew until it seemed every person in the building tapped on stairs, doors, glasses, lights, whatever they could. I'd been to enough weddings to know that sound. At my cousin's wedding the summer before sophomore year, everyone had clinked so much, I swear her lips never left her husband's.

Kierk didn't attempt to kiss me. Instead, we continued to smile and wave, leaving me to wonder if he didn't want to kiss me. Or if I wanted to kiss him.

I looked over my shoulder and smiled at him, but he wasn't looking at the crowd. He was watching me with an intensity that made me want to rip the mask from his face and see what was underneath. Kierk tilted his head forward. With his lips so close to mine they nearly brushed them when he whispered, "Don't feel like you have to do anything you don't want to, Sparx."

"It's all part of the experience, right?"

He grinned and glanced at my mouth, which made me look at his. The float hummed forward at a consistent speed. Slow and steady, yet my insides fluttered with the realization that the parade route would end, and this moment would be gone. I lifted myself on my tiptoes, inching closer to Kierk.

Journalist about to Get Way Inappropriate, Kissing a Source She's Lying To

At the last moment, I lost my nerve and instead pressed my cheek against his. From the crowd's viewpoint, it would look like a kiss. They would get what they wanted, and I wouldn't cross a line.

"Sorry," I whispered.

"Nothing to be sorry for." His breath tickled my neck.

"I know random hookups aren't your thing."

"Not yours either?" he said.

"Not really."

I'd never heard the crowd cheer louder. I swore I heard someone shout Kierk's name. I might've been anonymous at Carnivalesque, but Kierk was not. How many of them had gotten wind that he'd be in the parade tonight? Was Sweet Cheeks out there watching? What would they think if they knew why I was there? What would Kierk think?

I pulled away and looked down at the crowd. We waved to the last few people and tossed our final handfuls of beads before the float exited the massive factory through a garage door fit for a fire truck.

Harvey climbed aboard and shook Kierk's hand. "Not bad, milkshake man. And Sparx, you're a natural up there. Any time you want to join us again, let me know!"

"Thanks," I said, wondering if all the parades involved such intimacy.

"You back to the ballroom?" Harvey asked Kierk.

"No, I'm off for the night. Thought I'd show Sparx around a bit. If she's interested."

I met his expectant gaze and said, "That would be great!" before even thinking it through.

He smiled, and that was that. Kierk would be showing me around for the night. Despite it being exactly what I'd wanted, it felt entirely unexpected. While I'd planned to ask him some questions and explore the carnival, that moment on top of the float had distanced me from my analytical reporter side and left me feeling giddy and hopeful—like I was on a first date. With a really hot guy.

Problem was I had no idea if the moment, or almost moment, on the top of that parade float had been real or not.

It was Carnivalesque, I told myself.

Nothing was real.

SEVENTEEN

"I KNOW THE PERFECT EXHIBIT." Kierk tipped his head to the side, encouraging me to follow. "The place is particularly packed tonight because we have so many new exhibits for our Summer in Winter schedule."

A short walk brought us to banging sounds and lots of laughter. We turned the corner, and I half expected to see some violent display of medieval manhood, but I'd guessed wrong.

"Bumper cars?"

Small, glow-in-the-dark, circular cars with rubber rims sped through the dim room in flashes of colorful lights. When one collided with another, the masked carnival-goers inside lurched. Between the glow-in-the-dark cars and black lights, the room looked part night club, part amusement park.

Kierk led me to the line, which was surprisingly long.

"I can't believe so many people want to ride the bumper cars."

"First night," he said, as if that explained why grown

humans were so crazy about a ride usually reserved for children.

The line inched forward. We'd be there a while.

"What was here before?" I asked.

"Indoor sled riding."

I laughed. "How is that even possible?"

"Anything is possible with a little creativity. But don't worry, if you stick around here long enough, sledding will return."

The problem was once I published a story about the carnival, I'd be an outcast, and that meant I wouldn't be around long enough to sled ride with Kierk. The shock of disappointment pulled me a million miles away from the bumper cars.

"You okay?"

I forced a smile. "Yes. Definitely."

Masked people piled into the cars and, after getting settled and buckled, took off. Unlike the amusement park cars I remembered from being a kid, these cars swiveled in all directions and moved quickly. They lit up when bumped, which was often. And everyone riding them smiled or laughed like they'd never experienced anything like it before. That everyone wore masquerade masks only added to the appeal.

The room showed no remnants of indoor sled riding, and the number of cars and track pieces would take up significant space. "If you change the rooms—"

Kierk leaned toward me. "The exhibits."

"Right," I said, "the exhibits. If you change them so often, where do you store all of this stuff?"

"Different warehouses. You wouldn't believe how cheap they are in struggling river towns across the region. We try to keep materials as close as possible to minimize transportation costs, but my boss is willing to travel if an exhibit is deemed worthy."

"Bumper cars are worthy?"

He grinned. "Okay, skeptical Sparx. You try to ride around in bumper cars with a bunch of people in masks and costumes and not laugh the entire time."

I could tell from the noise in the room that my challenge was off base, even before Kierk had countered. "And how long will you use those floats?"

"Almost two months. Until Mardi Gras. We have an entire fleet planned for that parade."

"But all of these floats and sets and puzzles—it must take so much work," I said. And money. Hence the twenty-dollars-per-person entry fee, if you weren't VIP of course. With thousands of visitors each Friday and Saturday, the tally wasn't bad.

"You ask a lot of questions, you know that?"

"I seem to recall you mentioning that once or twice before."

He crossed his arms.

"But your point is well taken."

We descended into a thick silence. I wanted to ask more questions but couldn't. Shouldn't. Maybe I could tell him the truth. Maybe he would help.

No. We had rapport, but it wasn't solid enough to survive the truth. Not yet.

"You're dying over there, aren't you?"

I sighed. "Yes."

Kierk leaned against the wall, and the way he tucked his hands behind his back revealed some pretty spectacular arm muscles. I caught a few girls next to us staring. That moment behind the curtain at the top of the parade float flashed in my mind, and I didn't blame them.

"To answer your earlier question, my boss supports

opportunities for young people to explore their passions," Kierk continued. "The sets throughout the carnival, the floats, the designs, even the costumes result from partnerships with high schools, colleges, and universities across the region, including a few places in Ohio."

I worked to listen to his words and not watch his lips. "That's pretty amazing."

"It is. The carnival has been a pet project for so many people for almost a year. Now it's real."

We could have debated that whole "real" definition again, but that may have taken us to an awkward conversation regarding what had happened on the float.

"How do you maintain secrecy with so many people involved?"

"At first, nobody knew what they were building the exhibits for. Eventually, people began to figure it out, which, I admit, takes away some of the mystery, but there are confidentiality agreements for that. The best part," Kierk continued with infectious enthusiasm, "is that every person…*involved*…"

I got the sense "involved" meant the elusive "committee"—not that he would say so explicitly.

"…is able to embrace their passion: building, painting, sewing, crafting. You should see the number of masks our craft team created."

"Really?"

"Thousands."

"Wow. Can you create your own?"

Kierk tipped his head to the side. "What do you mean?"

"Is there an exhibit where people can make their own masks?"

"That's a good idea, Sparx. Might have to suggest that."

I felt too pleased with myself.

"So, what about you?"

"What about me?"

"What's your passion, Sparx?"

Writing stories that make people smile. Or think. Or wonder. Or dream. Piecing together words that in any other order would never carry the same meaning or power. The urge to allow those thoughts to spill from my mouth tugged at me, but I couldn't say any of that.

"I don't know," I lied, pretending to adjust my mask.

He gave my back a friendly pat.

"No worries. You're still young. You have time."

I simply nodded.

"Speaking of which," he said, "how young *are* you?"

"Seventeen. How *young* are you?"

He laughed. "Nineteen next month."

He waited for some reaction to that information, but I didn't give one. I couldn't be so presumptuous to act as if it mattered if we were two years apart. And like Colin's column had so brutally revealed, relationships with that kind of age difference only caused more stress than they were worth.

Ahead of us, a guy in a leather jacket and a solid black mask turned around and caught my eye. Then he smiled. With another change in riders, we moved closer to the front of the line. Around us, couples wrapped their arms around each other. The leather-jacket guy looked at me again. I pretended not to notice, wondering if it was the anonymity of the carnival that encouraged him to keep trying to catch my eye.

His boldness made me think of Harvey.

"Kierk?"

"Yeah?"

"You said Harvey isn't the kind of guy to have a girlfriend, right?"

He looked at me quizzically. "Are you interested in

him?"

I laughed. "Gosh, no. I mean, he seems nice enough, but no."

Kierk's wide, genuine smile made me believe our almost kiss might have been more real than I wanted to believe.

I shook the monumental distraction away. "I was just curious if that was the general way in the carnival? People are anonymous. If they don't like someone, they can ghost them with relative ease by changing their outfit or mask or just going to a different exhibit."

"I'm sure for a lot of people, the carnival can be that way. It's about the person though. Not the carnival."

"What do you mean?"

He hesitated. "Harvey had a girlfriend. He really liked her, but she betrayed him and basically messed him up pretty bad."

"Like…she cheated?"

"Not exactly. She's a writer for a college newspaper, and she took everything he'd told her in confidence about the carnival and published an article about it. We didn't want any publicity, which she knew, so…"

I might have stopped breathing. It couldn't be. What were the chances?

I guess, generally speaking, slim. How many people had worked on the carnival in the early months? A lot. But Sandra had needed someone more than a builder or designer. Her source had to know the inner workings of the carnival. Given the attempts at privacy, I could only imagine that circle was much smaller—it had included Darius.

The pieces of the puzzle couldn't be ignored. Darius and Sandra had been together. I hadn't found any other articles about the carnival, so it had to be. Her article had been the betrayal.

And I was doing the same thing to Kierk.

EIGHTEEN

"BUT IT'S NOT like that for everyone," Kierk said, as if the conversation hadn't taken a particularly painful turn. "Some people come here to hang out with friends or maybe even to meet someone real."

"Right," I said, only half listening. Kierk and I weren't together like Darius and Sandra had been. This wasn't the same. It wasn't.

He moved forward in the line, almost time to take our turn. "You're skeptical."

"I..." Couldn't speak. I'd made him my source without his knowledge or permission. Not the kind of journalistic integrity Northwestern would expect of their students. Or the kind I expected of myself.

"Tell you what," he said, "I bet that I can prove it's possible for you to really feel something for someone at the carnival."

The masked people suffocated me. I needed out of this room. Out of this place. What was I doing?

"Sparx?"

Kierk saying my name was like a pause button, sending all the negative thoughts into some holding pattern.

"You okay?"

I wasn't sure how to answer that probably because I didn't know the answer myself. *So don't use him,* a little voice said from inside my cluttered mind. Not the same voice that spouted the headlines, but somewhere close. I tried to listen as if an expanded explanation would magically follow. It didn't.

The line moved, and we were closer to our turn.

Don't use him. I'd write about my own experiences in the carnival. I'd talk to other people as sources. Kierk was just a friend I was spending time with. Not a source of information. Or at least I wouldn't make him one from this point on. It was all about my experience and what I observed. No more questions.

"I'm good," I finally said. "What were you saying?"

"I was saying that it's possible to feel something real here, and now that I'm saying it twice, I feel ridiculous."

I doubted it was possible, but I also supposed a firsthand account could be the story I was looking for. And whomever Kierk matched me up with could become the source for my story, which would mean not betraying Kierk's trust. "So, then I would bet the opposite?"

"Basically. But you have to be open to it. You have to try."

"What's in it for you?" I asked. "I mean, why do this?"

He shrugged. "Let's just say I believe in the philosophy of it. You always sound so skeptical about the carnival, like it's fake or something. I think if you let it, it could be the most real experience you've ever had."

He was right. I was skeptical.

"And I'm generally right about things," he said. "I like being right. I'm going to be right again."

"Fine," I said. "I'll take that bet. Not that you're going to—at all—but what do you want if you win?"

With a pensive look, he said, "Let me think about it. Not that you're going to—*at all*—but what do you want if you win?"

Why not shoot for the stars? All access to the facility, with a camera. Yeah, right. Maybe I could settle for a free milkshake. "I'll tell you mine when you tell me yours."

He laughed. "Deal."

"So, since you're my love coach, true or false: That guy up there in the black mask has been checking me out the entire time we've been in line?"

"True," Kierk said without even glancing the guy's way. The question had been a test of Kierk's observation skills. He'd passed.

The guy in the black mask climbed into a car with an empty one next to it. Since Kierk and I were at the front of the line, the exhibit worker asked if we were together. It was my chance to go have a moment with a carnival guy who was clearly interested.

"He's not the guy for you," Kierk whispered.

"Sorry," I told the worker and pointed to Kierk. "We're together."

A few minutes later when we'd climbed into our own cars, I learned Kierk had been as right about the bumper cars as he'd been about the beignets.

I floored my glittery cobalt-blue car and tore through the crowd with him hot on my tail. A girl with 80s-style big hair and an evil grin hit me head on, launching my car backward into Kierk's. He grunted when we made contact. Reeling from the impact and struggling to right my car, I ducked between two cars that crashed the moment after I cleared them, blocking Kierk's path to me. I headed for a corner and turned back to the chaos. Kierk sat vulnerable between a trio of battling drivers. He held up his hands in surrender, but I only shook my head.

"Sparx!"

I sailed into the side of his pink car, my momentum unhindered.

He flew sideways, vowing revenge, but the bell rang signaling the end of the ride. The cars' power faded.

I jumped up and reached for his hand. Pulling him to his feet. "You're right, that was fun."

He wrapped an arm loosely around my shoulders. "I bet it was, Sparx. I bet it was."

"I worked up an appetite."

"Wanna eat?"

"Lead the way," I said.

We traveled the usual nondescript, empty hallways designated for the staff. Crossing the threshold into the Starlight Café was like being transported through time and space to an outdoor bistro in a French Riviera summer. I stopped to take it in, and the people behind me crashed into us. Kierk called out an apology and pulled me to the side, so the traffic could continue pouring in.

The view had changed from the week before. Twinkle lights dangled from every elevated surface, enveloped the trees, and outlined the food tents. To avoid milking Kierk for information, I made mental notes of every detail. I'd resort to observation first and foremost—until I found another source.

"It's gorgeous," I said.

"It's one of my favorite places in the carnival."

"One? Not *the* favorite?"

"There's a lot you haven't seen yet," he said.

"I want to see it all."

He nodded as if the decision had been made. "Then you will."

The sky sparkled brighter than the man-made lights around us.

"You even managed to hang twinkle lights in the sky," I joked. "I'm impressed."

Kierk bowed. "The universe was good enough to comply with our first summer night request."

"How generous."

"Besides, what would the Starlight Café be without the stars?"

"What, indeed?"

I glanced at the long lines and sighed.

"C'mon," Kierk said. "I know a back way."

Of course he did.

Through a hidden hallway, Kierk pushed open a door to the kitchen of the Burger Hut. The smells of bacon and fried food wafted through the air making my stomach grumble even more. Three masked burger makers grabbed tickets from a machine that spat them out faster than they could make them.

"Crush, throw me a few patties," Kierk called. "Condiments, Sparx?"

"Lettuce, tomato, ketchup, mustard, and pickle." I thought better to hold the onions if I was about to meet the guy who could prove my misgivings about the carnival wrong.

Crush complied, and my burger took shape in front of me.

"Bacon?" Kierk asked.

"Always." I laughed.

He nodded. "Definitely."

Kierk stacked a double burger with an insane amount of fixings on his wrapper, grabbed two containers of fries, and called to a girl working the front of the hut for drinks. The epic line jump had us back in the Starlight Café, enjoying our food under the night stars, in fewer than five minutes.

"That's fast food," I joked.

"Sorry it's not fancy."

"I don't need fancy."

He smiled. "Noted."

"You mean for when you match me up with the perfect guy I'll fall head over heels in real love with?"

"As opposed to fake love?" he challenged.

Colin's face took shape in my mind. Fake love? Is that what it had been for us? I groaned because I knew the answer before I even finished asking the question.

Kierk found us a table next to an outdoor heater. Within seconds of sitting down, he tore into his burger. A couple jalapeños fell out with a splatter of mayo. I laughed at him, but he shot me a very messy smile, not caring in the least. He had this beautiful rhythm of massive bite of burger, little sip of Coke, and then a fry to wash it all down, which seemed a little out of order to me. I took a bite of my own burger and couldn't deny it was delicious, even if eating it with my face covered felt totally weird.

"Can I ask you something?" I said after a couple quiet minutes of eating.

"How did I know that bumper car guy wasn't right for you?" He tossed a fry into his mouth.

"You always know what I'm going to say."

He leaned close, smelling of fryer grease and Coke. "It's a gift."

"So…?"

"Dating is more about who you are than who you're with."

"Meaning?" I took another bite, careful not to drip a glop of sauce onto my dress.

"If you want to develop a lasting relationship, then you need to know yourself better."

"You're quite the philosopher," I said.

"By trade, actually."

A philosopher in a carnival built on philosophy. No wonder he was an advocate for the place. "Let's say I am ready. What then?"

Kierk sat back in his chair and crossed his arms. "I'll think about it."

"You're supposed to be helping me."

"I'm a philosophy major. Thinking is helping."

NINETEEN

AFTER DINNER, I took a quick trip to the restroom. In the stall, I scribbled everything I could remember from the night so far. No quotes from Kierk, just my observations. I hoped that would be enough to avoid crossing the new boundary I'd set for our sort-of friendship.

I had the choice to return to Kierk or wander off on my own. I could change my mask and my clothes even and become someone else. I could interview people about their experiences. I could work on my article. But I felt myself drawn back to his side.

When I returned to the table, Kierk was surrounded by Harvey and a gaggle of long-legged, silky-haired, sparkly-dressed girls. Kierk slid over on the bench when he saw me, and to the girls' dismay, I sat next to him. They redirected their attention toward Harvey, who received them with glee. I glanced at Kierk and swore he thought the same thing.

"Wanna go?" he whispered.

"Sure."

As we said our goodbyes, I realized the chill of the night hadn't touched me through the whole meal.

"How do you manage to control the weather?" I asked as we walked away.

"Magic," Kierk said deadpan.

I shook my head, not sure how to challenge his carnival humor.

"A very strategic system of space heaters. And fire pits. And a ton of body heat."

"Impressive. What's next?"

Kierk snapped his fingers. "Have you ever done a Scottish reel?"

"That's not a drug, is it?"

He laughed so beautifully that I didn't care if I'd asked a stupid question. "Let's go, Sparx."

After grabbing a bag of summer trail mix from the Burger Hut window and leading me through a few turns in the halls, Kierk pulled me into an elevator with another couple whose faces were straight attached to each other. I looked at Kierk, wide-eyed, but he only shrugged. On the second floor, three girls climbed on. The couple didn't stop kissing. When we got to our floor and exited the elevator, they stayed.

"Surely there are more private places in this massive carnival for that," I said.

"They're masked. In a way, that's as private as you can get. That's the beauty of Carnivalesque."

His declaration reminded me of something I'd recently read in a library book. "But isn't Bakhtin's concept of Carnivalesque focused more on a subversion of power?"

He stopped a peanut halfway to his mouth and gaped at me. "You've read Bakhtin?"

I helped myself to his trail mix, subverting authority in my own way. "Maybe."

His smile was wide and real and...wow. *Stay focused*, I urged myself. Any girl would need urging in the presence of that dimple right next to that tiny little scar.

"So…?" I prompted.

"Historically, the carnivals aimed to subvert authority by providing the attendees the opportunity to explore some aspect of themselves privately, away from the social pressures of their class and role in society."

I remembered reading about that. The royals would dress as peasants and vice versa. "But how does that connect to privacy nowadays? Nobody here's a king or peasant." At least that I knew of.

"True. But I'd argue that privacy is a bigger issue now than when carnivals rose to popularity in the middle ages."

I nearly choked on a raisin. "People were slaughtered for practicing the wrong religion. They didn't have the privacy to love who they wanted or worship as they pleased. They lived so closely together that if someone sneezed, the whole town could be obliterated by illness. You think they had privacy?"

"All good points," he said, but rather than appearing shamed, he nodded in respect. "But they didn't have the internet. They didn't live in an age where phones are used to document moments people are recording but not really living."

"Do you have a phone?" I interrupted, curious if his everyday behavior lived up to his high moral standards.

He grinned. "Why? Do you want my number?"

I hated myself for it, but I blushed and laughed out loud, playing right along with his flirtation. "So, you were saying?"

"The moments people have here are real. I know I haven't convinced you yet, but they are."

"People change their names, mask themselves, don't even know where they are, and alter their appearances with different clothes and costumes," I said. "Not to mention the outlandish experiences inside."

"Outlandish?"

"Indoor parades, outdoor meals in winter, grand balls. Dancing the waltz while a rock band plays, glow-in-the-dark bumper cars. Need I go on?"

"Don't forget the carnival games at the entry points, the mechanical bull ride, the potato-sack slide, oh, and the Tunnel of Love." He lowered his voice to a conspiratorial whisper. "That's glow in the dark, too."

I gulped at the thought of going into the Tunnel of Love with Kierk. "What I'm trying to say is…" I tried to recover. "How can anyone develop real relationships when they're hiding themselves?"

"We'd like to think people here are more true to themselves and more real than anywhere else. Research also shows that people carefully select images for their social network pages that represent the persona they're creating—not necessarily the real version of themselves. When we take away phones and cameras, we eliminate that urge."

"By your estimation, then, people can be whoever they want," I said.

"Exactly."

That might have been true, but did the girls at the carnival want to wear the short skirts and low-cut necklines, or did they believe that was the way to catch a guy's attention here? Did every girl, no matter her personality or body type, feel comfortable costuming herself and covering the face she'd spent the last nearly two decades showing the world? The carnival might have aimed to subvert power, but it seemed to me that leaving a phone at the door didn't erase years of social priming.

"Debate whether this world is real all you want, but you can't argue against this." Kierk opened the main doors to the

Milkshake Ballroom. We stood at the top of the grand stair-case, the sparkling decor of the room taking my breath away even more than the first time. On the dance floor below, two long lines of people faced each other. Couples took turns hooking their arms and spinning with their partners in the center of the row to a folksy tune and then spinning with someone on the outer line. Then back to the center. And then again and again. I hadn't spun once, and I already felt dizzy.

"This," Kierk pointed to the dance floor, "is reel." He winked. "Get it?"

TWENTY

I PRACTICED three religions as part of my Christmas Eve tradition. First, Dad and I went climbing. Second, we raided the grocery store shelves and prepared a feast of random milkshake concoctions. Third, I went to midnight mass with Dinah and her family while Dad worked a Christmas Eve bartending shift, which was surprisingly slammed every year. What was new about the traditions this year is that I spent them thinking about Kierk.

"I feel like we haven't talked in a while," Dad said during a break between climbs. "I'm sorry about that, sweetie."

"Don't be, Dad. I'm good. Busy."

He feigned a knife to his heart.

"That doesn't mean I don't like spending time with you."

He sat upright and smiled, quick to overcome his metaphorical injury. "Okay, then. What's been keeping you so busy?"

I took a swig of Gatorade. "Have you heard of Carnivalesque?"

His eyes widened. "You've been going there and haven't told me, young lady?"

"What's the big deal?"

"I've heard stories about that place."

"Such as…?"

"That it's a lecherous, underground…" His voice trailed off.

"Something you don't want to say?"

"You are still my baby girl."

"Dad, it's not like that. It's…" I looked around as though Kierk could hear what I was about to say and then wave his finger in his face with an *I told you so*. "…fun and exciting. And incredibly well planned and managed. It's basically an indoor amusement park slash theater slash dance slash escape room."

Yep.

I was totally drinking the Kool-Aid.

How could I not? I'd laughed more the night before than I had my entire life. In the Scottish reel, Kierk and I had hooked our arms at the elbows and spun together in the center of the lines, and then we'd separate, each spinning with someone standing in line. Then back to the center, and back to the next person in the line. So. Much. Spinning.

By the time we'd hit the middle of the line, I couldn't see anything but swirling colors and had totally relied on Kierk to keep me upright.

"Great," my dad said, stretching to prepare for his next climb. "I'll tell my editor."

I grabbed his arm. "Tell your editor what?"

"She knows I have a teenage daughter, so she wanted me to look into a story about it."

"For *The Pittsburgh Daily*?"

"Yeah, sweetie." He smiled. "What's going on?"

Dad had a hate-hate relationship with *The Herald*. Years

ago, an editor there had killed his story without paying him and had dropped his other assignments. My dad had never known why, but ever since, he'd pitched all his ideas to the other major newspaper in Pittsburgh and had built a close relationship with the editor there. Dad respected *The Herald's* summer program for teens and my dream of getting into it, but in general, it wasn't his newspaper of choice.

"Dad, I pitched the story to *The Herald*. Literally the competing newspaper." I could barely compete against the writers on my staff for *The Muse* cover. No way I'd defeat my father, a seasoned writer, for Carnivalesque.

His eyes were wider than the hand grips on the wall. "You pitched a story to a major newspaper and didn't tell me?"

I forced a smile and turned on that I'm-your-only-daughter-look-at-my-batting-eyelashes charm. "Sorry…?"

He lifted me into a bear hug. "Honey, I'm so proud of you. You need to tell me these things, but I'm proud of you."

"Thanks, Dad." I patted some chalk on my hands waiting for the inevitable question.

"But why *The Herald*?"

There it was.

"The summer program, Dad. And one of the editors is friends with Mrs. Graham. She came to talk to our staff and took pitches from us."

He kissed the top of my head. "When will you hear?"

I smacked my hands together creating a puff of chalk. "I sent her some of my best stories, and she's checking with the editorial staff. Hopefully soon."

"I have to get back out there before my old-man muscles get so stiff I hurt myself. Let's get one more climb in. We can talk about your story more on the way home."

"What about *The Daily*?"

"No way I'd ever compete against my little girl. But..." His eyes twinkled. "If *The Herald* editor doesn't get back to you soon, you can pitch to my editor at *The Daily* instead. I'm pretty certain the answer will be yes."

I hugged him so tightly his old-man muscles were in trouble. "Thanks, Dad."

———

One way or another, my Carnivalesque story would be published in a major city newspaper—if I managed to actually write it. I couldn't wait to tell Dinah.

I rushed to her house after dropping my dad at the bar for his shift and found her curled up on the basement couch watching *National Lampoon's Christmas Vacation* with Todd. I'd forgotten he'd be there. Although not sure how.

"Mackenzie!" she squealed and jumped up to hug me. "Are you hungry? My parents haven't put the food away yet."

"Actually, I am. My dad and I went climbing, and I haven't eaten."

"Say no more." She tossed the remote to Todd. "Be back in a bit."

No long gaze or embarrassing kiss. No hands reluctant to break apart. When we got to the top of the stairs, I pulled her aside. "Everything okay down there?"

She scowled. "His phone never stops beeping. And do you think he could silence it while we watch a movie together? He gave me my Christmas present and then actually asked me to pause unwrapping it so he could watch a stupid video one of his idiot friends sent."

Ouch.

She took a deep breath and closed her eyes. "Maybe I'm tired."

I thought she might finally be waking up.

"Whatever," she said, trying to shake him off. "Let's eat."

I followed her to the kitchen. "You haven't eaten yet?"

"I'm stress eating."

We piled our plates with cheesy potatoes, homemade rolls, and a myriad of fishes. Dinah's family's Christmas Eve Feast of the Seven Fishes was epic. Every year. So epic sometimes they had eight fishes. Or ten. I didn't count. I kept scooping and pushing the food around my plate to make room for more.

"So...you didn't tell me about your second carnival adventure," Dinah said once we were settled into the empty dining room. "Did you find anyone to go on the record?"

"Actually, I spent most of the time with Kierk."

"Again?" Her grin was too knowing.

"And I rode in the parade," I said, trying to change the topic from romance to the carnival itself.

"With Kierk?" Dinah asked.

She was good.

"Aha!" She laughed and somehow slurped seafood chowder at the same time. Without choking.

Her question took me back to delicious places I didn't want to go. The sight of Kierk's bare chest. The feeling of his lips so close to mine. And then the crash of my emotions at the reminder—it had all been a facade.

I shook the thoughts away and told Dinah that I'd need other sources. I wouldn't take advantage of Kierk, and given what I knew about Harvey and Sandra, Kierk would never consent to going on the record anyway.

"Wait. You met Sandra's source?"

"He's, like, Kierk's best friend," I said.

"The plot thickens."

"Next time I go I'm going to unthicken it." If that was even a thing.

"You like this guy."

"Not like that," I said. "I don't feel right betraying him."

"Right." Dinah tore a piece of roll and dipped it into her soup. "Like the time you revealed Claire Sanchez and Joe Riley were making out under the bleachers during lunch in seventh grade despite being friends with Claire and knowing that Joe was cheating on Leslie Knowles."

"That was different. We were in middle school. I was just learning journalism ethics." My audience had salivated at that story.

"What about last year when you broke the news that Michael Evans planned to quit the football team to play trumpet in the band?"

"He was the starting quarterback! It was big news."

"He begged you not to tell."

Suddenly, my appetite disappeared. "You make me sound like a brutal journalistic vampire."

Dinah pushed away her plate, too. "Not at all. I'm only pointing out that the story has come first for you for a long time. If you're even thinking about altering your plan for Kierk, that says something, whether you want to believe it or not."

"I…" I mulled over her accusation. Had I built a reputation for putting journalism first, above all else? Above my friend's ambitions with art? Above people's privacy, even when they begged me to keep their secrets? Was I willing to alter my journalistic beliefs for Kierk?

And if I was, what did that mean?

"And let's face it," Dinah went on. "You could have written a story by now, but you haven't. Why is that?"

"I don't know what the story is yet," I said, my words

not even convincing me. "I'm trying to write better stories, so they actually get read."

"Admirable," Dinah said, "but I still think you could have done that by now. You know that once you publish a story, you can't go back. That means no more Kierk."

"Do you really think I'm putting off writing a story because subconsciously I would miss seeing a guy?"

"Your words, not mine," she said with a shrug.

The seven fishes swam recklessly in my stomach. Mrs. Zimmerman popped into the room to say hello, ending the philosophical debate about Kierk and my article.

By the time Mrs. Zimmerman had finished chatting, we had just enough time to exchange gifts before mass. I went first, giving Dinah a framed photo of the two of us at *The Herald* tour from the previous school year and a sweater I'd picked up at her favorite store at the mall. She gushed about the sweater but didn't say much about the photo.

"I love it!" She pulled a necklace from under the sweater she had on. "It will go perfect with this."

It was a cursive letter *T* in white gold.

"Wow," I said.

"Amazing, right? Todd got it for me."

I could have guessed. A letter *T*. As if he'd branded himself to her chest.

She shoved a green gift bag into my hands. "Open yours!"

Glitter fluttered when I lifted the tissue paper. At the bottom of the bag, I found the culprit—a stunning black mask with green-and-silver sparkles. It would be gorgeous under the carnival lights. "Did you make this?"

Dinah grinned. "I have the glitter marks on my carpet to prove it! I know you like to wear white and green, but I thought maybe if you're feeling a little dark some night, you can wear this one instead."

Two green feathers flared outward above the right eye, and black satin ties dusted with green glitter hung at the sides. Dinah was an artist. A good one.

"It's amazing, D." I hugged her tight. "Thank you."

I couldn't wait to show Kierk.

TWENTY-ONE

CARNIVALESQUE WAS CLOSED the weekend of New Year's Eve. I'd have to survive the weekend without beignets, parades, ballroom dances, glow-in-the-dark bumper cars, and, of course Kierk. I wanted to ask him why the carnival was missing the opportunity to celebrate such an epic holiday. I mean, a New Year's celebration at the carnival? The dresses, the masks, the dancing, the floats! The word "epic" played on repeat in my head. Epic everything! They could even charge a holiday rate. It would have been packed.

But I couldn't ask Kierk because I had no way to reach him. I missed him.

Not *him*, but talking to him.

So, I guess, essentially him.

We'd become friends. So much so, he'd wanted to convince me that the place he loved so much was real and worthy of relationships that mattered. My skepticism had bothered him. If I bothered him, then that meant he cared. About me. As an ethical journalist, I couldn't take advantage of that.

The first week back to school after break passed uneventfully, and I found myself tapping my toes until Friday rolled around. My goals for the evening were to fill in as much of my Carnivalesque map sketch as possible. I'd already drawn the parade route with the Welcome Rooms that ran alongside it, the bumper cars exhibit, the Starlight Café adjoining the two buildings, the individual and group Welcome Rooms on the first floor, and the Milkshake Ballroom on the third floor. Kierk had mentioned the mechanical bull exhibit, a potato-sack slide, and—*cringe!*—the Tunnel of Love. Given the week off, who knew what new exhibits would be open at the carnival when everyone returned.

With my story deadline approaching, I still had several floors to explore—all the way up to the mysterious seven—and the many offshoots of the parade route. That in mind, I beat the crowd to the carnival, eager to get started. A new paintbrush icon on the map caught my attention. The corresponding description listed it as a craft room where attendees could paint their own masks.

That had been my idea!

Kierk had taken my idea to the committee. They must have spent the week off making the room a reality.

I hustled to the fourth floor to find a hallway similar to one in an office building. Maybe the space had been used as the factory offices once upon a time, not packed with masked carnival-goers squeezing past each other back then. Also, the strip of twinkle lighting along the baseboards was probably a new addition.

Crafty (and not-so-crafty) types filled the room. I paid ten bucks for a mask kit. Crossing the space to an empty table felt like traveling through a cloud of glitter. People threw it up into the air, allowing it to fall back down in even distribution on their masks, the wet paint catching the sparkles. I imagined Dinah honing that maneuver in her bedroom to create my Christmas present. I spied over shoulders and estimated about half of the masks could pass for actual masks on the walls of the Welcome Rooms. The other half...not so much. None of them were as gorgeous as my best friend's creation, a realization that sent pride soaring through me. If only she were here to enjoy it. Maybe after her parents read my article about the carnival, they would let her come.

But by then I wouldn't be welcome back.

I claimed a spot with a variety of paints, brushes, and glitter. Close proximity to the other artists could mean new sources.

During an hour of painting my mask, I interviewed three different couples and a group of guys who wanted me to join them at the parade. I politely declined and recorded everything I could remember in my tiny notebook under the table after they left.

When I was close to finishing my mask, another girl sat across from me. She was alone, too. As she worked, we chatted. She painted her mask a light pink, adding bright, glittery pink vertical stripes, each outlined in silver glitter. She finished it by outlining the eye holes with more silver glitter.

"That looks amazing," I told her.

"Thank you! I might paint another one. I'm kind of dodging my ex-boyfriend."

"No better place to dodge him than where you can change your outfit and mask."

"Yeah, but since we've been here so many times, our bands were linked. I filed to unlink them, but I'm not sure the request was processed yet. I had to sneak in here."

Linking bands? I'd never heard of that. Would Kierk and

I be linked? "How do you find out if you're linked to someone?"

"Scan your band at any tablet in the carnival. There's a little drop-down at the top right of the screen. You can search your links to see if they're here and, if they are, what room they're in."

Maybe that was why Kierk had told me to come find him the first night we'd met. He'd assumed I knew about the link.

"Excuse me," I said and headed for the wall-mounted tablet next to the door. I swiped my band and found the links the girl had mentioned. Sure enough, Kierk's name appeared. If I tapped it, I'd know where to find him.

My finger hovered. I shouldn't. I didn't want to be tempted to find him. Then again, I could use the information to avoid him and continue my observations and interviews.

"So cute that you're looking for me," someone whispered in my ear, and I jumped so violently I nearly knocked the tablet from its mount. Kierk laughed loud enough to catch the attention of everyone else in the room.

"Are you following me?"

"Actually no. Just got lucky," he said. "I'm here to check on the new exhibit. I walked by, and my name on the screen caught my attention. Green masks are kind of your thing, so I figured my mysterious carnival stalker had to be my pal Sparx."

"If your career in philosophy doesn't work out, might I suggest detective work?"

"Not sure that's actually a major, but I'll keep it in mind." His eyes twinkled through his usual red-and-black mask. "How do you like your exhibit?"

Heat flushed my cheeks.

"I won't lie. If I had your number, I would have called you over break to ask about your grand vision."

"That's why you would have called?"

He grinned, and I warned myself not to flirt. No guarantee I could handle the result.

"You hungry?" he asked.

"Always."

He gestured to the door.

"Wait. Real quick first—do you know how to unlink someone's band?" If anyone had the power to do it at the carnival, it would be Kierk.

"I do," he said slowly. "Were you trying to unlink with me?"

My earlier warning not to flirt went ignored.

"Feeling a little insecure?" I asked.

He pursed his lips and looked away.

"Okay, I quit," I said with a laugh. "Just teasing. It's for a friend, actually."

I pointed to the girl who had sat near me and explained how she was hiding out to avoid her ex. Kierk took in the information with a serious expression, nodding at all the right moments.

"It shouldn't take that long," Kierk said. "That's something we'll have to fix. Thanks for telling me."

"Can you help her?"

"Sure."

I introduced them, and within minutes, she had been unlinked from her boyfriend and free to move around the carnival however she wanted. She thanked Kierk and hugged him. I waved to her and looped my arm in his.

"You're a hero," I said.

"Don't patronize me, Sparx," he teased and led us to Little NOLA for our usual bag of beignets.

"How do you keep changing everything?" I asked him while licking powdered sugar from my fingertips. "Aren't you afraid you'll run out of ideas? Or money?"

I'd promised myself no more questions, but I found everything so fascinating.

"Money? No. We started at relatively low cost and work quite a bit on the barter system. Then there are our investors and the profit from entrance fees, entry games, and food and merchandise sales. Ideas are a little more complicated, but we have something cooking to keep them flowing, too."

"At the risk of drinking the Kool-Aid, it's all kind of amazing," I said.

"I knew you'd see it my way eventually," he said. "Have you been to the Ropes Room?"

"That sounds creepy."

He laughed. "Probably not the best name, but I promise nothing nefarious."

One more X to mark on my map. "Lead the way."

TWENTY-TWO

THE ROPES ROOM was across the parade route, one of the side rooms I hadn't had the chance to explore yet. Inside, a massive ropes course soared toward the ceiling.

"That has to be two stories high," I said.

"Three."

We parted to be fitted for harnesses. My fitting included a pair of shorts to wear under my dress—Carnivalesque planners thought of everything.

My heart rate increased with each step we took toward the stairs that led up to the first level. Kierk fist-bumped the guy tasked with spacing out people entering. I was practically drooling and bouncing on my toes by the time they finished chatting, and we headed into the course.

"You know this is going to be a repeat of the bead tossing in the parade, right?" I said.

"How's that exactly?"

"I'm going to destroy you."

He laughed that beautiful laugh.

In the mysterious Carnivalesque way, the committee had hidden a prize somewhere in the course. Both Kierk and I had a starting clue, but we'd have to scavenge to find the others. We started in different locations and raced each other. I used my climbing skills to reach challenging leads and balance on tight ropes while Kierk wobbled and even slipped a few times.

"It's like you're not human," he called when I sped past him for my next clue.

"I'm a superhero in disguise, actually."

"I thought I was the superhero," he said, referencing his rescuing of my mask-making friend.

"Oh, Kierk. I was only humoring you," I corrected. "You're the sidekick."

He stumbled from laughing. Pride tickled at my edges.

I claimed the prize—a certificate for free beignets—from the apex of the course and held it high in the air. Kierk clapped obnoxiously.

To get back down, I flew across a zip line and fell into a cushy mat. Kierk followed my trail a few seconds later. We sprawled on the floor and hydrated.

"You have wicked core strength," Kierk said.

I nodded, not able to hide my smile. "Thanks. Special-ized workout."

"Top secret?"

I took another sip of water. "Rock climbing."

His eyes widened. "That's really hard."

"You climb?"

"I tried once. It was a disaster. I was sore for days."

My heart fluttered. Had he been with Darius the day I'd met him? I dug through my memories, trying to recall the image of the guys sitting on the mats and searched for Kierk's face—or the half of his face that I knew—but I couldn't place him. Back then, he hadn't even been a face in a crowd. Now, he was…Kierk.

He finished his water and tossed the bottle into the recycling bin. "You up for another adventure?"

I stretched my arms above my head and thought about all the notes I'd have to make sense of in my tiny notebook. "Actually, I'm a little tired."

"Oh," he said, his shoulders slumping. "You don't want to watch the parade?"

"The parade's great and all, but there are so many people and it's so loud all the time."

"I know a quiet place," he said.

He stood up and reached for my hand. I could go home and call it an early night, but I still had a story to write. I reached for Kierk's hand, and he pulled me to my feet with such force I fell forward against him. We both laughed it off, but my fingers tingled from where I'd touched his chest.

Tingles didn't lie.

He led me through the crowds and across the parade route to the main building.

"Don't get me wrong," I said. "I appreciate the perpetual-tour-guide routine, but aren't you supposed to be working?"

"I am working." He opened a door and guided me into the employee hallway, away from the hordes of people.

"I get that, but I've lured you away…" I tried to count the number of times in my head. "…a lot. Aren't you going to get in trouble?"

"I'm what you call a floater. I help wherever we need it, but most of my work happens during the day."

"What do you do during the day?" I asked, curious about how the carnival appeared in the daylight.

"Setup. Teardown. Inventory. Scheduling."

"So, you're basically the manager of the carnival?"

He tipped his head side to side as if considering this. "I suppose you can say I'm one of them."

That made me feel even worse about all the information I'd mentally recorded for my article in his presence. Even after vowing to stay away and find a different source, there I was, spending all my time with him—again. Maybe I was the vampire journalist Dinah had pegged me as after all.

We got to the elevator the same time as two girls in short skirts and tall masks. They pressed the button for the third floor, and up we went. They got out, and Kierk hit the *Door Close* button. A tiny silver key appeared in his hand, and he turned it below the panel of buttons. We started going down but didn't stop at the first floor.

"There's a basement?" My heart had never known a beat so fast. There weren't seven floors to fill in on my map. There were *eight*!

"You wanted something quiet."

I squeezed his hand and hugged him until he laughed.

The doors opened to a dimly lit room that smelled of old books, leather, and, unfortunately, coffee. Shelves lined every wall, and seating areas with small Tiffany lamps were nestled throughout. I counted six other people as far as I could see. They were curled up on leather chairs and couches, sometimes nuzzling fuzzy blankets and holding steaming mugs, and they were all reading.

"There's a coffee bar over there." He pointed to the corner of the room. "It also has hot chocolate for those patrons with coffee aversions."

"This is amazing."

"I can give you your own key if you want."

"Seriously?"

He shrugged. "Sure. You've put up with me for this long, you should at least get a few perks out of it."

"I think I already have," I said—and hearing the words replay, cringed at the awkwardness. They could mean so many things. Kierk seemed confused at how to respond, too, so he continued with the highlights of the room.

"Feel free to grab a drink, a book, and a blanket. Find a spot to curl up and even sleep if you want. Your call. I'll be back to check on you in a bit."

"You're not staying?"

"Do you want me to?"

My gaze caught his, and for a moment, the masks were gone. In the silence of the room, I heard my heart. I heard his, too. I'd asked for quiet. I'd wanted to be alone. I should have told him to go so I could spend the evening working through my notes, maybe even writing a lead for the story and piecing together a few paragraphs. But then I thought of him leaving, and my heart twisted. If I asked him to stay, it could mean something. It *would* mean something.

"Yes," my mouth said before I could stop it.

He smiled. Like, really smiled. Like, full-blown, massive wattage, the room-was-no-longer-dim smiled.

My chest swelled until it couldn't fit in my body anymore. In danger of floating away, I avoided the power of his gaze while we grabbed drinks—water for me, coffee for him. He steered me toward the philosophy section.

"I thought since you'd read Bakhtin…" His voice trailed off. "You want to read something else?"

"No. I'm curious though."

"About?"

The question tickled the tip of my tongue, but I wasn't sure if it was okay to ask.

"What is it?"

"If this isn't okay, tell me, but I was curious if your name comes from Kierkegaard?"

His eyes twinkled.

"Not trying to invade your privacy or whatever. But

you're into philosophy, and Kierkegaard or Kierk—not really common names."

He nodded slowly. "This is dangerously close to talking about our outside identities."

"Yes," I said.

"Do you want to go there?"

The question felt weighted. If I said yes, then I was agreeing to something more with Kierk, something I probably wasn't equipped to agree to.

"I'll think about it," I said.

"Okay. You still want me to stay?"

"Sure," I said lightly as if the moment were carefree.

He scooped up a couple books and found an empty corner with an imposing but well-worn leather sofa. We took turns glancing at the couch and each other. Should I sit at one end with him at the other? Should we sit in the middle together?

"You first," Kierk said.

I sat toward one side, but not so far that it screamed I wanted distance from him. He did the same. He schooled me on the qualities of Aquinas, Locke, and Descartes while we sipped our drinks. The ice water lowered the temperature in the room a few degrees, or at least it seemed that way.

"You cold?" Kierk grabbed a blanket from a nearby shelf before I could answer. He draped it over me, the softness caressing the bare skin of my arms and legs.

"This is amazing," I said with a laugh.

"You look cozy."

I lifted the blanket for him to join me. He looked warm and—as usual—very, very good. Being physically close to Kierk triggered alarms and alerts in my body that being close to anyone else, even Colin, never had. My brain disregarded each one of them.

He rewarded my silent invitation with the bold smile

that I was beginning to think was reserved only for me, a revelation that set off more alarms.

Kierk slid closer under the blanket and raised his arm to the back of the couch. I reciprocated by sliding against him. His arm fell around my shoulders. I moved closer until my weight pressed against the warmth of his body.

"Is this okay?"

"Yes," I whispered.

He pulled me even closer to him and gave a small sigh as if relieved our bodies had found each other's edges so perfectly. I'd given in to my desire to be close to Kierk, and it felt so good to let go of every reason I'd had to stay away. I didn't even mind that he smelled like coffee.

He read me some of his favorite passages, and I fell asleep to the sound of his voice.

TWENTY-THREE

I PREPPED extensive notes about my carnival experiences for our Monday pitch meeting to show Lola that giving me a few more weeks would mean a better story. One with the depth of detail that would ensure every student in the school hung on each word. A story that I could actually make happen if I stopped spending my evenings in the carnival drooling on Kierk's chest.

When I'd woken up, his cheek had rested against the top of my head. A barely there snore had gurgled from his throat. His warm body had cradled mine, and the fuzzy blanket had cradled us both.

The moment—and the tugging and twisting it had evoked in my insides—had told me the web of trouble surrounding me was massive and growing so fast everything in its wake was in danger, including my journalism career.

Back in the newsroom, though, I wasn't Sparx, the masked mystery girl who'd flirted and snuggled with Kierk, the masked mystery boy. I was Mackenzie Davis. Reporter, writer, aspiring Northwestern journalism student.

"The story's going to be amazing," I told Lola, out of earshot of the rest of the staff.

"Better be," she said, not looking up from the pile of papers on her desk. "You've pursued it for weeks."

"What's a few more if it means getting it right, then?" Mrs. Graham interjected over Lola's shoulder.

My melodramatic editor sighed. Loudly. "Fine. A few more weeks."

"Definitely," I said. "Mardi Gras at the latest."

"Mardi Gras is, like, five weeks away. That's not a few more weeks."

"Sure it is," I countered. "And it's Mardi Gras. At the carnival. The wait will be worth it."

I pressed the issue partially because I couldn't imagine not being at Carnivalesque for Mardi Gras.

"I'm marking the calendar," Lola said.

"Mark it."

Lola opened her mouth to say something—probably something I didn't want to hear—but the chaos from the rest of the staff piling into the journalism lab intensified, demanding her attention.

"Turn it down, people," she shouted.

Dinah and I curled up on the couch, reminding me of the last time I'd curled up with someone. I'd planned to tell Dinah about it over s'mores the past weekend, but she'd changed our sleepover plans to hang with Todd and some friend he thought I should hook up with. Cue the eye roll.

The guys had left at eleven to go to a different party although Todd had known Dinah wasn't allowed. Dinah had gotten out the good ice cream and eaten her feelings while I'd walked the line between supporting her over video chat and lobbying how her boyfriend did not deserve her and she should dump his ass. Throwing in a romantic story about snuggling with Kierk hadn't quite fit the narrative.

In the meeting, Lola led a discussion about story ideas and assignments. Dinah's phone beeped. Twice. Lola stopped writing on the board, and her shoulders rose and fell with a deep breath. It beeped again.

"Everything okay?" I whispered, leaning toward Dinah to get a glimpse of her phone.

She turned the screen so I couldn't see it. "Fine."

Unconvinced, I watched her read the texts. She closed her eyes.

"Dinah?"

She shook her head, grabbed her things, and rushed out of the room. The meeting continued. I waited for Dinah to come back, but she didn't. When Lola wasn't looking, I slid sideways through the crowd, tugging my phone from my bag to call my best friend. It wasn't like her to bail on a meeting. I called her again.

On my third try, the ringing echoed through the halls. I picked up the pace toward the sound and found my best friend in the teacher's lounge, crying. I sat next to her, and she buried her head into my shoulder. "He wants me to go to the carnival with him. He's been asking, and I've said no every time."

"Todd goes to the carnival?"

"Every weekend."

Sometimes I thought of the chaos in my mind like the mission control room in *Apollo 13*—one of my dad's favorite movies: everyone rushing around, busy, too many details for there to ever really be silence. But in that moment, it was like when Tom Hank's character realized the life-saving oxygen the crew needs was venting into space. The control room went completely silent while there was a collective, "Oh, crap."

"I didn't know that," I managed.

"He's on the committee," she said quietly. "But please don't tell him I told you that!"

Todd Wilkinson on the committee? The revelation plummeted the committee's reputation.

"For what?"

"Carpentry, since he takes shop classes. He helps them build stuff."

My heart stopped. "Does he know I'm working on this story, Dinah?"

"No. I promise, Mac. I would never—"

My body sank with relief, and I raised my hands to stop her. "I know. Thanks for not telling him."

"He asked what you were up to a few weekends though."

If Todd found me at the carnival, then my time there would be cut short.

"I've been so embarrassed to even tell you. He comes over for a little while, but then he leaves and goes to the carnival. I'm such an idiot. I think he's gonna stay, and then he doesn't. And I fall for it every time."

"D…" I said, not wanting to pile on by agreeing and saying even worse things about her slimy boyfriend.

"I think he likes someone there," Dinah said, fresh tears falling. "The only way I'll know for sure is to disobey my parents and go with him."

"First of all, if he likes someone else, he is a loser who has no idea what a good thing is," I told her, but in the back of my mind, I reminded myself he'd been with Dinah longer than three months. That had always been his end point before, but he'd never been with Dinah before. Completely ignoring my best friend bias, I had no qualms arguing Dinah rocked every girlfriend category. Gorgeous—obviously. With long, light brown hair, she was beautiful in a quintessential, sweet way. Nobody could rival her loyalty or her honesty, and that included to her parents. If they didn't want her to go to the carnival, going was out of the question. "Do you want to go?"

"I'd have to lie to my parents," she said as if that was all the answer I needed, and knowing her, it was.

Suddenly, Kierk's point about privacy rang a little too true. Dinah's parents didn't allow her the privacy of the carnival, yet Todd had as much privacy as he wanted. I could have passed him at the carnival—he could have been the guy making out with a masked girl in the elevator right next to me for all I knew. Even if I wanted to keep an eye on him at Carnivalesque, I wouldn't know where to start.

"Guys suck," she said.

But not all guys. Kierk's masked face flashed in my mind, reminding me of those little sparks I'd felt when we'd snuggled and he'd read his favorite passages of philosophy. When he'd laughed that delicious, beautiful laugh, it had reminded me that a relationship could be more than comfortable. Dating Kierk would be more than what I'd had with Colin. Of that, I had no doubt.

"I'm sorry I didn't tell you about Todd being on the committee," Dinah said. "I've been an awful friend."

"No. You wanted to respect his privacy. I get that."

"Respect. Too bad it only goes one way." She closed her eyes and sighed. "I can't believe Todd gave me an ultimatum."

I hugged her.

"Over some stupid carnival!" She pointed at me. "I'm glad you're writing the article. All his friends go on about how hot the girls are. It's like *The Bachelor* with extravagant experiences and celebrations—a totally unrealistic way to date someone, but exciting or whatever."

Exactly what I'd told Kierk. The carnival world wasn't real. Neither were the experiences. As a result, people created unrealistic expectations for themselves *and* their relationships.

Thousands of high school and college kids went to the carnival every weekend, but the thought that Todd roamed the halls warned me my time was limited. Realistically, my mask would protect me, but as I'd argued many times, nothing at the carnival was real. Todd probably knew Kierk. Todd and I could run into each other, but even with a covered face, I was easily recognizable. Few people had strawberry blond spiral curls like I did. If Todd recognized me, any aspirations I had of writing about the carnival would be destroyed. Along with anything—real or fantasy —between me and Kierk.

TWENTY-FOUR

I RODE the trolley to the carnival Saturday night with a group of guys who talked way too loudly.

"Whoever thought of putting masks and hot outfits on girls was totally brilliant," one of them said. "I'll pay whatever they ask to come here every weekend."

"Last weekend," another chimed in, "there was this girl in a mini dress dancing up on me." He bowed his head and shook it like he was too overwhelmed to even continue speaking.

"Nobody was dancing up on you," one of his friend's teased.

"I'll show you tonight," he said. "I'll find..."

No interest in what he planned to find, I tuned them out. These were the kinds of guys Kierk insisted I could develop something real with? Or was that all a ruse because he believed I could develop something real with *him* if I gave it a chance? My head spun from all the questions—questions I'd have to leave unanswered.

At least until I finished the pieces I needed for the article.

That meant no Kierk tonight.

Fifteen minutes later, I had changed into a black cock-tail dress and a blue silk mask edged with sequins and feathers. Blue, not green. The mask may have been differ-ent, but my red curls, bold and flowing, dominated the look. I braided the top half to calm down the volume but wasn't sure that was enough. I swung by the store to grab a few blue hair pieces and wove the colorful strands in my braid, toning back my red hair and brightening my vibe. I barely looked like myself and looked more like me than I expected to at the same time. I checked my appearance once more in the mirror. Disappointment creeped through me at the thought that Kierk wouldn't see me in the look. The fact I wouldn't see him sent yearning through me. I had to focus on my article, and once that was done, I could figure out Kierk.

I let the Welcome Room door close behind me. For the next hour, I interviewed as many people as I could by care-fully sparking a conversation, and then when I felt confident they were cool with it, I'd ask if I could quote them for something I was writing for school about the carnival—technically not a lie. They all agreed, and my notebook filled with more stories and quotes about the carnival than I'd ever be able to use.

From the top of the grand staircase in the Milkshake Ballroom, I watched the dancers below turn, twist, and laugh. I closed my eyes and let the music flow through me. My stomach grumbled, so I bowed my head and decided one last visit to the Starlight Café was in order. I ordered a sandwich the size of my head. With no empty tables, my only option was to invite myself to sit with someone else.

Two girls slumped into one of the outdoor couches around a welcoming fire pit. The couch was big enough for one more, so I introduced myself as Gina—the cover I'd used all night. Their names were Chanel and Steel. At first glance, I pegged them as pretty, friendly, and exhausted.

"Sit with us," Steel said.

They pushed aside their food to make more room on the table.

"Thanks."

"Is that the Capri sandwich?" Chanel asked.

I nodded.

"I had it last weekend. It was delicious!"

"This whole place is so Mediterranean," Steel said. "Makes me think of summers with my grandparents."

"Your grandparents live in the Mediterranean?" I asked, cutting my massive sandwich in half.

"No. They took me there for vacation. Monaco was my favorite."

Kierk had nailed the ambiance so accurately that people who'd spent time in the region felt at home. My lips curled in pride.

"Do you come here a lot?" I asked them.

"Any time we can!" Chanel said. "Guys are so much sexier in masks."

Steel laughed. "Agreed."

"And you can hook up without judgment or expectations," Chanel added—definitely a point to add to my article, possibly exploring the social judgments and expectations that come with hooking up with a person outside the carnival.

"Do you ever wonder what they'd look like without them?" I asked.

"Terrifies me to my core," Chanel said. "So I try not to find out." Steel high-fived her.

The girls chatted about the food, the entertainment, the guys, the clothes. I took a few more bites of my sandwich, glad my interviews were finished and I could sit and enjoy.

Steel pointed across the café. "Perk up, Chanel. Incoming."

Three guys approached from the funnel cake booth, carrying a stunning temptation with powdered sugar, straw-berries, and whipped cream. I was able to place Harvey—with his flirtatious grin, dark skin, and muscular arms—and Kierk, next to him. They tended to be a package deal.

My heart soared. I'd get to say goodbye after all.

"How's it going, ladies?" Harvey asked, setting the funnel cake in front of them. "I brought you something."

Chanel and Steel smiled at his gesture and tore off tiny pieces while I studied the guy behind Harvey. He squeezed himself next to Chanel and put his arm around her waist. In one movement, he pulled her toward him. I'd seen him pull that move a million times before. At the lunch table. At the movie theater. Even in my own living room.

Of course, every other time, it had been directed at my best friend.

"I have to go," I said, jumping to my feet. "Nice meeting you all."

I coughed while I spoke, hoping to cover the sound of my voice, but Todd was too immersed in Chanel's eyes to notice me.

"You, too, Gina," Steel called.

I glanced over my shoulder once more to confirm the guy with his lips on Chanel was in fact Todd Wilkinson. My chest burned for Dinah, and tears clouded my limited vision from the mask's glimmering eye holes. The thought of telling her…the thought of *not* telling her… I needed air.

I pushed through a door and found myself on a patio open to the elements and far from the system of heaters Kierk had devised. It felt as frigid as expected on a western Pennsylvania winter night—like the slap in the face I needed. I should have confronted him right there. Why had I run? To protect myself and my story? What about protecting my best friend? I leaned against a metal railing and let the tears fall.

"Gina?"

I shot upright.

"Sorry. I thought you were someone else."

Kierk. I'd totally forgotten he'd been at the table, too. I slid my fingers under my mask and wiped away tears, not that he could probably see them anyway, then turned to face him with the fakest smile I'd ever sent in his direction.

"Kierk, it's me, Sparx."

He hugged me. "Thought so. You looked different, but still like you."

"What I was going for," I lied.

"Is everything okay? You really ran out of there. Unless you don't want to talk about it. Don't feel like you have to tell me anything."

Kind of ironic, considering how little I had told him. I'd never been honest with him. Given Todd's dishonesty, that revelation had me feeling like the biggest jerk ever. I didn't want to lie to Kierk, but the truth didn't exactly bubble in my throat either.

I rubbed the cold away from my arms, unable to look at him. Silence grew between us as if every benign comment we could make would be a burst of air blowing up the massive balloon of tension.

"What are you up to tonight?" he asked.

Oh, finding people to interview to reveal the inner workings of the carnival for a newspaper article you'd never sanction.

"I was hungry. Hadn't gotten further than that."

"I didn't realize you knew Chanel and Steele."

"Just met them, actually."

He nodded. "Oh."

More silence.

"Is everything okay?" he asked.

"Totally."

"I know we got kind of close last week in the library, but if that makes you uncomfortable, we can forget it happened." His lip twitched, making me wonder if he meant what he'd said. And making me hope that he didn't.

"Just like that?"

"It's Carnivalesque. Anything is possible."

Maybe for him. I'd spent the entire week replaying what it had felt like to fall asleep in his arms. "Just a harmless snooze, right?" I suggested, even though I didn't believe that for a second.

Nothing about my feelings for Kierk had felt harmless.

His gaze intensified as I stood on a tightrope above a bubbling volcano. I could tell him right there. I could admit our time in the library had been more—at least for me.

Despite the fantasy of the carnival, falling asleep in his arms had sparked feelings that felt so real. Of course, if by some stretch they were real and Kierk and I had a chance, then my article loomed, eager to destroy that chance.

Either way, I couldn't be with Kierk. Ever.

"Right." He pressed his lips together and nodded. "Good thing because I have big plans to find you someone worthy tonight."

"What plans?"

"The reel?"

The thought of all the spinning threatened the Capri sandwich in my stomach. "I just ate."

"Point taken."

"What about the maze? We haven't done that yet," I said.

That delicious grin of his appeared. "I don't think you're quite ready for the maze."

"I'll take your word for it."

"One of these times though."

But time was running out.

I shivered at the same moment a massive, floor-length winter coat draped over my shoulders. "Where'd this come from?"

"We have a closet over there for anyone who needs them." Kierk tilted his head toward an open door and tied the coat at the front. "Better?"

I found myself looking into those genuine eyes of his. They moved closer. My hands pressed against his chest. When my gaze fell on his lips and refused to move, I knew I was in more trouble than I thought.

TWENTY-FIVE

WITH ME LEANING against Kierk on the cold balcony, the week could have passed. The year, even.

I shook myself back to reality and gently pushed back from him. "Better. Thank you."

He cleared his throat. "Good. I've been thinking about our bet and how I can win it."

Win the bet? Wait. If I felt something real for him, then he'd win the bet. Were his flirtations a ploy to win? Maybe I'd been right to believe nothing in the carnival could be trusted. Sadly, not even Kierk.

I'd finished the interviews for my story, so the bet didn't really matter anymore. But how could I explain that to him?

"There is a thing, but only if you're ready."

"Sure," I said.

He glanced at his watch. "We might have just enough time to get there."

He took my hand, led me around the back of the building, through the float entrance, and across the massive, empty space that housed the nightly parades. "Not sure if you know this, but for centuries, men and women trusted their gut instincts about love. They might attend a celebration at court and perhaps even be masked like we are tonight. Across the room, they'd lock eyes with someone. They'd talk, flirt, dance. It was that easy for them to fall hopelessly in love and marry immediately after."

"Seems a bit rash," I said.

"In our contemporary context, sure. But for them, no. They married young."

It sounded romantic and idealistic, but I wasn't convinced it would win him the bet. "How's that relevant to what we're doing?"

He winked. "We're going to a ball at the King's Court. I hope your food has digested enough for you to dance."

We found our way to the back of a short line, relatively speaking by Carnivalesque standards. While we waited, my date master explained I'd go into a fancy version of a woman's locker room, answer a series of questions on a touch screen, and then change my clothes to a specific costume based on the result.

"Aren't I already in costume?"

"Not one appropriate for the eighteenth-century French court."

"You're not serious."

"I am."

"Are you going to wear one of those weird white wigs?"

"And cover up these gorgeous locks? No."

I laughed out loud. "I've never known you to be so vain."

He offered a combination smirk/shrug that oozed appeal. As usual. It made me think of what Chanel and Steele had said. Was Kierk without the mask attractive? Or was it his carnival identity that gave him the confidence and swagger?

A question I'd never answer.

We scooted forward in the line. Only a handful of people waited ahead of us, so Kierk talked fast.

"Not sure if your high school did this, but the King's Court exhibit essentially relies on a matching software."

"Like student council does on Valentine's Day?"

"With the questionnaires?"

I nodded.

"That's it. You'll be matched to three other carnival-goers based on how you answer your questions. When you leave the dressing room, you'll be assigned three dance part-ners. They're your 'matches.'"

"Meaning?"

"If you like one of them, you exchange an invitation to meet somewhere else in the carnival."

"Like a date?"

"Exactly."

So the carnival was also a matchmaking service. Maybe Dinah had been on to something with her comment about the carnival being like *The Bachelor*.

"We have space for two more," a guy called from the front of the line.

The group in front of us, which had way more than two, wanted to stay together, so Kierk's hand shot up, and he pulled me to the front of the line. As we went our separate ways to dress and take the matching quiz, he winked.

I had this overpowering urge to grab his arm and pull him back to me. How had everything gotten so compli-cated? I was in this bet with Kierk to find something real in the carnival, and I couldn't even figure out if the feelings I'd had in quiet moments with *him* over the last few weeks had been real. The thought of starting that process over again with a stranger exhausted me. And what was the point? If I couldn't tell the difference with Kierk, how could I be expected to tell the difference with someone else?

And if I couldn't make sense of any of this in my own head, how could I possibly articulate it in an article that would become the clip I needed to score a place in *The Herald*'s summer program? It was like deciding you were going to organize your T-shirt drawer: A simple, manageable task, but then somewhere along the way you started reorganizing every drawer, sorting clothes to donate, repositioning the furniture in your room, and for fun, adding in a massive scrapbooking project of every photo you'd ever taken your whole life. Convoluted. Messy. And totally confusing what you'd originally set out to do.

The opulence on the other side of the door—so grand I half expected Marie Antoinette to appear and powder my nose a pristine white—distracted me from my thoughts. The walls, chandeliers, drapery, and furniture were gold. Two rows of mannequins wore period clothing, and the masked women in contemporary cocktail dresses surrounding them painted a stark contrast.

"The King's Court and the dressing rooms were modeled after the Palace of Versailles," said a smiling door attendant wearing a low-cut dress that fanned out to either side. "You're our last one, so we'll go ahead and get started. Attention, everyone!"

At least fifty girls roughly my age huddled around her, listening to a version of the same instructions Kierk had given me. The dresses would be assigned after we took our matching quizzes, so we should get started on that first, she said.

Everyone took a tablet to type their responses, which was when it occurred to me that the tablets would have to be connected to the internet. I checked mine quickly—it was! As I answered the questions, I took screen shots and emailed them to my Jackie Goerman email. My heart raced. I looked over my shoulders. The other girls cooed over the details in the room design and chatted. I hit the Home button and searched for a camera icon.

Oh. My. Gosh.

I found a comfortable chair with a great view of the dresses and nonchalantly snapped a picture—making sure the flash was off first. The angle caught a glimpse of the upper part of the walls and ceiling, so no faces would appear in the photo.

Snap and email—pictures for my article complete.

"A few more minutes!" the room attendant called.

I quickly tapped choices for the questions, without even reading all of them. Another lie I'd have to tell Kierk. I dropped the pictures into the tablet's trash.

My heart didn't slow to a normal pace until I logged out of my email, cleared the history, and returned the tablet to the pile.

———

If the dressing room decor had been a ten, King's Court maxed at about two hundred. Clearly an impressive drama club or art club or both had been involved in designing and painting the walls with their high archways and even sparkling gold paint that gave the impression similar to the palaces I'd studied in an art history unit sophomore year. Sculptures, busts, mosaics, and a painting of cherubs, gods, and goddesses on the ceiling accentuated the decor.

The room attendant had assigned me a pale periwinkle dress with golden accents and a gold mask. No green, yet totally princess-worthy. I thought the golden tiara might have been a bit much…until I put it on my head. Where was my prince charming?

Giddy with the excitement I only felt at the carnival— like a five-year-old playing pretend—I found spot number twenty on the ballroom floor as the place filled with eigh-teenth-century aristocrats.

Like the French revolution had never happened.

The guys wore either tight full-length pants with jackets or white socks with tight pants that ended below the knees and, again, tight jackets. Everything was tight. And kind of delicious-looking.

With the epic skirt of my dress, I felt too wide to fit through a doorway. Contemporary guys did not want a girl to have hips three times the size of her actual body, but the creators of this exhibit had missed that detail.

One more look at the guys, and I desperately wanted to find Kierk in the room and laugh at his costume.

"Welcome, ladies and gentlemen. If you would please face the throne."

We all did, tentatively looking to our rights and lefts. I wondered who my first match would be.

"Ladies, bow to the gentleman on your right, and dance!"

The guy to my right had a buzz cut that I was fairly certain wasn't a popular look in the King's Court. He resem-bled the sun in his bright yellow suit and the shade with his cool demeanor. He took my hands and spun me around the floor awkwardly. So much for prince charming. He led with such jerky movements, I barely had the chance to think about where my feet were going or whether I could stay upright. He never spoke, only watched me with intense eyes and turned and dipped me so fast I was sure he planned to kill me with dizziness.

The announcer called the end of the dance, and we hadn't even exchanged names. Lucky that.

I repositioned to my mark—space twenty—and waited for my second match to find me.

He differed so much it was comical to think the software

had selected both partners for me. With dark curls enveloping his golden mask, he bowed and extended his hand. I slipped my gloved hand into his, and he pulled me toward him so quickly I thumped against his chest with a laugh. He smiled, and off we went. Any chance he got, he spun or lifted me, but unlike partner number one, his movements were so fluid I could have been twirling at a palace, with a royal.

"I'm Zag," he said.

"Sparx," I answered, and he lifted me into a spin.

"I like your laugh, Sparx."

"Thanks."

He let go of my hands and broke into the robot. When I laughed again, he bowed, and pulled into another dance.

"So laughing's your thing?" I asked.

"Laughing's everything."

The bell rang, and Zag grabbed his chest as if the timer had intentionally wounded him. I laughed as he'd expected me to and waved goodbye.

A hand reached for me as the bell sounded. Two spins later I recognized that smirk. "Kierk?"

TWENTY-SIX

KIERK GRINNED. "Well, I'll be. Sparx and I are a match."

"You did that on purpose!"

"I swear I didn't," he said, holding up his hand as if he were promising to tell the whole truth in a courtroom.

Even if he hadn't pulled strings in his Kierk way—which I was convinced he had—the computer had matched him with a profile I'd given zero thought to. This did not prove Kierk and I were a match.

We danced to the edge of the ballroom, and he led me to the refreshment table. I stole an appreciative glance at his tight clothes as he explained how he'd thought I might want a snack.

"You know me so well," I teased.

We took turns piling our plates with finger foods and bite-sized desserts.

"It was a risk," he said, "considering you just ate."

"That was, like, an hour ago." My protest fueled his laughter, and he dropped a bacon-wrapped scallop onto my plate.

"The selection's amazing." I held the scallop between

my teeth and pulled it from the toothpick with a groan. "How do they not make people pay to get in here?"

"Oh, we paid," Kierk said. "Or I did."

"You paid for me to get in?"

He shrugged like no big deal, but didn't that make it kind of like…a date?

"How much was it?" I asked.

"Taste the cheesecake, and give me your best guess."

Drizzled with strawberry sauce, the little squares screamed *expensive*.

"Do you want to talk about what upset you before?"

The memory of Todd and Chanel turned the dessert in my stomach. Guilt mixed with the acid there forming a dangerous concoction. How had I danced around the ballroom without thinking of my best friend and the impending doom hanging over her? On the other hand, if I stayed at the carnival forever, maybe I'd never have to tell her.

No. I had to. Somehow.

Maybe Kierk would have good advice, being a philosopher and all, but telling Kierk would be like blending my carnival and non-carnival worlds. Something I should have been particularly concerned about, yet my mouth opened and the words tumbled out. "I saw my best friend's boyfriend here with another girl."

"Wow." His hand paused with a bacon-wrapped scallop halfway to it. "You sure it was him?"

"Positive."

"And obviously your friend doesn't know."

"She suspects something, but no, she doesn't officially know. Yet."

"You plan to tell her?" His tone sounded accusatory.

"She's my best friend."

"I get that, but the carnival's about privacy."

I almost choked on a mini key lime pie. "You're not

seriously condoning her boyfriend cheating on her and using the carnival to do it? Isn't that the kind of thing that should piss you off?"

He shrugged. "Maybe."

"Maybe to the first question or the second?"

He scrunched his eyes closed as if doing so might help him remember which question came first. Or maybe he didn't want to answer at all. "The second."

I exhaled.

"This might not be what you want to hear…" he said.

I could have bet on that.

"But clearly your friend and this guy don't belong together. Otherwise, this wouldn't be happening."

"Obviously, but if I don't tell her, how will she know that?"

Kierk pointed to the exit as the crowds bottlenecked in that direction. "Sorry. Quick time-out. Tap your band and answer whether you'd like to see any of your matches again. I'll meet you outside the court."

I thought about my matches as I changed out of my Marie Antoinette garb and back into my black cocktail dress. One? No. Although the immediate rejection made me feel bad. A little. Two? Maybe. Could the ambitious-and-cynical parts of me work with someone who was always interested in a laugh? Then again, did my ambitious-and-cynical parts need exactly that?

Jeez. Was I actually considering dating any of these people? Ridiculous.

I decided to pass on all my candidates. If Zag invited me on a date, then I'd consider it, but I was"t going on a limb to invite anyone myself.

I found Kierk in the lobby finishing his appetizers.

"I made you a fresh plate," he said when he saw me. "Just in case."

"Thank you."

"You should tell your friend," Kierk said between bites of his chicken wing.

Being on the same page as Kierk brought me an eerie sort of calm. "Thanks."

I tapped my band on the screen, and an invitation appeared. "Look at that. Mystery Man Number Two would like to see me again."

"That's great," Kierk said in a way that had me questioning whether "great" was the best word choice. I considered challenging him on the lie, but something had shifted when I'd decided to invade Todd's carnival privacy and tell Dinah the truth. Yet another reminder that Kierk valued the world of the carnival over reality. And I didn't. It was a reminder of how fundamentally different we were. No manner of attraction or masquerading fun could change that.

"Are you gonna go?" he asked.

"Yeah," I said without a second thought. "That's the point, right?"

"I guess it is. What will you do?"

Kierk had always made our plans, so I hadn't thought of that. "You don't have a rock-climbing wall I haven't seen, do you?"

"No," he said, intrigue lacing the single word. "Would you like one?"

"That would be incredible. People would love it, don't you think?"

He smiled, but I couldn't tell how true it was. What was happening? Were we being friendly? Was he angry I'd planned to see another guy? Was he really considering building a massive exhibit based on the fact I wanted it?

"I'll take it up with the exhibit committee," he said, so I guessed so.

———

When the computer had prompted me with Zag's invitation, it had included a photo of him wearing a deep red mask and the description of his clothing—black shirt, black jacket, black pants. Very unlike the centuries-old getup he'd worn when we'd met. So no way was I prepared for the hotness that dripped from him as he waited for me at the elevators with a rose in his hand.

"You look like Damon Salvatore standing there," I said.

"Sparx!" He kissed my cheek and handed me the rose. "Funny you should mention that. I took an online quiz last week called *Which vampire are you?*"

"And…"

He looked appalled. "That's more of a second date reveal."

I laughed—as I'd tended to do with him for the whole five minutes we'd spent together. No matter how the evening went, I had no preconceived notions that Zag and I would be together in a month. Or in a week, even. All I wanted to keep straight in my head was the details of the experience, so I could write my article. After all, that was why I'd come to Carnivalesque, I reminded myself.

Given the distractions, the reminder was regularly necessary.

"Thank you for the rose. Where did you find one in the carnival?"

"I have my ways," he said with a wink. "Your message said you had something in mind for our *date*?"

Date. Right. That was what I was on. Deep breaths.

"Have you been to the roof?" I asked.

He held out his arm so I could loop my hand around it. "One of my favorite places. Shall we?"

Zag cracked jokes in the elevator, the subsequent

laughter calming my nerves. The crowds had already shifted to the factory building for the upcoming parade, so the hallways were mostly empty. On the roof, he draped his leather jacket over my shoulders, and we gazed at the stars. The sky sparkled like I'd never seen anywhere but the carnival.

The time I spent with Zag was fun, enlightening, and romantic, yet all I could think about was Kierk four floors below. Had one of his King's Court partners asked to see him? Had he said yes? Todd didn't leave my mind either. He was somewhere in the carnival with Chanel, while Dinah sat at home wondering if he was doing was she was afraid he was doing.

The bell rang for the parade. "Wanna head down and check out the floats?"

"I can't," I said.

Being part of the packed crowd on the parade floor had been on my list of must-do Carnivalesque experiences, but my best friend needed me more.

"There's actually somewhere I have to be."

TWENTY-SEVEN

AFTER I LEFT THE CARNIVAL, I parked outside of Dinah's house for an hour, working through what I should say. Two details stopped me from knocking on her door.

First, I'd never liked Todd. If she didn't want to believe me, she could simply chalk up my accusation to my disdain for her boyfriend.

Second—and the more selfish detail that I hated to admit —if she didn't believe me, then I was outing myself with Todd. He'd know I was at the carnival. He might figure out Mackenzie Davis was Kierk's friend Sparx. He'd assume I was working on a story because I was always working on a story. To spite me, he wouldn't stop digging until he had proof he could take to Kierk.

And then I'd be done with the carnival.

Dinah had been right, and I couldn't deny it now that I had everything I needed for my story. Losing my connection to the carnival meant losing Kierk. Spending time with Zag that night had made it clear—just because a guy was fun didn't mean he was Kierk.

After the hour sitting in the cold, I drove home and

climbed into bed.

———

Sunday I went to The Climb with my dad, courageously navigating the most complicated paths in the place. Then I avoided my best friend like the coward I was. I knew I had to tell her. That was the simple part. The complicated part was how to do it.

I continued lying to myself all day Sunday. Dinah was at church. She was busy. She was with her family. She didn't have time for me to ruin her life. I avoided like a true professional—all the way to Monday morning when my phone rang promptly at 8:00 a.m. A Pittsburgh number I didn't know lit the screen. The thought crossed my mind that it could be Kierk. Maybe. Somehow…?

"Hello?" I said tentatively.

"Hi. I'm calling for Mackenzie Davis."

"This is she."

"Good morning! This is Liz Valentine from *The Herald*."

I sucked in a breath, and the world around me stopped except for Liz's voice. She said words like "editorial team" and "love your story" and "are you interested?".

"We have some time with this," Liz continued. "We have a weekend special scheduled in about five weeks on regional attractions for our teen readership, and your pitch fit perfectly. Do you have any questions?"

Lots. How would Kierk react to seeing the story in print? Would I really be able to violate his privacy by writing it? Could I ever be considered professional again after even asking those questions…even to myself?

"I do, actually," I said, refocusing on Liz's voice and the opportunity I'd thought I'd wanted for months. Years, even.

"So far, my work at Carnivalesque has been observation-based. Given the private nature of the environment, I haven't openly interviewed an official source…"

My voice trailed off as I realized I didn't know how to frame the question I needed to ask.

"You're curious about our expectations regarding comment?"

Phew. There was a reason the woman was an editor. "Exactly," I said.

"I won't lie, Mackenzie. While much of the article could likely be observation-based, we will need comment from appropriate parties about what teens can expect there. But you have some time to work on that."

The enthusiasm in her voice annoyed me.

"So, are you interested?"

In a credit in *The Herald*? "Yes. Absolutely."

I'd be able to tell my dad his daughter was about to be published in a major newspaper as a high school student. And see the look on Lola's face. But the enthusiasm didn't quite overflow. An image of Kierk in his black-and-red mask, with his heart-crushing smile, filled my vision.

"Mackenzie, one more thing," Liz said.

"Yes?"

"There's no guarantee, of course, but this assignment could be a stepping stone for a wonderful summer program we run for teen journalists. You remember me talking about that when I visited the school, right?"

"I do," I said as if that had been the first I'd heard of it. As if I hadn't been counting down the years until I could apply. As if the last few months hadn't been completely consumed by finding the perfect article that would score me a spot in that very program.

"I read your award-winning story from last year, and I think you have real talent. I'm rooting for you."

TWENTY-EIGHT

I THOUGHT it was safe to say that both my professional compass and my moral compass might have been broken. I'd accepted an assignment to write an article for *The Herald* that would violate the trust and friendship between Kierk and me, and I still hadn't told my best friend that I'd seen her boyfriend kissing another girl.

After school I packed up my things and hurried to Dinah's locker, but she wasn't there. Part of me viewed it as a sign that now wasn't the time to tell her. Another part of me said, *You know where she lives.*

I drove the few miles to her house rehearsing what I'd say. I wouldn't back down. I'd break the news. She'd believe me. I'd hold her while she cried. We'd get some ice cream. She deserved to know.

Her parents' cars were gone. Good. Some privacy. I rang the bell, and she threw the door open.

"Hey! I wasn't expecting you. Come in."

I followed her to the kitchen. Slices of bread covered the center island. She scooped peanut butter onto half of them.

"What are you doing?"

"Church youth group tonight. I'm in charge of sandwiches. Wanna help?"

"Sure," I said. She had somewhere to be. I couldn't drop news like this when she couldn't spend the evening crying into her ice cream.

She passed me the jelly. I dropped dollops onto my slices. She slammed the knife down, and I jumped.

"I have to tell you something," she said, although I was pretty sure that should have been my line. "Todd told me he loves me."

I gaped at her rosy cheeks, bright eyes, and brilliant smile. "When?"

"Yesterday. We went out to dinner, and he told me after the appetizers."

"Oh."

"I know, right!"

He'd made out with Chanel one night and then declared his love for Dinah. I couldn't let this go on any longer.

"Mac?"

"Huh?"

"You can at least pretend to be happy for me."

I put down the jelly. "No, I can't."

"I know Todd's not your favorite person, but you're my best friend, and—"

"He's cheating on you," I blurted out, at the same time that she said, "I'm in love with him."

We stared at each other. Dinah Zimmerman could not be in love with Todd Wilkinson. He didn't deserve that.

"What do you mean he's cheating on me?"

"I saw him at the carnival. With another girl."

"He didn't have his mask on?"

"No. He did, but I was a few feet away from him. I heard his voice. I recognized his body language. I know it was him."

"You don't know, Mac. You can't know."

"I've watched him grope you in public for months. I'm pretty sure I know what it looks like."

"He does not grope me in public."

"I didn't mean it like that, D. Listen, I know this has to be hard to hear."

"Hey, babe," Todd called from the entry hall. "I'm here."

Oh no.

Todd came into the kitchen. I mentally pleaded for her not to tell him what I'd said. I knew I should have been focused on Dinah's feelings, but if she told him, he'd know I was at the carnival. If Todd knew I'd been at the carnival, could he figure out why? And would he tell Kierk and completely blow my cover?

I'd taken a risk telling Dinah what she'd deserved to hear. I prayed she'd realize that and protect me in return.

"Mac tells me you were kissing some other girl at the carnival," Dinah blurted.

I pinched my eyes shut.

Todd slowly turned his gaze from her to me. "What the hell?"

"Is it true?" Dinah persisted.

"Of course it isn't true."

"It's true," I said.

He crossed his arms. "And when did this kissing allegedly happen?"

"Saturday night."

"He was with his sister Saturday night," Dinah said. "They went to visit his grandmother."

With Dinah's eyes on me, I snuck a look at Todd. The smug look on his face told me everything I needed to know. "If he's willing to lie to you about cheating on you, don't you think it's possible he lied about where he was going?"

"You're way out of line, Mac," he said. "I get that you're miserable over Colin dumping you, but you can't make everyone else miserable, too."

Oh no he didn't. "I am not miserable about Colin."

"Right," he said with a sad smile—a fake, sad smile that I wanted to slap off his fake face. "It's okay, Mac. I forgive you for this."

"*Forgive* me? Are you serious?"

"We have to get to church," Dinah said. "Mac, maybe you should go?"

I should go? The best friend who'd told the truth and now had a target on her back?

"Fine, I'll go. But be careful, D." I turned to Todd. "And you…"

He looked at me with an icy glare.

"Tell Chanel I said hello."

A flinch in his jaw told me without a doubt the masked guy with his tongue down Chanel's throat had been him.

TWENTY-NINE

TODD WAS SUCH A SNAKE.

My stupid headline voice was right. I was a snake in a Mardi Gras mask. I lowered my head into my hands. How could I hurt Kierk the way Todd was hurting my best friend? I sorted through my notes for the article, and no matter how I pieced together the details, I couldn't write a story without him being part of it.

I needed more from the carnival, and if I could manage to be brave enough, I had to tell Kierk the truth.

Friday night, I stepped off the trolley more nervous than I'd been since my first time at the carnival. I bought a bag of beignets when the line was short and ate them while walking a few laps around the buildings, taking in details I might have missed before and diving into the privacy of Welcome Rooms to record tidbits on my tiny notebook.

When I passed the King's Court, I watched couples flirt in the same places I'd stood with Kierk. Where he'd given me a fresh plate of food. Where we'd waited to see if any of my matches wanted to see me again. Where I'd left him to go date Zag.

I felt the square notebook through the light fabric of my dress. No matter my hopes with Kierk, I'd created the perfect storm of doom for us.

"Sparx!"

The sound of my name made me jump. I looked up to find Kierk walking toward me. I could tell him now. I could end things. I could walk away.

"I've been looking for you everywhere." He looked around as if expecting someone to appear. "You waiting for Zag?"

"No."

Even Kierk's mask couldn't contain the wonder of his smile, which convinced me walking away from him would be harder than ever. "You have a second to come with me?"

"A second?" I teased.

"Might be a little longer than that."

I stood, ignoring the thoughts urging me to work on my article or tell Kierk the truth. "Sure. We off to the parade?"

"You could say that."

Yet he led me in the opposite direction, and when we rounded on the bank of elevators, he pressed the Up button. The parade wasn't up.

"Where are we going?"

"It's a surprise."

The elevator opened, and he pulled me inside. He bounced on his toes, unable to stand still for a second.

"Must be a good surprise," I said.

"You have no idea."

I laughed and rested my hands on his shoulders. "Stop bouncing. You're shaking the entire elevator."

The elevator dinged what seemed like 7,088 times louder than it normally did. Kierk gestured for me to exit first. He tapped his band next to a door with an image that could only be for a maze, and the intrigue was nearly enough to supplant the awkwardness hovering around me like an aura. Almost.

"You're finally bringing me to the maze?" My voice sounded normal. I think.

"The maze is great, but no. To get where we're going, we have to go through the maze. So, close your eyes."

"What?" I laughed.

"No peeking."

I obliged, and he pulled me straight, then to the right. Straight some more. Left. Straight. Then he spun me until I giggled, and it continued like that. A beep told me he'd tapped his band to open another door. Cool air greeted us.

"Can I open my eyes yet?"

"Not quite."

We took a few more steps.

"Are we outside? Is this a balcony? Are you going to throw me off?"

Kierk pressed my hand against his chest. "I'm hurt. Don't you trust me?"

"Of course I trust you." Talking about trust with Kierk squeezed my chest as if it were a sponge.

"You can open your eyes now."

Surrounded on both sides by windows, the darkness of the forest was even more pronounced. Beyond the reflections of fluorescent lights on the glass was nothing but trees and night sky. He tapped his band to open a door at the end of the skywalk. "This…is the best view in the house."

The cold air and the epic noise that greeted us told me without a doubt where we were: the factory building. I'd seen the skywalk that joined the two buildings every time I'd entered Carnivalesque, but I'd never imagined how high it must have connected with the factory. We stood on a large balcony that was closer to the ceiling above than the floor below.

Straight ahead were a series of hand holds that made me feel at home.

"Surprise," Kierk whispered.

"A climbing wall is part of the parade tonight?" I couldn't believe it.

"Yep. From what I understand, they're lead climbing—not that I know what that means."

The wall was wide enough that the three climbers could traverse without getting too close to each other, and the large balcony below would serve the belayers well. Above the wall was another balcony, much closer to the ceiling, and it seemed that was where climbers would top out. My heart jumped at the height. And the noise. And the spectacle.

"How did you—?"

"You wouldn't believe it if I told you," he said. "It's totally safe, and we have some professional climbers for the parade."

"Professional climbers?" I didn't even realize how much I'd wanted to be out there until he'd made it clear I was only there to watch.

"They're wearing glow-in-the-dark outfits with lights sewn into them. For a few minutes during the parade, we'll dim the lights and the ceiling will become the show. It's gonna look amazing."

"Sounds…great." Too great for me to stand on this balcony and watch.

Two climbers stepped into harnesses—white and lime green. They matched their costumes with the lights and the glow-in-the-dark patches Kierk had mentioned. I fantasized about dragging one of them out of there and taking his place. After the week I'd had with Todd and Dinah, a climb was the perfect medicine. Tomorrow I'd have to hit The Climb the second it opened.

"They're total professionals," Kierk said. "I mean, they'd have to be to make this climb, right?"

"I could do it." The words had leapt from my mouth without my mind's permission, yet I didn't regret them. I could do it. I'd bouldered every indoor rock wall in the city and wasn't a stranger to lead climbing either, although I didn't do it as frequently. When grown men collapsed against the mats in exhaustion, I scuttled around the walls and ceilings as their entertainment.

Kierk's expression showed a mix of pride and something else I couldn't recognize. Maybe smugness.

"You sure?" he asked. "Falling would kind of ruin the exhibit."

"You don't think I can do it? You've never even seen me climb." Or maybe he had. That was a revelation for another time.

Kierk reached into a closet off the balcony and pulled out a bright orange, glow-in-the-dark, light-up climbing suit. "I think we should probably change that."

I hugged the climbing suit to my chest. "You're not serious."

"Oh, I'm serious."

Adrenaline ripped through me, rockets shooting in all directions.

"You'd better get changed," Kierk said, pointing to the closet.

I ducked inside and tugged my dress off in seconds to

slip into the climbing outfit Kierk had given me. I pulled the snug one piece up over the front of my body, but my left arm kept getting tangled on the lights on the sleeve.

"You ready, Sparx?"

"No."

"We need to get going. The parade's about to start."

"One more sec." I tugged and managed to tighten the cord around my forearm even more.

"Sparx!"

"I need your help." If my body could have handled any more emotion or energy, it would have spiked out of control when Kierk's eyes landed on me. With one arm in the body suit, the other tangled up outside of it, it was hard to say how much he could see, but my bare back and the lace of my bra was definitely on the list. "I'm stuck in the cord for the lights."

"Oh."

His fingertips touched the bare skin of my shoulder and I shivered.

"Sorry. You must be freezing up here."

He worked quickly, twisting and turning the wire until my arm was free. He guided it into the sleeve and zipped the back of the suit. I turned, resting my hand on his chest, without any good reason other than I wanted to, and thanked him

"Kierk!"

Harvey's harsh voice sent us jumping apart yet again, Kierk muttering something I couldn't hear over the raucousness of my heart beating.

"You ready?" Kierk asked.

I nodded.

He laced his fingers in mine and didn't let go until I stood under my section of the wall. A familiar woman with perfect hair handed me a harness.

"I'm Barbie," the woman said. "I'll be your belayer. I'm assured you have significant climbing experience."

"Good luck, Sparx," Kierk said, stepping away. "I'll let you two get focused."

I nodded to him, replaying *Barbie's* voice in my head. When Kierk was out of earshot, I whispered, "Barb, is that you?"

She studied my eyes closely as if my name were written on the lids in eyeliner. I'd braided my hair again in my attempt to disguise myself from Todd, but Barb wasn't fooled. She looked around before whispering, "Mackenzie?"

I laughed, most of my anxiety from climbing a new wall with new routes in front of Kierk high above the ground with the most massive audience ever abating. "You're belaying me?"

"We thought it would be best to put the strongest belayer with the newest climber." She laughed. "Knowing it's you, I'm not so nervous anymore. Better news—you even have a liability waiver already on file."

"Look at my luck," I laughed.

"We do have you set up to top rope rather than lead since we didn't know your experience level."

The crowd below screamed, and the lights flickered. "That works for me. The parade's about to start," I said. "We'd better get into position."

"Are you sure you can climb with that mask on?" Barb asked. "Is it safe?"

"I'm so used to it, I forget I'm wearing it now."

"If you're sure," she said, adjusting her own mask.

"We'll be fine."

I knotted the rope into my harness, and Barb checked it for safety. We double-checked each other, our fingers confident yet also fumbling the slightest bit. To stay connected amid the noise, Harvey secured a communication device over my ear, the microphone close to my cheek.

"Can you hear me, *Barbie*?"

"Loud and clear, *Sparx*."

I bounced on my toes and studied the holds as I waited for the signal to start climbing. I wanted to grab the first one and get moving. Harvey flipped a switch on the back of my costume, and through the corner of my eye, I saw colorful twinkling lights that, had my suit been green instead of orange, would have made me look like a Christmas tree.

"Because of the balcony, the crowd below won't be able to see you until you've gained a little height on the wall," Harvey's voice said into my ear. "We have a couple minutes until the lights go out, so go ahead and get started!"

The moment I grabbed a hold marked with a glowing pink, a calm settled over me. I climbed, each hold like a step in my own personal maze. How could I, Mackenzie Davis, make my way across this massive wall? Which routes were suited to my height and strength? How could I live the beauty of the exhibit?

The answers came easily. I moved around the wall for several minutes before the lights in the factory dimmed and the crowd below erupted. The holds also glowed in the dark, and the two professional climbers and I moved around to a drummer's beat. Each note challenged us to stay within the rhythm.

One of the other climbers let his legs dangle, and the crowd played along. Their fearful gasps turned to laughter when he swung his legs back upward and continued his climb. His core strength had to be amazing.

The committee was smart to call the mini worlds within the carnival exhibits: we were living a work of art.

I stretched my forearm and fingers, then reached for a hold for more, communicating with Barb in my ear piece the whole time. I felt her moving below me, anticipating my fall path and knowing exactly where to stand so that I was safe. I zigged and zagged until with one final hold, I topped out and pressed a button that sent an orange light and whistle blaring to life. I signaled to Barb to bring me down and leaned back into the rope. Seconds later, I settled onto the balcony below, my arms burning from the workout and the adrenaline.

The climb might have exhausted me physically, but mentally it had rejuvenated me like every other exhibit in the carnival ever had. The parade. The bumper cars. The Scottish reel. So much passion and excitement, and Kierk had been a part of them all.

Kierk with his gorgeous abs and undeniable charm. He could spout philosophy and debate with me so easily. He loved a thrill and could also chill in the quiet of the basement library. He listened enough to me to create multiple exhibits based on my ideas.

He could be anything and everything all at the same time.

Barb's hand landed on my shoulder. "That was impressive, Sparx."

"Thank you," I said, eager to be free of the ropes and harness.

I thought of Kierk. His laugh. The way he made me giggle on the inside—and sometimes on the outside, too. His sense of adventure. The way we'd almost kissed in the parade, and how I'd wondered what it would be like to kiss him for real. How he was always there. How I always wanted him to be. And I couldn't wait anymore.

With the exhibit ending, the crowd of Carnivalesque staff hovered around on the balcony, clapping and cheering. I searched their faces for the one I wanted to see the most.

And naturally, he was there.

"That was ridiculous." His smile was as big as I'd ever seen.

I might have muttered my agreement. I might have even fallen into his arms. It didn't matter how I got there, only that when I pressed my lips to his, like so many things in the carnival…it was magic.

THIRTY

BEFORE I COULD SETTLE into the kiss, Kierk pulled away.

"Shit, Sparx." Kierk pulled me to the closet-sized room and helped me to a chair inside. "Your whole body's shaking."

"It's the adrenaline."

He nodded. "And the kiss…?"

His words stabbed me.

"Was because I wanted to."

With the parade noise muffled in the distance, we sat quietly, watching each other. As if he wanted me to say more. I, on the other hand, wondered why he was so far away, why he'd pulled away so quickly when I'd kissed him.

Had I made an absolute idiot of myself?

The privacy of the carnival felt particularly brilliant in that moment. I could change my mask and my dress and disappear to wallow.

"Kierk, the guys need the room to change," Harvey called from a crack in the door.

"I should go," I said.

"Are you feeling up to it?"

My hands shook so badly, I wasn't sure I could get my climbing suit off, let alone go anywhere on my wobbly legs.

Leaning on the strength of the chair, I stood and turned my back to him. "Can you unzip me, please?"

"Um…sure."

Every time his warm fingertips brushed my skin, my body betrayed me. The zipper caught.

"Sorry," he whispered. "I'm trying to do this with my eyes closed."

Well, hell. He didn't even want to see my bare back. "Harvey!"

The door opened. "Yeah?"

"Mind unzipping me?"

"It would be my pleasure, but…Kierk?"

"I can do it," Kierk said.

"You sure because—"

Kierk cut Harvey off. "I got it."

The zipper screamed its discontent over the situation, too.

"Thanks," I muttered.

The door closed behind Kierk, and I changed quickly, as if doing so could help me outrun my thoughts. Kierk had flirted with me. We'd almost kissed in the elevator. I couldn't possibly have read things so wrong. He'd created two exhibits for me. The climbing exhibit had to have cost a fortune, and he'd had it installed so quickly. Barb is a good business woman. She would have charged a rush rate.

He'd done all of that for me?

And when I kissed him, he freaked out?

Not able to make sense of any of it, I hurried into my clothes, still shaking from the adrenaline of the climb.

Dressed and masked, I left the closet and tapped my band next to the door that would take me back through the maze. I hesitated, afraid to get lost. The only thing I wanted less than being lost in a maze for an hour was to see Kierk.

I spotted him in the skywalk. He leaned against the wall like he had when we'd waited in line for the bumper cars my second trip to the carnival. His arms were tucked behind him, the edges of his biceps showing where his short sleeves ended. He'd been looking down, but when I'd opened the door, he'd raised his gaze ever so slightly.

We watched each other for a few seconds, but didn't speak. Probably better that way. I hurried past him.

"Sparx, wait."

"I'd rather not."

It was totally unprofessional, what I'd done: Falling for a guy at the carnival instead of doing my job and writing about it. I'd spent almost all my time with him instead of doing my work.

I was my mother's daughter after all.

To make matters worse, Kierk didn't even feel the same way.

"Please," he said, following me.

The maze door opened. The lights in the room rotated between strobe, blue, and black. I tried to let my eyes adjust, but all I could tell is that a few of the walls were more permanent, rising all the way to the ceiling while others were dividers probably used to reroute the maze and keep it fresh. I automatically went right, wishing I hadn't been blindfolded the first time through.

"Sparx!"

I turned. "Kierk, I'm sorry that I misread things between us, but I feel so stupid. Please. Leave me alone."

"Don't feel stupid. You caught me off guard. I..."

He took my hands, but I pushed them away. I took a left and then another quick right through the maze. A group of girls ran by us like a train, each with her hands on the waist of the girl in front of her. I tried to use the distraction to take a few quick turns and lose Kierk, but he stayed with me. He wrapped an arm around my waist and pulled me through a series of bends that took us to a dead end.

He ran his fingers through his hair. "What happened on that balcony..." he said. "I've wanted that to happen from the first day I met you. But..."

As his confession settled over me, the first day we met came into focus. The girls chasing after him. How he said he didn't do hookups. He was looking for something more. He wanted something that mattered. I'd told him he couldn't find it in the carnival. I'd bet him nothing real could ever start in a world where everything was pretend.

"But you want something real." I stepped toward him, a voice inside my head—muffled but definitely there—warning me that it couldn't work, that too much could come between us. That I was there for a story, not for him.

Standing so close I could feel his breath on my cheek, I was terrified to be humiliated. Again.

"Kierk?"

"Yeah?" He ran his hands down the length of my body, stopping when he pressed the little notebook in the pocket of my dress into my leg. Confusion swept across his face.

Instinctively, I moved away. "I should go."

"Wait!"

Miraculously, I found my way through the people and out of the maze. I didn't stop until I was sitting in my car, wishing things could somehow be different.

THIRTY-ONE

I WOKE up the next morning to a headache and the memory of running away from Kierk in the maze.

I pulled the blanket back over my head.

"Macky?" my dad called. He was up early. I curled down the corner of the covers and one-eyed the clock: 11:00 a.m. Not so early after all. "Time to climb."

"Dad, I don't want to climb." I wrapped the pillow around my head, covering my ears.

"We leave in fifteen minutes," he called back loudly. And then he shut the door at about the same volume.

MACKENZIE DAVIS WILL NOT CLIMB THIS MORNING

MACKENZIE DAVIS WILL STAY IN BED AND WALLOW

MACKENZIE DAVIS MIGHT THROW EVERY LAST CARNIVALESQUE NOTE INTO THE NEAREST OPEN FLAME

———

An hour later, I stood at the base of my favorite bouldering wall. I started on the hardest course, one I'd completed with ease many times before.

Except this time I fell. Twice.

"You okay?" Dad asked when he managed to hop down safely instead of taking the much quicker route I had.

"I'm fine."

"You seem distracted."

I grunted.

"That's teenage daughter speak for *you don't know what you're talking about, Dad,* when of course I know exactly what I'm talking about."

He did.

"You wanna talk about it?"

Right there in the foam that had broken my fall, I did something that surprised me: I told my dad about the time I'd spent with Kierk. And he listened like the incredible dad I knew he was.

"You clearly like this guy, so what's the problem?"

"He doesn't know about the article."

He sighed. "Look. You're my daughter, so we won't debate journalism ethics or professionalism here, okay? Truth be told, highly professional men and women since the beginning of time have screwed up a time or two in the name of love."

"Thanks, Dad."

"But you know this is absolutely unethical, right sweetie?"

I punched his arm lightly. "Dad!"

"Right, right." He wrapped an arm around my shoulders. "You know what you have to do."

"Tell him the truth."

He kissed the top of my head. "Exactly."

"I don't know if the truth matters if I can't even write the article."

"Writer's block?"

Or writer's fraud. "All I could think of was scoring the big story and competing with Lola's article in *The Herald*."

"You know that competing only sets you back. You spend too much time worrying about the people around you instead of focusing on bettering yourself. Just do you."

I'd heard the advice many times before. Intellectually, I got it. In practice, the message felt a little elusive, especially in an internet world where the victories of others were constantly rubbed in your face.

"Maybe Lola was right. I'm not capable of making a story matter. Of finding the story behind the story." I wasn't the writer my dad thought I was after all. Or the writer I envisioned myself to be.

Dad smiled sadly. "I'm sorry you're struggling so much, honey."

"Me, too."

"What does Dinah think about all of this?"

I groaned. "Dinah and I aren't really talking. Not since I saw her boyfriend with another girl in the carnival. I told her, and she didn't believe me. She took his side."

"Oh," Dad said with raised eyebrows. "That must be hard. I know how closely you've both worked on your stories together over the years."

"Yeah. But since she quit the newspaper, that's not really a thing anymore either."

"How long has it been since we talked?" Dad said with a dramatic expression.

Against my better judgment, I laughed.

"Tell you what. Why don't you freewrite about this boy and all your emotional attachment to the carnival? You have to sort through it, so it doesn't overwhelm you anymore, and then you can focus on the heart of the story you want to tell. It might help with the writer's block."

I couldn't imagine facing how my heart felt about the carnival…or Kierk. But at the end of the day, it was my only option.

"Get up there and climb before your old-man muscles get all twisted up," I said with a smile of gratitude.

"Hey, now. I'm the only one who gets to pick on the old-man muscles." He moved through his next climb in his dynamic style, proving he was far from old.

"He looks good up there," Barb said, sitting next to me.

"Hey, Barb."

"Hey yourself." She looked around as if about to spill military secrets and then leaned toward me. "That was a pretty impressive climb at the carnival."

Modeling her low tone, I said, "It was an impressive wall. How long did it take you to build?"

"We were able to use pieces we already had, so it wasn't too much trouble. Wait. Is it okay that we're talking about this?"

"Sure." I hated to lie to Barb. I respected her too much, but I had no intention of writing about the climbing wall in either of my articles, so it felt fair. "Is the wall still there?"

"Sure is. I don't think they intend to use it frequently, but they have the option now. The project manager for the carnival wanted it for a special girl." She raised an eyebrow at me.

"Kierk?"

"I believe that was his name. By the looks of it, you know him well?"

She was good at prying.

"Look, Mackenzie. I saw your falls this morning, and I saw you last night when you shed your harness. I've always felt that, well, you're a special kid. Maybe because your mom hasn't been around—I hope that's okay to say. Or maybe it's that you remind me of my own daughters. Or maybe because I respect so much how you devour the challenges in this gym. Climbing teaches you amazing life lessons."

"Like if you fall, get back up?"

"Definitely. But also, sometimes the right path isn't always clear. Sometimes you have to study the wall, try one option, then choose another. It takes time."

"Thanks, Barb."

"Any time. Why don't you get back out there and give it another go?"

THIRTY-TWO

Pittsburgh region's new teen hot spot, Carnivalesque, lives up to the chatter that made the media-shy experience the most popular weekend hangout for...

CRAP. Highlight, delete.

I tapped my fingers at the keys, not pushing them down, but to hear the clacking sound as if some progress existed. Deep breath, I could do this.

In a place where there are only a few rules, a mysterious mask is non-negotiable as teen carnival-goers explore creative exhibits...

Explore creative exhibits? That meant nothing to people who hadn't been there, in other words, my audience for the article. This time, I took pleasure in deleting the sentence letter by letter with efficient yet forceful successive taps on the key.

No brilliance poured out. I closed the laptop screen and

rested my head against it. I climbed into bed with my feet at the head and tapped an unidentifiable tune against the wall with my toes.

My dad's words played in my head. I should freewrite about Kierk. I should let all the excess go so I could trim away and find my focus. Kind of like when people purged their belongings to find their center. Ooh. Maybe that would be a good article idea. I wondered if anyone in the school was into that sort of thing.

And I digressed. Yet again.

"Macky," Dad called up the stairs. "School."

Excellent, a chance to see Todd and Dinah all smug and smoochy. And for Lola to ask questions about the carnival story: When would it be done? What was it about? How could she be sure it wouldn't suck?

I had no answers for her, but I got dressed, I got myself to school. And that was about as productive as I could be.

MACKENZIE DAVIS SCRIBBLES IN NOTEBOOK THROUGH EVERY CLASS, FAILS TO WRITE THE PERFECT LEAD

What was Kierk doing? How had he reacted to me running off? Did he expect me to come back this weekend? Would he tap his band on the computer screens, hoping for my name to pop up on his links? Or had he decided I was more trouble than I was worth?

He'd designed more than one exhibit for me. A moment of confusion wouldn't change his feelings. Right?

Freewrite, and get it out! It was Dad's voice again, even though he wasn't anywhere near me in the library.

I opened a blank document and typed, *Kierk.* The cursor flashed at me until the bell rang.

———

TUESDAY PASSES LIKE MONDAY: NO WORDS FOR
STRUGGLING REPORTER MACKENZIE DAVIS

———

WEDNESDAY—SAME

———

THURSDAY REMINDS MACKENZIE DAVIS ONLY ONE MORE
DAY UNTIL THE CARNIVAL OPENS AGAIN

———

FRIDAY—MACKENZIE DAVIS TAKES ADVANTAGE OF THREE-
FOR-FIVE ICE CREAM AT GROCERY

———

I made it through Friday night with ice cream and a healthy
binge of streaming television shows. Saturday morning, I hit
The Climb alone, but Barb didn't leave it that way for long.

"Looking good out there," she said, handing me a cold
bottle of water after I'd emptied my own.

"Liar."

She grinned. "Anything on your mind?"

I rested my head against the wall and sighed, hoping
tears didn't follow.

"Oh, Mac."

I could pretend the boulder in my chest wasn't there. But
something about the brightness in Barb's eyes and the softness of her smile made my lips move. I poured the drama
into the space between us, word after word, story after story.

"That's a lot to carry," she said.

Thus, the boulder.

"I'm an old woman," she said, and I rolled my eyes. "Old enough to know that when it's real, you can't ignore that. Everything you've said about this Kierk sounds pretty real to me."

"But isn't my passion for journalism real? My dreams of getting into the summer program and a good college? Aren't those things real, too?"

"Sure," she conceded. "Sometimes, though, looking back at my life, I wish I'd chosen people more and stuff less."

"I don't even know his real name."

"True. But let me be cheesy for a second."

I covered my eyes in mock horror.

"I get the sense you know his heart."

Maybe. At least I thought I did. "This is what I said about the carnival from the beginning. You don't know what's real and what isn't."

"Honey, that's how the world outside the carnival is, too. You never really know. You have to trust how you feel."

Even if I agreed, I couldn't make sense of what I was feeling.

———

I skipped the carnival Saturday, too. If I didn't know what I'd say to Kierk anyway, what was the point of going? I had all the pieces I needed for my article, even if I couldn't piece them together.

Monday morning reminded me I had two weeks until Valentine's Day, which happened to be Mardi Gras, two major reasons to be at the carnival with Kierk. The holiday also marked the deadline for *The Muse* story and a few days shy of my deadline for *The Herald.* I'd spent the last week trying to force words. Why not try the opposite?

Instead of writing, I climbed every day after school, avoiding the questioning gazes from Barb. I worked ahead on school projects and assignments.

Motivation to Write Still Eludes Mackenzie Davis

After lunch Friday, I spotted Lola down the hallway toward me, and, like in a tense movie scene, we moved toward each other. I swore I could hear old western music playing, and I half expected her to stop and pull her cardigan back over her hip to reveal a shining pistol she'd use to duel.

I totally needed to spend less time in the room when my dad watched movies.

To avoid the inevitable onslaught of questions about how well my article was going, I ducked into the nearest bathroom. And plowed right into Dinah.

"Oh," I said. "Um, sorry."

"Yeah. Sorry."

We danced that who's-going-to-step-where waltz but didn't laugh at the awkwardness. I pressed my back against the wall, creating room for her to pass. She nodded and reached for the door. I leaned against the sink and thought about running the cold water until I was soaked through. After a few seconds the door still hadn't opened.

"You okay?" Dinah whispered.

"No."

"Do you want to talk about it?"

"Does Todd allow that?"

"It's not like that, Mac."

Frustration, anger, and sarcasm mixed, creating a dangerous concoction that spewed from my mouth before I could—or wanted to—stop myself. "Well, it's not like I have my best friend anymore either. Even when we were friends, you spent all of your time with him. When you didn't have plans, you had to make yourself available for the possibility of having plans. And then when I told you the truth about what you already suspected, you believed him. You sided with him. So no, Dinah. I don't want to talk about it."

Instead, I went to the nurse and got a pass to go home and sleep away the afternoon.

———

Friday night, I shot upright in a dark room with an idea. A glance at the clock told me it was 7:00 p.m.—perfect. I tucked the tiny silver key Kierk had given me into my pocket and headed to the one place I knew would give me the inspiration to write.

If I avoided interruptions.

"Excuse me," I said politely to a girl in line in front of me. She turned and smiled. "I have a kind of crazy request. I'm trying to avoid an ex tonight, and I'm not sure if we've been unlinked yet. I see you're with a big group of your friends. Would you mind switching bands with me? I can totally find you later and switch back."

"I don't know…"

"What's the problem?" one of her friends asked.

I reiterated my story, partially borrowed from the mask-making carnival-goer I'd met in the Craft Room weeks earlier.

"I get it," the friend said. "Totally sucks. Tell you what, we have an extra." She dug around in her bag until she found a band, sticky on the edge from a rogue piece of gum or candy. "Sorry about that."

"No problem." It would get me inside without Kierk seeing. And I definitely didn't want him to see what I was about to do.

THIRTY-THREE

THE AMBIANCE of the carnival settled over me like the crisp flap of opening a Sunday morning newspaper. Without a trace of green on my mask or dress and an extension of blue hair from the Welcome Room Barbie closet covering my natural red, I moved through the carnival, breathing in the alluring scent of beignets, hoping I'd have the chance to enjoy them again.

Scanning the borrowed band, I took the elevator down to the dim library, where I could work distraction-free. I chose the couch I'd curled up with Kierk on because I relished personal torture. A Kierkegaard philosophy book sat atop the stack on the table next to me. Could he have been there? Reading? Enjoying the quiet? Had he snuck away for only a minute to go to the bathroom or check on something upstairs?

I hid my notebook behind the couch pillows and waited, but ten minutes later, I was still alone.

Notebook in hand, I finally scribbled the story of a skeptical girl who'd come to the carnival and met a guy who'd opened her mind to the silliness and adventure in the world around her. While she'd looked at the carnival with criticism, he'd twirled her into experiences that had helped her feel the world. I massaged my cramping fingers. The stress of the last two weeks faded into the comfortable pillows beneath me. Breath by breath. Moment by moment.

I'd needed to be here—at the carnival—to write about Kierk. It was our place. At least, it had been. Who knew what the future held?

Rested and emotions purged, I picked up my pen once again and finally wrote a workable lead for my story in *The Herald*:

> *The invitation-only teen hotspot Carnivalesque requires patrons wear masks to find their true identity.*

Maybe it wouldn't last revisions, but it was a start. I kept writing.

> *The approach may seem contradictory, but the carnival's philosophical foundation relies on the teachings of Mikhail Bakhtin who believed, "...[look up direct quote and insert later]..."*
>
> ~~*Bakhtin's concept*~~ *For hundreds of years, civilizations across the world have celebrated carnival or some incarnation of it—Mardi Gras, Carnivale, Feast of Fools.*
>
> *[Seek comment from Carnivalesque staff about why these festivals are appealing on a fundamental human level.]*
>
> *Perhaps it's this fundamental human connection that's drawn thousands of teens across the Pittsburgh region to* ~~*the carnival*~~ *indoor masquerade every weekend since it opened in November despite relatively nonexistent marketing.*
>
> *[Interview a few people about what attracts them to*

*the carnival and then transition into a discussion of some
of the exhibits and the parade.]*

"What are you writing?"

A creepily familiar voice in my ear made me jump and
smack my head against his.

"Ow."

"I'll second that," he said, rubbing his temple.

That was when I recognized his sneer and his disdain for
the world. Okay, maybe that was too far.

Todd.

He grinned at me in a way that made no sense. Todd
Wilkinson did not grin at Mackenzie Davis that way mostly
because he knew she—I—had no interest in his sleazy
charms. Acid crept up my throat at the realization he'd been
flirting with me. I closed my notebook and picked up the
Kierkegaard book. "Just an essay for school. Thought the
ambiance might help get me in the mood."

His body stiffened at the sound of my voice. "You're
doing school work here?"

I nodded and buried my face in the book.

Todd lowered it and studied me. "Mackenzie?"

I feigned surprise. "Hi. Good to see you."

"Like hell." He lurched forward. "Give me that
notebook."

I tucked it into the pocket of my dress. "If you want an
essay about Kierkegaard, you're going to have to write it
yourself." I was sweating, well, everywhere. I stood. "I have
to go anyway. I'm meeting someone."

"Kierk?"

Dammit, Dinah!

"I saw you with him the night you met Chanel. You go
by Gina, right?"

"Right," I lied.

"So, Gina. Show me what's in that notebook, or you're going nowhere."

"You have the authority to search my things?" I asked.

"Damn right I do."

"And what are you searching for? You think I'm plagiarizing a book you can get at any library in the area?"

"I think you're writing an article about the carnival for *The Muse*."

MACKENZIE DAVIS GETS STUCK WITH EMPTY THOUGHT BUBBLES ABOVE HER HEAD

"So that *is* what you're doing," Todd said.

I forced my mind to develop a cohesive thought. Like now. "You think I'd write about the carnival? With Kierk's permission?"

His grin faltered.

"Do you think Kierk would endorse an article about the carnival? Kierk? The believer in privacy above all else?"

"Uh, well, everything you do in life is for the newspaper. I figured…"

"Don't think too hard, Todd. You'll hurt yourself."

He glared at me.

"I'm not showing you my notebook," I said. "If you have the authority to see it, call Kierk down here, and he can tell me himself. Otherwise, I'll be going now."

I tried to walk away, but he stopped me. "What if I do call him?"

I faced him and crossed my arms, daring him. I was bluffing, but was he? If we were both bluffing, whose bluff would out-bluff the other?

A tall girl wearing a dress about three inches shorter than my best friend would ever wear appeared next to Todd.

"I got our hot chocolates," she said, and then, noticing me, added, "Who's this?"

"I was wondering the same thing," I said.

"Just a friend," Todd said, his jaw tight. The girl seemed mollified, but I, on the other hand, wasn't stupid enough to buy that the other girl was "just a friend."

"I wouldn't want to disrupt your evening," I said. "I'll make sure I tell your girlfriend you said hi next time I see her."

He glared through his mask, but without another word, the cheating bastard so not worth my best friend's time let me go.

THIRTY-FOUR

AFTER SPENDING MOST of the weekend twitching over the fact that my best friend actually believed Todd and the possibility that he might tell Kierk about the night in the carnival library, I gave in to the realization that shit was totally hitting the fan in my life and if I was lucky, I'd be able to avoid the splatter.

"All right, people!" Lola hollered over the bustle of everyone settling into their seats for our Monday after-school staff meeting. "Our Valentine's Day feature crashed and burned. I need something fast. Ideas. Go."

Silence.

Lola pinched the bridge of her nose and sighed in a way that you'd think was for dramatic effect. On the contrary, she was perfectly serious. "I promise the front cover. Some-one, show some ambition. Please."

The front page. The cover had eluded me all year. Tempted, I logged into my account in our software system and opened the file with the carnival story I'd written about me and Kierk—being very careful not to share identifying information about the two of us. I'd planned to appeal to

Lola and Mrs. Graham to run the article with an anonymous byline. Otherwise I'd out myself before I could finish my second article for *The Herald*. Anonymous bylines lacked credibility, though, so that could be a tough sell.

My article for *The Muse* was more of a personal essay about how one relationship might blossom in the carnival and whether that would make it real or not. Hiding my identity might be futile anyway if Todd saw the article. He'd tell Kierk, and I'd be banned from the carnival. But what if he'd already told him? What if the writing was on the wall for me? Could I give up an opportunity like this for no good reason?

I was proud of my piece. The words reached through the screen and grabbed me. I'd spent the weekend rereading and rewriting until the images and emotions were exactly as I wanted them. It had transformed from a freewritten purge to a cohesive piece with a message. I wondered if it could resonate with our readers. Or better yet, be picked up by other publications.

I formatted the article into our online notes system we used to submit stories. Twenty inches. Perfect. With the addition of the photos from the King's Court I had stored in my email account—I uploaded those, too—Lola would probably be salivating.

My hand itched to rise, to tell Lola I had the perfect story for her about the facade of teen dating with Carnivalesque as the prime metaphor. I could click Send, and that would be it.

The front page. Above the fold.

But I thought of Kierk, and I couldn't—not before confessing to him face-to-face. I'd be doing to him exactly what Colin had done to me—turning our private experiences into public discussion. Not to mention the carnival had helped me find my true self, my lonely true self. Even if it had been the right thing, I'd lost Colin. Dinah and I weren't talking, and Dad was busier than ever. All I had was writing.

Now that the words were in the computer system and would eventually be published, though, I couldn't wait anymore. I had to tell him what I'd been up to.

———

That Saturday night in the Milkshake Ballroom, it took me only five seconds to find Kierk. Without a doubt, the masked man behind the milkshake bar was him. He moved with ease, so at home in the small space. He'd flip a bottle of chocolate and pour it into the blender with one hand while dropping a scoop of strawberries in with the other. Friendly with the customers, he never returned the flirtations directed at him by piles of girls in all directions.

I thought about going to talk to him, about kissing him, about what it would be like to date him. I thought about the look he'd have on his face if he found out about the article.

And yet I couldn't walk away.

I waited until he cleared tables to approach the bar and set my sights on a seat next to a few girls I didn't know. The seat put me in the middle of the group, totally camouflaged and also partially hidden from Kierk and Harvey's view by the pillar at the corner of the bar.

"Mind if I sit for a few minutes?" I asked them. "Been dancing forever."

They let me take a seat.

"Oh, he's coming," one of the girls said, and sure enough Kierk headed toward the bar with a tray of glasses.

"Someone else order something so we can talk to him again."

The girls looked at me. "What are you drinking?"

"You order if you want a reason to talk to him." My heart stayed in my chest long enough to get the words out.

The girls didn't think twice. They leaned over the bar. Nobody could miss the low cut of their dresses as they splayed their upper bodies over the wooden bar top. I couldn't bring myself to watch Kierk to see if he reacted to their obvious affection.

"Hi, ladies!"

I recognized Harvey's voice right away.

He worked his way through the group, hugging a couple of the girls and kissing a few others on their cheeks. He slipped behind the bar to shake hands and one-arm-hug Kierk. Then he turned back to them. "Ladies, I'm sorry to tell you but my boy Kierk here is off the market."

His declaration was met with groans and whimpers. From the girls. From me, he nearly got a patron in cardiac arrest. Kierk was off the market?

"I know. I know," Harvey said in his usual big-man-on-campus way. "I'd be happy to console you for however long it might take to get over this news."

Kierk leaned back against the bar with a good-natured grin on his face. The girls had major cause for disappointment. It was all I could do not to hop over the bar and kiss the smirk off him.

Which was why I'd told myself to never come back here. I had no control. None.

I wasn't there to be with Kierk. I was there to tell him who I really was—Mackenzie Davis the journalist. Mackenzie Davis, the girl who'd agreed to write not one but two articles about Carnivalesque. Two articles that would soon be published.

I'd violated his privacy—everyone's privacy, really—and like Harvey's ex, I'd be outcast.

"So where's your girl tonight?"

Kierk didn't answer.

"Uh-oh. She didn't show? Again?"

"She's probably busy."

Harvey nodded. "Right. After you declared your love—"

"I didn't declare my love," Kierk said, looking around to see if anyone could hear their conversation. I turned away yet leaned closer against the bar.

"You might as well have. You can have any girl you want—what's so special about this one?" Instead of waiting for a response, Harvey tapped the computer and grabbed Kierk's arm. In a single motion, he'd scanned Kierk's band.

"What are you doing?"

Harvey smiled. "Finding out what Sparx has been up to."

Even the blood stilled in my veins. Instinctively, I covered the band on my wrist, not that that would help me. Since I'd planned to see Kierk tonight, I'd used it instead of my dummy band. A decision that fueled regret in that moment.

"She's here!" Harvey said.

"Shut up," Kierk said, turning the screen toward him. "No." He pushed it away again. "I'm not gonna be a hypocrite about this. I'm the first person to advocate privacy, and I'm gonna watch her every move? Close it."

"Are you sure?" Harvey asked. "You might want to know that—"

"Close it!"

Harvey sighed but complied. After a few seconds of them both cooling down, he said, "Look, man. Maybe it was just a carnival thing."

"I freaked her out."

I wanted to spin in my stool and tell him he hadn't. That I'd wanted more, too. That I wanted to see him every day. But I couldn't do it. I couldn't tell him.

I hopped off my stool and pushed through the crowd, searching for the closest exit. The long hallway blurred. Before I reached the end, someone yanked me backward.

"Wanna tell me what you were doing back there?"

Panicked, I looked over Harvey's shoulder, expecting to see Kierk.

"He's not here. He has a problem violating your privacy. I don't."

Not sure what to say, I didn't speak a word.

"You're hiding something from him."

I wiped at the tears that escaped the confines of my mask. "Harvey, I need to go."

"Fine. Go. But if you're not into him, leave—and don't come back. He likes you way more than he should."

THIRTY-FIVE

I PACED the hallway outside the Milkshake Ballroom with Harvey's words replaying in my mind. Kierk liked me more than he should. Relief and anxiety warred inside me. Relief because I hadn't submitted the article and anxiety because I had to tell him the truth. Once and for all.

After I came clean, I'd never see Kierk's beautiful smirk again or hear him talk about philosophy and exhibits and how much the carnival matters to so many people. He'd never again kiss me with more passion than on-screen kisses of the year.

How had I screwed up so badly? How had I set myself up for failure from the moment I'd met him? How had I taken a guy like Kierk and squandered our chances?

It wasn't that I *needed* Kierk. It was that I'd wanted him. I wanted him.

MACKENZIE DAVIS IMAGINES BIG SCREEN ROMANTIC
MOMENT, GAINS COURAGE

I tapped my band to open the door, marched across the ballroom, and found Kierk and Harvey still behind the bar.

"Hey," I called.

Kierk turned at the sound of my voice, but Harvey scowled. Kierk picked me up and spun me around. In his arms, I no longer cared what Harvey—or anyone—thought. It was just Kierk and me—how it should be.

"Harvey, man the bar," Kierk called over his shoulder. His friend saluted him, and Kierk and I ran behind one of the curtains in a corner. "I didn't think you would show after last time."

"I didn't think so either, to be honest. I'm sorry about running out on you."

"Forget it."

"Seriously?"

He hugged me, pressing his face into my neck. "Seriously."

"Kierk, I have to tell you something."

"Me, too," he smiled. I thought back to what I'd over-heard Harvey say to him earlier. "You go first."

"Sure." I took a deep breath. It was hard to know where to start. "When I came here that first day, it wasn't why you thought."

He squinted at me. "Not to get covered in powdered sugar and watch the parade from an old, wobbly lift?"

"No," I said, taking another breath. "I wanted to know more about the carnival. I wanted to learn about it, so I could…" *Write about it. Just say it.*

"That's why you asked so many questions."

I nodded. *To write about it.* The words wouldn't even form on my tongue.

"That fits perfectly with what I have to tell you."

Confused, I didn't respond.

"We have a new exhibit tonight. A live one, you could say."

He took a deep breath and rubbed his fingertips over my cheek, flirting with the edges of my mask. His hands trailed down my neck and the center of my bare back. He tilted my head, so we were staring into each other's dark eyes. "Do you want to be my date?"

I closed my eyes and pressed my forehead against his shoulder. *I'm writing an article.* Just say it!

MACKENZIE DAVIS CONTINUES LYING TO HERSELF, HAS GOTTEN VERY GOOD AT IT

I'd tell him tonight. I would. Just not right now. Now, I'd have one last night with him before I had to let go.

"Yes," I whispered.

He brushed his lips against my cheek, and it felt as though every bone in my body exploded into ash. With no other support, I fell into him, my lips finding his. Being with him like this could be interpreted as agreeing to his terms. To being more than a carnival hookup. I hadn't come for that, but I obviously couldn't walk away from it either.

"Yo, Kierk!" Harvey snuck up behind me. "It's time for the thing."

"No need to be vague, Harvey." Kierk looped his arm over my shoulder. "This is Sparx here."

Harvey nodded with a tension that only he and I understood. "Okay," he said. "It's time for a group of masked misfits to roam the city."

Harvey led the way through the crowd to one of the group Welcome Rooms where roughly a dozen other couples waited for us. Kierk led us to one of the couches, sat on the arm, and pulled me toward him. Not exactly sitting on his lap, I leaned against him, and as the people around us chatted, I reveled in how powerful he felt against me. How strong I felt when we were side by side. How hours ago I'd been in the real world where I didn't know his name or his face, but here, nobody could deny how close and comfortable we'd become.

I was living two lives, and I liked this one so much more than the other.

Harvey settled the group to give instructions, and I scoffed.

Kierk's breath was warm on my neck. "What?"

I tilted my head back over my shoulder. "Can't believe someone put Harvey in charge!"

He grinned. "I did."

"What were you thinking?"

"That I wanted to be with you and if I was in charge, I wouldn't be able to do that."

"You didn't even know if I was coming."

"I hoped you were." His arms tightened around me.

"All right, kids," Harvey called. "You're the elite. I know. Don't pat yourselves on the back too hard."

Everyone cheered. Harvey grabbed a couple of boxes from a closet and threw them into the center of the room. "Some might even say you represent the nobility among us. Anybody know what happened to nobles at the carnival?"

Instinctively, I raised my hand. I'd read every book, blog, and website I could find on the historical aspects of carnival. I'd watched documentaries. All to research an article that nobody in that room could know I was writing. I played off the movement by scratching my shoulder and scooting closer to Kierk.

When nobody answered, Harvey dumped one of the boxes. Stacks of tattered clothing poured over the ground. "They pretended to be peasants."

"I'm not wearing those rags," a girl across the room

called. I swore it was Chanel. And the guy standing next to her looked familiar, too. I turned away before Todd could make eye contact with me. He could ruin my perfect night with Kierk or tell Kierk his suspicions about me writing an article for *The Muse*, all while cheating on my best friend and getting away with it.

"Ladies and gentlemen, we come to the carnival to find our true selves. We explore aspects of our identity in a safe, anonymous space. We learn about the power society holds over us and how we can reclaim that power in our own ways. Of course, anyone wishing to can bail out of the experience."

A few of the couples glanced at each other as if they should consider it.

"If you want to go on the field-trip challenge—not to brag, but it comes with quite the prize—I suggest you open your envelope and get moving."

THIRTY-SIX

"WHERE'S OUR ENVELOPE?" I asked.

Kierk pulled a black envelope from his pocket. The number three was written on it in gold letters. He tore it open and handed me the note inside.

"*When a woman kills like she does,*" I read aloud, "*acclaim soon follows. Secrets lie in wait behind closed doors or perhaps down the circular staircase.*" I gazed at Kierk. "Please tell me you're good at riddles."

"Terrible, actually."

I groaned.

"Unless our mystery woman was a famous philosopher."

"A famous female philosopher? Who murders people."

He went palms up. "We're screwed."

He ran his fingers along the exposed skin on my back, and I sank against him. "I want to have an adventurous night with you," he whispered. "That's all."

A few of the couples tore through the piles of peasant clothing.

"We better get changed before the options are even bleaker than they are now," I said.

"Agreed."

Ten minutes later, we looked like extras from a period flick: Kierk in his beige tunic and brown leather boots, and me with my brown skirt and golden corset that succeeded in boosting as corsets did.

"Wow," Kierk said. He tried not to look at the blinding light that was my overspilling chest.

"Let's solve this puzzle, shall we?" I said.

The group shifted outside, where a row of black sedans awaited us.

"Is this for real?"

Kierk laughed. "Let's hope so."

We climbed into the second car, Kierk behind the wheel and me in the passenger seat. "Where's Harvey?"

"Every couple gets their own car," he said, turning off the bright GPS screen.

"Isn't that a bit much?" Not that I didn't appreciate being far away from Todd and Chanel.

"That's what we're here to find out. Tonight's an experiment for a new...let's call it a traveling exhibit."

"Meaning?"

He put the car in Drive and off we drove, passing the cul-de-sac where the busses dropped off and picked up.

"What happened to nobody knowing the location of the carnival?"

"That's changing. It has to. People put tracking devices on their clothes and their phones. Ideally, Carnivalesque would be hidden forever, but technology prevents that."

"But you've known where it was all along."

He grinned. "You could say that."

He turned onto the highway, relaxed into his seat, and reached across the console for my hand.

"Where are we going? Shouldn't we figure out the clue first?"

"Theoretically…"

"And as a philosopher, don't you essentially live your life in the theoretical realm?"

"Ouch, Sparx! There's someplace I want to go to figure out the clue. I thought that would be an adventure in itself."

"Okay. Tell me about this traveling-exhibit idea."

"We can only do so much with the carnival's limited space, but the city's too close to ignore. We can keep surprising our clientele by creating puzzles and unique experiences across Pittsburgh. It's also an opportunity to attract corporate clients looking for rapport-building exercises."

"Do you think people are getting bored with the carnival already?"

"Not at all," he said. "But the mark of a good businessperson is the ability to stay ahead of the trends."

We passed the bright lights of downtown Pittsburgh, a compact city center with an excess of hills, bridges, and potential for mystery. I read our clue again, but nothing specific came to mind.

"Did you create the puzzles for tonight?" I asked.

"Unfortunately, no. The committee wanted fresh feedback, so one group created the experience and another is experimenting. We'll take turns though. Next time, the groups will swap."

I thought back to the twenty-plus people in the group Welcome Room dressing as peasants. "How many people are on the committee?"

He drove in silence for a moment, and I worried I'd gone too far, that he wouldn't answer my question. "About sixty."

"Sixty people. Are you serious?"

He merged onto a road I recognized, and the bright lights of traffic filled the car. "Yep."

"I didn't expect that many people to be involved."

"That's only the core planning committee. We also have volunteers who work to bring the exhibits to life, but we already talked about that."

"Right."

"I've been thinking about something, and I have a question for you."

"Okay…"

"How are things with your friend? Did you tell her about her boyfriend?"

I exhaled. "Yeah. It didn't go well."

"I'm sorry."

"He denied it, of course, and she took his word over mine."

"She's not ready to face it," he said.

That summed it up. Part of me couldn't blame her. There were things in my life I didn't want to face. Kierk squeezed my hand.

"Thanks for asking," I said.

He nodded. "Of course."

I was quiet for a moment. "Kierk, can I ask you something that might be a violation of carnival privacy or whatever?"

He considered it. "You can ask."

But he wouldn't commit to answering. "Is Harvey's real name Darius?"

His gaze spun to mine.

"It is!" I said.

"How did you know that?"

I took a deep breath, knowing what I was about to reveal flirted with the boundary between us. "He gave me my first invitation."

Kierk laughed. "He was flirting with you, no doubt."

I looked away and watched the darkness swirl with a

mix of streetlights outside the window, trying to hide my smile.

"You didn't, like— You two weren't *together*, were you?" His voice registered actual horror.

"No!" I fell into giggles. "But yes, he flirted with me. The thing is, though, I think you might have been there."

He shook his head. "I'd remember you."

I wasn't so sure. "Have you ever been to The Climb?"

He gasped. "That was you on the wall, scooting all over like it couldn't be easier!"

"That was me," I said with pride.

"I don't know how to tell you this, Sparx, but I asked you to marry me."

Now we were both laughing.

"I'm crushed you refused," he managed through laughter.

When we recovered, I exhaled a deep breath.

"What are you thinking?" he asked.

"That's the ultimate question to violate someone's privacy, don't you think?"

"You don't have to answer."

But I wanted to. "I'm thinking how that day you were a face in a crowd. I can't even focus on you and see you in the memory. It's weird to think that one day someone can be a nameless face in your life and then, well, they're something completely different."

He squeezed my hand. In the past few weeks, something had changed in both of us. When I'd first asked questions, he'd answered, but with some caution and skepticism. I got the sense that in the car alone with him, I could ask anything and he would answer truthfully.

I should have left the moment where it was. I shouldn't have said another word.

But I did.

"Kierk… The carnival's so secretive about things. Why do you answer my questions so openly?"

His genuine smile suggested his response was the most natural thing he'd ever said. "Because I trust you."

My smile was forced. Shame flooded my bloodstream.

Kierk parked the car on the street next to a gothic skyscraper climbing into the night.

"Is this where we can find the next clue?" I asked, desperate to focus on anything but my lies and manipulation.Or milking him for information he didn't want to give.

"Nope. Open the glove box."

I pressed the button and it popped open, revealing a tablet connected to the charging cable inside. "Technology!"

Kierk laughed. "Solving the puzzles without Google would be impossible."

"Then what are we doing here?"

"If we're going to brainstorm, we might as well do it in one of the most academically inspiring spaces in the entire city. Don't you think?"

"And who says this is the most academically inspiring building in the city?"

Kierk's eyes widened so huge behind his mask that I couldn't see his lashes. "Only everybody."

I wasn't convinced such a survey had ever occurred. My expression must have communicated as much.

"Have you never been to the Cathedral of Learning?"

"Um…"

"Never?"

"I drove by it once on my way to a concert," I said.

Kierk grabbed his chest. "You wound me."

"Like you don't like music."

He got out of the car, walked around, and pulled my door open. "Let's go, my uncultured friend."

"I resent that," I said. I climbed out of the car into the chilly night. "I've seen the Monet at the museum."

"At least that's something," Kierk teased. "What about the Bernini bust?"

In my best interest, I didn't answer.

Kierk laughed and threw his arm around my shoulder. "Let's go."

We emerged from the cover of the trees and saw the cathedral, lit up in its gothic glow. "It's beautiful."

"Wait until you see inside."

We pushed through the revolving door. "What if people see us?"

"The place is going to be packed. People will definitely see us."

He wasn't lying. With high-vaulted ceilings and stunning archways, the grandeur ripped my breath away.

"This is the most academically inspiring building in the city," I said.

"I might have heard that somewhere before."

I took in a three-hundred-and-sixty-degree view from the center aisle, not wanting to miss a single curve in the stone, a spike on the gate leading to the bank of elevators or a gothic lantern hanging low from the stunning ribbed ceiling to light the wooden tables and chairs where students leaned over texts, wrote in notebooks, and typed away at artificially lit computer screens. They focused on their work as if not surrounded by architecture that could grip their insides in a single glance.

Kierk rested his chin on my shoulder. "When I went to school here, this was my favorite place to study."

"You studied here?" Standing in the foreign but gorgeous space amid hundreds of strangers, a prickling down my back reminded me I knew very little about the man next to me.

A few students looked up at us curiously. Maybe something to do with wearing a mask in the middle of their study hall.

"We should go," I muttered.

"Yeah." Kierk pointed back toward the revolving door, and we hustled out of view into the hallway that surrounded the common room.

"What do you think security will do if they see us here?"

"Throw us in jail, masks and all." I swatted his arm, and he laughed. "It's a college campus. There's nothing they haven't seen."

I pulled him down the hall. "I don't want to find out, though, okay?"

"Sure." We walked along the outer stone hallway with archways that provided peek-a-boo glances at the common area. Everyone was still hard at work. Kierk could have been among them.

"Why don't you go here anymore?"

"I dropped out," he said with a shy smile. "College is a pretty incredible thing, if you know what you want to do."

I couldn't see Kierk quitting anything. "But you didn't?"

"Not even close."

"But you said your passion is bringing creative ideas to life."

"Sure. But how? Like, as an engineer? Then you're in the science department forever. Or do I want to bring stages to life in the theater department?"

"You could double major in engineering and theater."

"Nobody does that."

"What about philosophy?"

He didn't answer.

"Oh, I see," I said, not able to ignore the frustration coming to life inside of me. "You spend your days bringing miracles to life for people to experience every weekend because you're concerned about what everybody else does?"

He grinned in that way of his that made me droop into a puddle on the floor. "You think there are miracles at the carnival?"

"You created an outdoor café under the stars in the middle of winter, Kierk."

The pride on his face made me want to kiss him. So I did, right there in the hallway, I ran my fingers along his back and neck, learning his curves and muscles. He jiggled a key from his pocket as he deepened the kiss and pulled me closer to him. A crash of metal sent us jumping apart.

"I dropped the keys. Sorry."

I laughed. "That scared me."

"Me, too. Come on," he whispered. "And keep it down."

"Stop dropping things."

He gave me a sideways grin and shook his head.

We ran to the bank of elevators, and he tapped the number three on the touch screen. Up we went, giggling in the elevator over I wasn't sure what. We ran down the hall to a wooden door with a stone crest above it. Kierk looked in both directions. We were alone in the hall.

"Keep watch," he whispered.

"What are you doing?"

"Shh," he said with a laugh.

"We are so going to jail," I mumbled, but to avoid it if possible, I kept watch. The lock clicked, and Kierk pulled me inside where it was pitch black. He closed the door quietly and flicked three switches beside it.

"Oh. My. Gosh."

"I know, right."

A small room with a formal table at the center lit up before me. Regal chairs with the same patterned red uphol-stery as the walls lined the table. Two bright chandeliers hung low over it. Their light sparkled in the windows that separated us from the cool, black night.

I set the tablet on the table and looked around. "What is this place?"

"The Austrian Nationality Room," Kierk said. "The cathedral has, like, thirty rooms that celebrate nationalities from around the world. The chairs are upholstered in royal red damask, and the style is reminiscent of the Baroque period. Look up at the ceiling."

I did and was struck by the brilliant colors.

"The murals are inspired by the Latin novel *Meta-morphosis*."

I wandered the room slowly, taking in the knickknacks in the display cases and the grandeur from every angle.

"That's a replica of the most famous sculpture found on Austrian soil—the Venus of Willendorf."

The faceless woman's middle, breasts, and legs were voluptuous. "She's…curvy."

"She represents the ultimate body type of the time. She was a symbol of fertility."

"Interesting," I said, considering how differently society viewed the female form now. "You know a lot about this room. Did you have class here?"

He laughed so adorably that I turned to look at him. He pointed to a paper mounted next to the door. "It's all right here."

"You sounded very in the know."

With a serious nod, he said, "I read really well."

"You do." I walked toward him slowly. "I like the chandeliers. What does it say about them?"

I hoped my flirtatious saunter unsettled him like his smirky grin untangled every bit of my control.

He watched me and then glanced back at the tourist guide. "Um…they're Lobmeyrs."

He glanced at me, so I grinned. "Lobmeyrs are my favorite. Anything else?"

"They're similar to the ones in Vienna's Palace."

"Oh, really? So, it's like we're in a palace right now?"

"Kind of…"

I teased my fingers up his neck, and he lifted me onto the pristine table. Our hungry lips found each other as if they hadn't been touching only minutes before. Every curve and edge of my body found a place to fit within his, and I couldn't quiet the nagging voice in my head that said, *It's not always like this. People don't always work this well together.*

Kierk's pocket rang.

THIRTY-SEVEN

I JUMPED BACK FROM HIM. "What is that?"

Kierk pressed his pocket. "Um…"

"Because it looks a lot like you're silencing a phone… but phones aren't allowed at Carnivalesque."

"It's not a phone."

"You know," I said, "phones interrupt real-life experiences."

"You're killing me, Sparx."

I hopped off the table and made my way to the window to check out the view. "What's over there?"

Kierk wrapped his arms around me and looked over my shoulder. "That's the Monet."

"I got really turned around in here."

"Me, too." He kissed my neck. "Every time."

"Who was on the phone?"

"Harvey. He has interesting timing."

"You think he was calling because we've made no effort to actually solve the clue?"

"What clue?"

I elbowed him in the gut.

"Right. The clue," Kierk said. "Read it one more time."

I pulled the envelope from his pocket and smoothed out the black paper. *"When a woman kills like she does, acclaim soon follows. Secrets lie in wait behind closed doors or perhaps down the circular staircase."*

"I got nothing."

It seemed like the circular stairs were important somehow. "Does the cathedral have any circular stairs, by chance?"

"Behind a latched door in the Early American Room. Not a lot of people realize that, but I've been there. It's kind of creepy, actually."

A creepy excursion could be fun. Oh! I wondered if the carnival would do creepy Halloween exhibits in the fall. But...I probably wouldn't be welcome to see it.

I shook the thought away. "Let's check it out."

"I'm not sure the key works for that room. It's kind of a special room. Haunted."

I popped my hip to the side and rested my hand against it. "Where's your sense of adventure? What would the committee think?"

"You want to break into a haunted room that multiple grown men have gotten stuck in more than once?"

"Stuck?"

He nodded.

"Maybe we shouldn't sneak into locked rooms while masked at night. So, we need to find a female killer who became well known for it. And somehow this connects to a circular staircase. You think she killed people by pushing them down the stairs?"

"Or maybe throwing them over the railing?"

"Nice."

Using the carnival's tablet, I searched for famous female murderers in Pennsylvania and scrolled through a resulting list. Most of the killers were male. I kept scrolling, but any decent human could only take so much of throat-slitting, stalking, raping, murderous tales. I passed the tablet to Kierk. "This is depressing."

He glanced at the screen and cringed. "I get that. Why don't we search the keywords?"

I held up the clue again, wondering if we should give up and get a Primanti's sandwich or something. "Woman. Killer. Acclaim. Secrets. Circular staircase."

He tapped in the words as I spoke them.

"Maybe we should add Pittsburgh, too," I said.

He nodded.

"And put *circular staircase* in quotes."

"Right." He hit the Search button and grinned.

"What?"

"Mary Roberts Rinehart. She was an acclaimed mystery author. She killed people for a living—fictionally speaking. And..." He scrolled. "One of her most well-known titles was *The Circular Staircase*."

I hugged him. "Brilliant! Did she live in the city? Maybe the clue is at her house."

"Not that I can see, but there's a park named after her."

"Where?"

He did some more tapping and scrolling. "Crap."

"What?"

"You were right. We should have figured out the clue before we left."

"Why?"

"The park's in the direction we came from. All the other teams must be ahead of us." He pulled the cell phone out of his pocket. "That's probably why Harvey called. Now we'll have to backtrack and be behind the rest of the group."

Truth be told, I didn't really feel bad about that. My goal wasn't to win a competition. I just wanted to spend more time with Kierk, and the Cathedral backdrop did not disappoint. We hustled down a stairwell to the first floor and out the nearest revolving doors to the massive patio with the well-lit gothic cathedral behind us. He tapped the screen and held up a finger to his mouth in the universal sign for *Shh*. I laughed, as he'd expected. He smiled.

"Harvey, hey! …We just solved it, actually… No, we were not doing other things."

I giggled.

"No, that was not Sparx giggling… Okay, fine. We're in Oakland." His eyes brightened, and he grabbed my hand. "Really?" He looked across the lawn to the museum. "Perfect. We'll see you there." He hung up the phone.

"What is it?"

"We got lucky," he said. "Most of the other groups are heading to the Museum of Art. Harvey's going to text me the clue everyone picked up at the park, and then we'll walk across the street and actually be ahead."

"Definitely lucky."

We walked toward the crossing zone.

"So does your key open the museum, too?" I teased.

"No, but my dad knows some people in the administration there."

"What does your dad have to do with it?"

He stopped on the sidewalk.

"Is everything okay?"

He shook his head and kept walking. "Yeah, it's fine. Thought I forgot something." We walked in silence for a few seconds.

"Kierk… Your dad…?"

"Oh, right. Since this is an experiment, the committee planned to use clues for only facilities they could get into without a cost. People can rent out the museum, but a bunch of the guys on the committee know my dad, so they probably asked for his help in setting up the clue. We should cross here."

His response sounded totally plausible, yet it didn't ring true to me. Not entirely. When someone held back on an interview question, I knew it. The idea that Kierk might be lying to me didn't sit well, but I couldn't exactly judge, considering I'd been doing the same to him. And within hours, I'd have to find a way to tell him the truth.

I watched the concentration on his face—what I could see of it—as we crossed the street and snuck around the back entrance to the museum. He took care to point out the curb and any changes in the smoothness of the sidewalk so I didn't trip. His thumb caressed my hand. He pointed out the dinosaur statue, as if I could miss it, and the nighttime view of the cathedral behind us. He wanted to keep me safe, to help me experience every moment, to be at my side as I did. I nudged him with my hip, so he stopped walking and caught my eye. He didn't look away. He didn't speak. He seemed to realize that I needed those silent moments to work out the emotions tugging my heart in a thousand directions. A tear fell behind my mask, and I prayed he couldn't see it. That he didn't realize my chest burned with the beautiful, painful realization that I'd carelessly fallen in love with him.

I'd set out to expose the carnival life—maybe even the pressures of dating and falling in love for my generation, especially in a world that fabricated experiences and filtered images—yet what I felt in my core was more real than a fantasy world could ever claim. And it wasn't worth risking for a news story.

Mrs. Graham had been right, as usual. I'd have to take on other assignments to make up for the time I missed. I'd have to work double time. But I'd find a different big story for *The Herald*. I'd fail Journalism this grading period, but

I'd figure out a way to bring up my grade at the end of the year. I might miss out on the editor position next year. I might even miss out on the summer program, but I wouldn't publish a word about the carnival.

I was okay with whatever happened because what was happening with Kierk felt nothing short of magic. Maybe sometime in the future, I'd tell Kierk what had brought us together—when we were solid enough that it wouldn't tear us apart. We'd laugh about how the carnival had changed my perspective.

I hugged Kierk for a reason he didn't know.

We laughed our way through the dimly lit museum on the way to our next clue.

THIRTY-EIGHT

THE NEWSPAPER RACKS were full by seventh period on Mardi Gras, which happened to be Valentine's Day, too. Although it was a Tuesday, the carnival would be open—and packed—for the celebration.

I grabbed a copy of *The Muse* and tucked it into my stack of books—not much to fuss over seeing as I hadn't written an article in months. Still, I was proud of my decision not to publish the Carnivalesque story. It felt good to let go of all the stress and pressure. To quiet the chaos in my mind. To enjoy the guy I'd fallen in love with.

ALERT! MACKENZIE DAVIS CAN'T STOP SMILING

I collapsed into my chair and glared at the clock, willing it to move faster. The day needed to end.

"I can't believe it!" Dallas said, slapping his copy of *The Muse* onto his desk. In typical high school fashion, half the class crowded around to read over his shoulder. The other half were above such behavior.

"Someone wrote about Carnivalesque!"

Wait. What?

I moved to pull *The Muse* from my pile of books, but my hands stopped and started like an online video that wouldn't load. There, above the fold, in the right column was the headline

True or False? Dating in the Teen Hot Spot Carnivalesque.

My headline. For *my* story. Saved on *my* computer.

I read the headline again, but wish as I might, the words didn't change.

How had it ended up in print? I'd never filed it. Lola hadn't even said she'd planned to run it. I read the byline to be sure. *Written by Mackenzie Davis.* It was mine. A story finally on the front page, and I wanted it buried from anyone's view.

Clusters of kids hovered over newspapers around the room. Even the teacher sat at her desk reading a copy. Heads turned my way. The questions began.

Mac, what's the carnival like? Can you get me in? I've wanted to go there forever. I thought the carnival was, like, super secretive. How did you get them to tell you all this? My friend got blacklisted for having his phone on him, but his parents insist they can reach him every second.

My face and neck burned so hot I thought I might go up in flames. The bell rang, and the rest of the class filtered into the hallway, leaving me to burn up into the atmosphere all by myself. How had this happened?

"Mackenzie, dear," my teacher tapped me on my shoulder. I didn't feel a thing. "The bell rang. It's time for your next class."

What was my next class? I piled my books and notebooks in my arms, placing the newspaper on top. I stared at it and walked into a few desks, a couple doorways, and at least one wall. A few centuries later and moderately bruised, I found my way to Mrs. Graham's office.

"Mackenzie, are you all right?"

"My story," I held up the paper. "How? I didn't…"

"Oh no," Mrs. Graham said, somehow interpreting my entire existence. "Sit down. Lola, get in here!"

Lola appeared, looking blissfully unbothered. "Yeah? Oh, hey, Mac. Great story!"

Kierk would see it. Maybe he had already. Someone from Homer would forward it to him. Probably someone on the committee. Would he know it was me who wrote it?

"Are you okay?"

"I didn't want to print it," I said.

Lola looked to Mrs. Graham and then back to me. "The story was filed."

"How did this happen?" Mrs. Graham asked.

I didn't answer. How could I? I had no idea how it had happened.

Mrs. Graham frowned at Lola. "Did you discuss this with Mac?"

"No," I said, the dull numbness subsiding and being replaced by a growing fire. "She didn't."

"Don't be so dramatic. You filed the story yourself. Look." She pulled up the computer system and showed me the file date and time. Sure enough, my name was listed as the one who'd filed the story.

"That's not possible," I said.

The date was from the week before. During our staff meeting. When I'd had the story and photo saved in the system but thought of Kierk and decided against sending.

"I searched the filed stories, as we're trained to do," Lola continued defending herself, "and found this. The only story worthy of the cover."

Her compliment fell flat.

"It's sensitive material," Mrs. Graham said. "You have to be more careful with some stories than others."

"I decided this weekend I didn't want to publish the story after all."

They both stopped squabbling and stared at me. "At all?" Mrs. Graham asked at the same time Lola said, "You what?"

I crossed my arms. "You heard me."

"You begged for this story. You worked on it for months. How do you expect to pass Journalism without it? Or earn a space on staff next year let alone the editor position we all know you want?"

"Easy, Lola," Mrs. Graham said. "This is a good learning experience for all of us. Mackenzie, you have my sincerest apologies. I'll implement a system immediately that confirms story submission. Lola, you can help me with that."

I nodded numbly, but that wouldn't help me now.

I glanced down at the copy of *The Muse* on Mrs. Graham's desk. All I'd wanted all year was a story on the cover that resonated with people. That got them talking. But not like this. Not when I had so much to lose.

I lowered my head onto one of the desks.

"I should have..." Lola muttered. "It's just that we've been talking about it forever. I was pressed for time at deadline. I...I don't know why..."

I lifted my head, surprised to see this version of Lola. Unsure of herself. Concerned for approval. Wary of possible consequences. She'd screwed up in a big way, but I was likely to pay the price.

IN EPIC FAIL, MACKENZIE FILES NEWS STORY SHE MEANT
TO DELETE

In Other News: Those Buttons on the Computer Screen Should NOT be Side by Side

I'd woken up that morning thinking only of seeing Kierk at the carnival celebration that night. We were scheduled to ride in the parade as the king and queen of Mardi Gras. If I went to the carnival, I had no idea what I'd be walking into.

My dad had been so right. I should have told Kierk everything weeks ago. No matter the consequences, he deserved the truth from me.

After giving me some time to wallow and a pass for the classes I was missing, Mrs. Graham pulled me aside. "Mackenzie, I know this didn't go as you planned, but you wrote a beautiful piece. It was cohesive and well developed."

"Thank you," I managed.

"Are you planning to go to the carnival tonight?" Lola asked.

It could be my only chance to Kierk my side of the story. "It's Mardi Gras," I said, as if that explained everything.

"I'm going with you," Lola said.

"Why would you come with me?"

"Editors protect their writers. Or at least they should." She shoved a stack of papers into her bag and tied a scarf around her neck. "And I realize I screwed up big time here. I was in a rush and should have talked to you about using your story before I pulled it. Even if you had filed it."

"Thanks, Lola."

She waved away my kindness, which made her visibly squirm. "I'm all yours as soon as I find someone to write a weather story about the record-breaking snow this winter."

I laughed. Staff writers hid from weather stories more than any other benign crap that could grace our pages. "Good luck with that."

"Look, Mac. I know I can be competitive." I raised my eyebrows at her. "Okay, very competitive."

Somehow, I managed a slight smile.

"But," she said, "that doesn't mean I'm a complete jerk. I have your back, no matter what. I promise."

"Lola, that's really nice of you, but—"

"I got you into this mess, and I know you want to tell your boyfriend the truth." She studied me. "Am I right?"

I shrugged. Even if Kierk had been anything close to being my boyfriend, he wouldn't be for much longer. I'd published an article about our relationship, without him knowing. He would probably feel as embarrassed, hurt, and angry as I had when Colin had done that to me—a moment that would come in the next couple of hours, if it hadn't already.

"Besides," Lola rambled on, "I've never been to the carnival, and given the article, this will likely be my last chance. So, what do you say?"

Her motives may have been partially selfish, but I believed the she wanted to be show her support, too. Besides, if I drove myself, I might chicken out. "Pick me up at five. And Lola?"

"Yeah?"

"I'll write the weather story for you."

THIRTY-NINE

DURING THE DRIVE to the carnival that night, I told Lola where to go for the parade and then where to meet me in the Milkshake Ballroom afterward. I leaped from the car before it had even come to a complete stop, desperate to find Kierk. I scanned my dummy band when I entered the carnival— just in case the committee had connected the dots between Jackie Goerman and Mackenzie Davis, the evil journalist villain.

Nobody at the carnival knew Sparx had arrived—I could be anyone. Exist anonymously. My heart terrorized my chest the moment I entered the ballroom. I couldn't bear anything other than the adoration in Kierk's eyes I'd become so accustomed to.

I'd come clean and explain the whole story—if he'd let me.

I strode right up to the bar and shouted over the music, "Can I get a boring chocolate shake, please?"

My legs nearly gave way when Kierk hustled around the bar and spun me in a hug that I would have sworn I'd feel for decades.

So, he didn't know. Yet.

"Sparx," he whispered, and then our lips found each other's.

Harvey's booming voice next to us finally tore us apart.

"Well, if that's what you get when you order a chocolate milkshake, I might have to let a few admirers in on the secret," he said.

I shot him a look that I hoped said, *Don't mess with me.*

Kierk smirked. "We need to get dressed for the parade, right?" Before I could answer, he motioned for Harvey to join us. "Let me know if you hear anything about Mackenzie Davis, okay?"

A desert climbed into my throat and sucked up every ounce of moisture.

"You think she'll come here tonight?" Harvey whispered.

"Guess we'll find out."

She was holding his hand.

One good thing: If they were looking for Mackenzie Davis, Kierk hadn't connected that she was in fact Sparx. That meant I still had time to tell him the truth. But not much.

"You mind closing up for me?" Kierk asked.

Harvey saluted him. Kierk took my hand, and we were off, running through the ballroom to the elevator. He pressed the button and then kissed the back of my hand.

"You okay?"

"Mm-hmm," I mumbled.

"You nervous about the parade?"

"Actually, I was wondering if we could skip the parade."

He laughed. "Are you serious? Skip the Mardi Gras parade? It's going to be over the top. More than we've ever done before."

"There's something I really want to talk to you about. It can't wait."

"Okay… Give me two seconds."

He hustled back to the bar and said something to Harvey, who looked confused but then shrugged and picked up a walkie-talkie.

"Come with me."

Kierk took my hand but kept distance, too—nearly cold, but not quite. He thought I was going to break up with him. He had to. I squeezed his hand.

Every time we passed a security guard, I held on to Kierk more tightly. They all nodded to him without glancing at me.

Kierk tapped the up button on the elevator. "There's a place I've always wanted to show you, but it's kind of isolated. Is that okay?"

Privacy to break the news? "That's perfect."

His shoulders lifted a little as we stepped into the elevator. "Great. Close your eyes."

"Kierk…" My tone must have been enough to curb his playfulness because we stood side by side, staring at the inside of the elevator door in silence.

The elevator dinged open to the mysterious seventh floor. In all our time together at the carnival, we'd never gone up to the top floor. Unlike the levels below with their long hallways and office-like design, the seventh floor appeared residential with a massive ornate wooden door and a hall table decorated with fresh flowers as if we were at the penthouse of a fancy apartment building. Kierk slipped a key into the door, but it was too dark inside to see much until we took a few turns and he flicked a light switch.

The room had that antique style that couldn't be replicated in our time. Authentic. Each window was stained glass, the floors and bottom half of the walls were real wood

—not that weird paneling stuff from my grandparents' generation—and bookcases with glass doors covered three of the four walls.

"Did you learn how to teleport?"

Kierk squeezed my waist. "I knew you'd love it."

"What is it?"

"The original owner's library. He was such a workaholic that he built apartments to sleep in while he was here."

I ran my hand along the top of the bookshelves, peeking inside at the titles. None struck me as familiar. "Did he live far from here?"

"No. But he had a ton of money and…"

I got the sense he had more to say. "And…?"

His neck and cheeks reddened. "Legend has it that he had a mistress. He kept her here and his wife at his mansion."

"Oooh. Intrigue!"

Kierk laughed. "But it's a cool room, right?"

"Definitely. I would not have expected this here."

"It faces the back of the building, so unless you were in the woods, you wouldn't even notice the windows are more ornate than the floors below." Kierk snapped his fingers. "Oh, speaking of hiding, check this out." He opened one of the glass doors. "Push the wall behind the books."

"Push the wall?" I asked.

"Yep."

I did, and it gave. "Is that a secret passage?"

"A storage closet to hide his stash during the Prohibition. Records show that he spent a lot of time in here with clients and other prominent businessmen drinking alcohol and smoking cigars."

"Outlaws," I teased. *Like me,* a tiny voice said in my head and threatened to grow louder.

"Exactly."

I walked around the room, picking up random knick-knacks as if to inspect them. Really, I was procrastinating long enough to unjumble my thoughts. The silence between us ballooned into an undeniable awkwardness that demanded more silence.

"Sparx, I know you have something to tell me, but I want to say something first, if that's okay."

I nodded.

"When I think about the fact I've only known you a couple of months and realistically have spent a few hours with you—"

"More than a few," I interrupted.

"Even still, you've never seen my face. You don't even know my real name."

"Do you want me to know your real name?"

"I do," he said. "I might be completely out of line here, especially not knowing what you have to say, but I've been thinking a lot about it, and I want to be with you. For real."

I squirmed. "Like…outside the carnival?"

"Not the reaction I hoped for." He grimaced. "Please don't tell me you're here to break up with me."

"It's not that. I…I…" *Would love that. Yes, let's go to movies and dinners. Come climbing with my dad and talk philosophy and the academic stuff he loves. Come see all the newspapers around my house, the award-winning articles my father and I wrote over the years framed on the walls.*

"You…?" His smile was an invitation to tell him anything.

The words couldn't form in my head, let alone reach my mouth. I thought of Kierk every day. When I was in school, I fantasized about masking myself and challenging him at the bumper cars exhibit or devouring beignets at his side or running from him in the maze. Or kissing him atop a parade float.

"Being with you at the carnival has been magical. Adventurous. Romantic." I let my gaze fall on the stained-glass window as heat crept up my neck.

"That all sounds pretty good to me." Kierk ran his fingers through my hair and tilted my head back so our gazes had no choice but to find each other. "I'm in love with you, Sparx."

I pinched my eyes shut, my body feeling as though it was splitting in two. Half felt utter elation that Kierk felt the same way about me that I did about him. The other half muttered, *No, no, no.* How much worse was what I was about to say now that I knew how he felt? How much more brutal the betrayal?

"And unless I'm completely off here, I think you're falling for me, too, or at least I hope you are. If this thing you have to tell me is bigger than that—bigger than us loving each other—then tell me. Otherwise..." He ran a fingertip along my cheek to my chin. "Do you love me?" he whispered.

"Yes," I breathed back.

That beautiful grin of his appeared, and I was done. His lips found the curve of my neck, and I shivered as I slid my fingers down his back, passion sending wickedness through me. I ripped his shirt over his head, accidentally shifting his mask in the process. My heart jumped. We paused there for a second, both of us breathing heavily. I could lift my hand and slip the mask over his head or let him adjust it. He waited for me to decide.

One thing was certain: I didn't feel ready to remove my mask for him—not until he knew the truth.

Gingerly, I repositioned the mask on his perfect face, ignoring the way his lips pursed in disappointment.

"Kierk," I said, quietly. "I heard everything you said, but I still have something to tell you."

His shoulders slumped. "Why do I feel a sense of overwhelming dread in my stomach?"

Because despite how brutally I'd made a fool of him, he was incredibly smart and intuitive. Not to mention perfect.

The clock on the mantle told me I had fifteen more minutes to get to the ballroom to meet Lola before our deadline. I'd need more than fifteen minutes to break this news. To make Kierk understand. Before I could say more, the door opened, and a man stepped inside the room. He gaped when he saw us wrapped up in each other, Kierk shirtless. Unlike every other employee I'd met at the carnival— besides Sweet Cheeks, whom Kierk had admitted was the only "older" staffer—this man wasn't a teenager. Far from it, actually. I knew that for certain because instead of wearing his mask, he held it in his hands.

"Perhaps your friend should leave," the man said and disappeared into a room down the hall.

I'd never been caught in a compromising position with a guy, probably because I'd never been in a compromising position. Even worse, right when I was finally mustering the courage for the big reveal.

Kierk pulled his shirt back on and escorted me to the elevator.

"I'm so sorry. Is that your boss?"

"You could say that," Kierk said.

"Your boss? Like *the* boss of the carnival?"

He pressed the down button. "Nobody knows him, Sparx. You really have to keep this between us. The only reason he didn't have a mask on is because this is a private suite. Nobody else has access."

Nobody other than Kierk. His trust anchored me to the floor.

"Sparx!" Kierk snapped his fingers in front of me. Somehow the elevator door had opened. "I'll meet you in the ballroom as soon as I can. Ten minutes tops."

The elevator doors closed. His boss. Unmasked. I could search the internet for prominent Pittsburgh businessmen. I'd look at their photos and learn the owner's identity. I had it within my grasp to answer one of the most intriguing questions of the year. Even the committee members didn't know the boss's identity. And by morning I could have a phone number and address to request official comment for *The Herald* story.

But…Kierk.

When the doors to the ballroom finally opened, a part of me wanted to slow down, to take in the beauty of the place that I'd made my weekend home—because it would be my last night there.

People were everywhere: dancing upstairs and down, milling along the railing, piled around the tables. Too many people in which to even imagine finding Lola. Kierk would be there soon, too, and I wanted him to be able to find me.

"Ow!"

Someone had grabbed my arm.

"Let me go!"

Harvey pulled me into a corner, his eyes baring down on me. "Tell me you're not Mackenzie Davis."

I froze, my mind working double-time. If Harvey turned me over to security, I'd never get to tell Kierk myself. I had one choice.

To lie.

"Why would you think that?"

"Because someone from her school who's on the committee told security that she spends most of her time in the carnival with Kierk. You're the only one I know who fits that description."

My brain could not think of a lie fast enough. Or at all. "I…"

"This is gonna kill him. You know that, right?"

There was no point in digging myself in any deeper. "I'm sorry."

"You're sorry?" He chuckled unkindly.

"I want to tell Kierk the truth. I do, but I need your help."

"No."

"He deserves to hear it from me."

He cupped his face in his hands.

"Harvey, please."

"Fine. Come with me."

Behind the milkshake bar, he swiped his own band and tapped the screen. "He's up in the residential suite."

"I was there with him," I said, leaving out the details about their boss coming in. If Harvey knew his boss was a few floors away, he might abandon his efforts to help me. "He told me he'd be down in ten minutes tops."

"You don't have much time—security will be here any minute. They're doing rounds looking for you and Kierk. He doesn't have a walkie-talkie on him, but if someone gets to him first, then you won't have the chance to tell him anything."

I'd go back upstairs and face him there. "Swipe your band for the seventh floor."

"I don't have access."

I wiped my head around wildly, looking for a solution.

"Look, Sparx—"

"Harvey, I need a few minutes with him. Please."

"I don't think any number of minutes is going to matter. Take it from someone who's been there."

Sandra—his girlfriend who had written an article about

everything he'd revealed when the carnival first opened. Harvey was right. This was going to kill Kierk.

He pressed his fingers against his temples. "There's a Welcome Room in the corner. Hide in there. I'll send him your way when he comes down."

I jumped up and kissed his cheek. "Thank you, Harvey."

"I'm not doing it for you. I'm doing it for him."

FORTY

I PACED in front of the wall of masks in the Welcome Room, chewing at my fingernails. I needed Kierk to find me before security did and to listen to what I had to say.

Somehow.

I tore through all our memories, but none of them provided me with answers for how to navigate this situation. It was probably why I'd chosen not to tell him before. No way of telling him ended with us together. This would be it.

I slumped into a chair.

I was losing so much: The way my insides twisted at the sight of him and how my heart expanded with every smirk. The tingle of my skin like a racing fire across my body when he touched me. Even if it was fantasy, not reality, I wanted it in my life. I wanted him in my life.

I jumped at a knock. "Sparx, you in there?"

With a deep breath that did little good, I opened the door and pulled him inside. He kissed me a quick greeting, then brushed my neck with another kiss as he hugged me.

"Sorry about that," he said. "You are sworn to absolute secrecy about him. I vouched for you."

My throat closed. He'd vouched for me—the girl who had written the article he and his colleagues despised. By the time he pulled away, tears streamed down my cheeks.

"Are you crying?"

"I…"

"What is it?" Kierk asked.

"I'm not… It's just…" I glanced over his shoulder and through the crack in the door into the ballroom. Across the room, beyond the lines of masked, spinning couples, three bouncers interrogated Harvey. Instinctively, I knew they were looking for me. Harvey shrugged at them and went back to mixing milkshakes. The trio turned and scanned the room. Harvey caught my eye and shook his head so inconsequentially nobody else could have seen it, but it was the warning I needed.

"Everything okay?" Kierk asked.

I took a mental picture of the love and adoration that painted every stroke of his face when he looked at me, knowing it was all about to disappear.

"You shouldn't have vouched for me."

"Okay…"

"Kierk." My words, my breath caught in my throat.

"You're scaring me, Sparx. What's going on?"

The tears poured now. "I lied to you."

He straightened, finally taking me seriously.

"I'm so sorry."

"What do you mean you lied?"

"I wanted to tell you. And it doesn't change my feelings. Everything we did here, everything we said, I meant it. These last few weeks have changed me in the best ways. You've changed me."

"You have a boyfriend."

"No," I whispered. My body ached from the impending impact. I searched my entire vocabulary for the words that would make him understand, the words that would buy me a few more minutes to explain, the words that would save me from this web I'd allowed to spin so strongly it suffocated me. No words came. Some writer I was.

"You look terrified. Sparx, please. Tell me."

"You once asked what my passion was?"

He nodded.

"I want to be a writer. A journalist. There's this program. And Northwestern. And it's all I've wanted. It's my dream."

"A writer. That's great." Confusion spread over his face, though, and I could see him working out the details. The realization would never come to him; he'd have to be dragged to it. He trusted me that much.

I stifled a sob. "But I didn't mean to. It just happened. I chose you, I did. I promise I did."

"I'm confused."

I took a deep breath and then exhaled, "I'm Mackenzie Davis."

Recognition found its way to his eyes slowly, and then his face formed a shape I'd never seen in all the hours I'd looked at him.

"Kierk?"

He pulled his hands away. "You wrote that crap about the carnival? After all that we've done here, I thought... How could you... This whole time...?"

I bowed my head at his inability to form a sentence. The malady had stricken me every time I'd considered telling him the truth.

The guards passed the Welcome Room again, pausing to search the crowd. I couldn't bear to look at Kierk any longer. My heart implored my mouth to explain, but my body was caught in a storm with the twisting and uprooting power of a tornado, the flooding insistence of a hurricane, and the blinding frigidness of a blizzard. I was no match for the unnatural disaster I had created.

I stepped out of the room, and the only thing I could say to the guards was "I'm the one you're looking for."

FORTY-ONE

I SWALLOWED my tears until they formed a dangerous lump huge enough to cut off my breathing at any second. I couldn't have done a worse job explaining things to Kierk. Seriously. Epic disaster.

The guards pulled me into a nondescript room. An unmasked Lola sat at the table. Her arms were crossed, and her attitude was maxed to about 178 percent.

"Hey," she said.

"Lola." I turned to the bouncer. "Why don't you let us go, and we'll be on our way."

The guard pointed to Lola. "She took a photo."

I swiveled on her. "You didn't."

She shrugged. "Oops."

Someone knocked on the door. The bouncer opened it, and despite the mask, I had no doubt the tall, domineering figure was Kierk's boss.

"Miss St. James," he said, sitting across from us. "Editor of *The Muse*, I presume?"

Lola smiled at him with pride. "Glad to hear you follow our work."

He smirked at her as if she were a toy and then studied me. "You're the girl who wrote the offending article."

I tried to be irritated by his description, but my body had had its fill of emotions at that moment.

"Clearly you don't know good journalism when you see it," Lola said.

A figure loomed in the doorway. I didn't need to look to know it was Kierk.

I couldn't bring my eyes to his. Ever again.

"I'll escort them out."

"Kierk—"

"I'm in charge of incidents like these, am I not?"

"Given the circumstances—"

"It's my job."

His boss nodded. Lola and I looked at each other. "So... are we going, then?" she asked.

Kierk nodded and gestured for us to stand. His boss didn't even look at us while we left the room.

When Kierk turned his back and ordered us to follow him, Lola leaned over and whispered, "Mac, he is fine as—"

"I can hear you." Kierk led us through the usual places. Like a carnival version of torture. *This is what you had before you went and messed it up.* The Starlight Café, the beignets and bumper cars. The parade, the climbing wall. All moments of brilliance. All lost.

A massive garage with parade floats and the fleet of black sedans we'd used for the excursion sat behind the building. Kierk climbed behind the wheel of one. "Get in," he said.

Lola climbed into the front seat. I nearly told her that was my spot. But it wasn't. Kierk glanced at me in the rearview mirror before he started the ignition. Then we sat there.

"What are you doing?" Lola asked.

"Waiting for your bags."

As if on cue, Harvey appeared from the same exit we'd used and tossed them into the trunk. I watched the carnival get smaller in the back window as Kierk drove away.

He drove us to the trolley station in silence. Lola pointed out her red Volkswagon, and Kierk pulled up beside it. My heart betrayed me with another crack when the car stopped.

"For what it's worth, Mac didn't mean to publish that story. I published it without first confirming it with her," Lola said. "You should also know that her choosing not to publish that story meant she would fail her journalism class and lose any hope of becoming the editor next year, which has been her dream for as long as I've known her."

I put my hand on her shoulder. "Thanks, Lola. But let's go."

I grabbed our things from Kierk's trunk and dropped them into Lola's, rounding the car to the passenger side. With my hand on the door, I stopped and looked back at Kierk. After all my resolutions to tell him, I'd done it too late and in the worst way possible. He deserved more. Way more.

I headed back to his car.

"Mac, what are you—"

I held up a finger, signaling her to wait a minute, and tapped on Kierk's window. He stared out the windshield for a few seconds before sighing and rolling it down. My words and thoughts and desires twisted inside me like a pile of climbing equipment, knotted and waiting to be sorted.

"Never mind." I walked a few steps away before turning back. "Someday, I hope you'll try to understand."

He shook his head. I stood next to his car, feeling pathetic and probably looking worse. Short of ripping off his door and forcing him to hear me out, what could I do?

Absolutely nothing.

"Let's go, Mac," Lola called.

"Sparx, wait." Kierk threw open his door and stood next to it, half of his body still inside.

I stopped, a thrill of hope untangling a few of the ropes.

"I realize I'm totally embarrassing myself here. I'm pathetic and I know it, but, I mean, did I imagine everything?"

"No," I said quietly.

"Why did you do it?"

"I want to go to *The Herald*'s summer program this year and get into Northwestern's journalism school."

"So, this is all about school?"

"It's a big deal for me. I'm sorry I never told you."

I couldn't tell what he was thinking, but whatever it was, his hopeful expression transformed into anger. "You didn't tell me a lot of things."

"No," I said quietly.

"I have to go," he said.

Before I could protest, he slipped back behind the wheel, and the black sedan disappeared into a trail of red taillights.

FORTY-TWO

LOLA DROPPED me off at my house with a string of apologies. As soon as she disappeared from sight, I dug my car keys from the bottom of my bag and drove to Dinah's. I parked in front of her house, tears wetting my shirt. The light in her bedroom was low but on. I tapped a message into my phone again and hovered over the Send button. Closing my eyes, I pushed it, and seconds later, Dinah opened the door in purple unicorn pajamas, a look of concern on her face.

"I know we haven't been talking," I said, "but I didn't know where else to go."

She wrapped me in her arms and pulled me inside. "You can always come to me."

I cried harder.

Moments later, I sat at her kitchen island with a bowl of salted caramel pretzel ice cream.

"You wanna tell me what this is about?" she asked.

"Well, I'm in love with Kierk, who is wonderful and perfect and now knows that I've lied to him since the moment we met."

"Oh no, Mac. I'm sorry."

"He wanted to take off his mask for me!" Another scoop of ice cream down my throat.

"He did?"

"Before he found out who I was." I swung my spoon in the air to emphasize my point. "Sparx was great. Mackenzie Davis ruined everything."

Dinah rested her hand on my shoulder. "Look, Mac. Todd told me about Kierk. He believes in the rules of the carnival more than anyone. He practically wrote them. If he was willing to move beyond them—to give up his privacy and to take off his mask—he's definitely in love with you, too. At the very least he can forgive you."

I took another bite. "Yeah. He amitta ta fall—"

"Swallow and then speak."

I did. "Sorry. He admitted to falling in love with me and then basically told me to get the—"

Dinah's eyes widened so much I thought she'd seen a ghost. But I got the idea—no swearing. Parents. Yada yada.

I slumped into my chair, mulling over my reality. Kierk had loved me. He'd trusted me so completely, and I'd cut him deeply. Probably too deep for him to ever trust me again. I stuffed an entire scoop of ice cream into my mouth, dripping on my shirt and the table in the process.

"What a mess." Dinah reached for some napkins.

I held her hand and gave her a look that I hope she understood as *I'm sorry* and *thank you* and *I missed you*. Despite the distance that had grown between us, Dinah Zimmerman was my best friend. That meant I could brokenly stumble into her life at any moment and she would grab a tube of super glue, just like I would for her.

"Me, too," she whispered. And then I cried some more.

"D?"

The question on the tip of my tongue was like standing

on the precipice of the highest, most challenging climb I'd ever make. "Do you think I'm an idiot to hope?"

"I want you to be happy, and if there's any chance you and Kierk could be, then no. I don't think you're an idiot to hope."

"In my head I know there isn't a chance, but I'm not sure my heart will listen."

We ate our ice cream while the truth settled over both of us, and my bites of salted caramel suddenly became a little more salty.

―――――

Wednesday, I woke up with the kind of hangover one would expect from indulging in Fat Tuesday, living a split identity, and getting dumped. I shut off my alarm and pulled the covers over my head. Hours passed, evening came. I made two trips to the kitchen and left the scraps from the food I'd retrieved on my nightstand table.

―――――

The next month passed like a turtle crawling through my calendar. Okay. It had been only two days, but it had felt like a month.

"Macky, get out of bed," my dad said on Thursday afternoon.

"I'm good here."

He ripped the covers away. A fitting metaphor for the article ripping my shield of safety and comfort away. Yes, world. I was fully capable of bringing every moment of life back to my…let's call it a misstep.

"Give them back."

"We're going to The Climb. Now."

"Dad, I really don't want to go."

"I don't care. You've missed two days of school and you barely eat anything. You desperately need to shower. Get up this instant, or I'm calling your mother."

I didn't think I could deflate any more. My body was a pancake against the bed, and my father knew it. My mother would question every detail. She would insist a teenage girl should live with her mother and plead with me to move to London, or at the least apply to colleges there. She wouldn't work her life around me and live here, but she had no problem with me molding my world around hers. Calling my mother would set me down a slope so slippery the best traction equipment couldn't stop my fall.

"Fine," I said.

MACKENZIE DAVIS COMMITS TO GETTING OUT OF BED, SHOWERING, LEAVING THE HOUSE

"Fifteen minutes. Shower, brush your teeth, and let's go." I groaned. "And Macky?"

"Yeah, Dad?"

"I love you."

———

Barb greeted us in the lobby of The Climb. She only needed one glance at my puffy cheeks to transition into mother mode. "Your father told me you were upset, but I didn't know it was this bad."

Dad's cheeks flamed red. Oh my gosh. Were they... friends? Or something more? I'd completely missed it. I'd been too wrapped up in myself to notice much at all.

Barb ushered me into her office and closed the door. She

did all the right things: handing me tissues, rubbing my back, hugging me, criticizing teenage boys.

When my tears finally stopped, she said, "Why don't you get out there and climb? It might help work out some of these emotions."

"Thanks, Barb," I managed. "You've always been good to me."

"And I always will be."

My shoulders slumped even more at that. She'd never given me reason not to believe that, and in this emotional moment where my life and my body felt entirely broken, her solidness bolstered me.

Kierk had thought he could rely on me. He'd given up his time in the carnival for me. He'd shared his philosophy and beliefs with me. He'd kissed me, like... I shook the thought away.

He'd believed in me.

A group of guys congregated in the corner, laughing and talking about their plans for that night—Thirsty Thursday. I searched their faces for a scar like Kierk's—hoping but also dreading that he might be there. *He's not,* a quiet voice said. In the carnival, Kierk had emitted an electricity. The only thing electrical in The Climb was the lights. Would that electricity fade now?

My dad handed me a granola bar and a Gatorade.

"Thanks."

He nodded. I peeled back the wrapper and took a bite.

"Were you really going to call Mom?"

"You've never scared me like this."

I'd never felt like this.

"Is there anything I can do to help you?"

I shrugged, and he pulled me into his arms. "You really like this guy, huh?"

"Doesn't matter."

"Honey, it always matters."

Not if you messed it up too badly to fix it. "Can we not talk about it, please?"

"Sure."

I kissed him on the cheek and shifted into climbing mode. The first few holds slipped through my fingers. My rubbery legs struggled to push the lifeless blob that was my body upward. At some point, though, muscle memory engaged, and I thought of nothing except the next colorful hold. Red. Blue. Orange. Red. Yellow. Blue. Yellow. Orange. Motion was a reminder that through the numbness, somewhere, there was life.

My life.

Orange. Yellow. Green. Red. Green. Blue. I didn't allow myself to think about anything but the colors until I reached the perch where I'd first seen Kierk. Dad and Barb chatted on the ground, glancing at me every few seconds. I waved to show them I was okay. Not sure they bought it. I wasn't sure I did either.

Dinah had texted me that morning that kids at school were still talking about my story. I had more notifications from people asking how they could get an invitation than I could even respond to—like I could help them with that now.

I'd written a story people wanted to read—on page one, above the fold—yet I'd messed up even more than when I'd written a boring story about the planters. Lola had been right: It wasn't the story. It was the person writing it.

I took the long, hard way down. Not wanting to interrupt Barb and my dad or actually look closely enough at their flirting, I swiped the home screen of my phone. I ignored the scores of social media notifications and found a voice-mail from Liz Valentine.

"Mackenzie, hi! You're probably in class, but I wanted

to check with you. Is it possible for you to come to the Herald *offices after school for a meeting? Four o'clock. One of our editors was able to set something up with the manager of Carnivalesque. I thought it would be great for you to meet face-to-face. I'll text you the details. Please let me know!"*

"What is it?" Dad said, suddenly standing next to me.

"It's the editor from *The Herald.* She wants me to come to the offices today to meet with the editors and the manager of Carnivalesque."

"I'll drive you," Dad said.

I felt suddenly energized. I'd made a mess of the first article for *The Muse.* For *The Herald,* I'd get it right.

"I have to go home and prepare."

FORTY-THREE

THE HERALD OFFICES were in the North Shore of the city, near the football and baseball stadiums. Unable to find a place close by to park, my dad dropped me at the front entrance. I smoothed my pencil skirt and scarf before pulling the door open and heading for the elevators. From the outside, I appeared calm—I thought. Inside, a battle raged between the part of me that wanted to see Kierk and the part that hoped he wasn't there.

To distract myself, I focused on my plan. I wanted a full interview and tour of the facility—with photos. If the manager wouldn't go for that, I had a list of five questions, in order of importance, to ask on the spot. If he was willing to go further, I had additional questions. I already had a rough draft of the article as a jumping-off point. I always found when I sat down to write, even if I'd thought I'd asked everything, something else always came up. I might not have another opportunity, so I wanted to be prepared for that, too.

I marched into the newspaper office feeling confident and ready and introduced myself to the receptionist.

"Right this way Miss Davis."

I followed her through a very gray maze of cubicles. Many were empty, but some housed reporters typing faster than I could ever had imagined possible. Others wrote in long, narrow notebooks while talking on the phone. After the week I'd had, I shocked myself at the smile spreading across my lips.

Until I heard *his* voice.

"If you'll wait here, Liz will be with you soon," the receptionist said, leaving me outside of a gray conference room with a gray door and gray paint. By the sound of it, Kierk was already inside.

"Dad, we don't have to do this," he said. "The carnival is still packed to capacity every night. We don't need publicity."

Dad?

Kierk had access to everything. He supervised everything. He knew everything.

It made painful sense—among all else, why my treachery had hurt him so deeply. His dad owned the carnival.

I fell into the closest chair. Fresh tears warmed my eyes, but I dabbed them away. I couldn't cry. I'd ruined everything between Kierk and me. I wouldn't ruin the chance Liz had given me, too.

"The mystery of the carnival was the hook to get people inside," Kierk's dad said. "Now that it's doing so well, we can adjust our tactics."

"Because of your business arrangement with the paper?"

"Among other reasons. After your girlfriend wrote what she did, others will do the same. They'll sneak in and violate the privacy of patrons."

"She's not my girlfriend." His words had been spit into my face.

I shouldn't have been hearing this. It was another violation of Kierk's privacy. I stood up, wondering if it would be
best to go back to the reception area.

A phone rang inside the conference room. "I have to
take this," Kierk's dad said.

I glanced around, but there was nowhere for me to
disappear to. I moved as far away from the room as I could,
studying the screen of my phone. Mr.—whatever his name
was—paused in the doorway. I could feel his eyes on my
back. After a few seconds, he said, "No, nothing. I'm here.
What did you find out?" and walked past me and down the
hall.

My chest rose and fell so carefully as though the conference room and the hallway were on the precipice of absolute
disaster. Even a deep breath could set me tumbling into an
abyss.

Mackenzie Davis Weighs Her Terrible Options

Option one: look into the conference room and see Kierk
from a distance before Liz appeared and sat me down right
next to him.

Option two: I could leave. Tell Liz I wasn't feeling well
or something.

Option three: I could invent a time machine.

Slowly, I turned until a view of the conference room was
clear through the vertical glass window beside the door. I
raised my eyes to Kierk's, contradictions exploding in my
mind like fireworks. To see his face without the curve of a
black mask over his cheek bones, which were perfection,
felt almost wrong. The scar on his lip had stood out as so
prominently in the past, but without the mask to cover the
rest of his face, it could go undetected.

He took a breath so deep that his chest swelled, and I

wondered if he envisioned himself on a precipice, too. He didn't smile at me, but he also didn't look away.

I glanced down the hallway—still no sight of Liz or his father. With courage I didn't know existed, I stepped through the doorway into the room.

"Hi…" he said.

"Hi." With only a few chairs and a table between us—no masks—his beauty shocked me. I'd laughed with Chanel about how terrifying it might have been to see someone from the carnival in real life. What if they looked better with half the face covered?

A laugh escaped my mouth.

Kierk smiled, and my heart shattered. "What's funny?"

"You're gorgeous," I said without a thought.

He laughed for real then, rolling his eyes at the same time as if frustrated I'd made him laugh at all. "Of all the things I thought we might say to each other, that was not one of them."

"It just came out."

"Excellent," Liz said from the doorway. "You're here." She looked around the room, realizing Kierk's dad wasn't present. "Where's Mr. Scott?"

"Stepped away for a phone call. I can grab him."

Liz nodded and then shook my hand. "Mackenzie! Good to see you again."

Kierk's shoulders stiffened when Liz said my real name, but he shuffled out of the room to find his father.

"My colleague, Jeannette, will join us in a moment as well. She's friends with Mr. Scott and set up this meeting."

I nodded.

Jeannette, Mr. Scott, and Kierk descended on the room at the same time. I turned over my reporter notebook in my hands, my stomach knotting even tighter with each rotation.

Finally, Jeannette took my hand. "Mackenzie Davis, the

young journalist who managed to break through the carnival's defenses and live to tell the tale. I'm Jeannette."

I couldn't bear to see Kierk's reaction to her words, so I focused on her. "Nice to meet you."

But then my choices were to formally greet him and his father or appear incredibly rude and unprofessional—not much of a choice.

Mr. Scott extended his hand. "Breaking through the carnival's defenses—that's one way of looking at it. Ms. Davis, pleasure to see you again."

"You've already met?" Jeannette asked.

Sure, if you called being caught entangled in his son's arms in the residential suite of the carnival meeting someone.

"Twice, actually," Mr. Scott said.

My cheeks warmed.

"This is my son," Mr. Scott said, "Soren."

Soren. Like Søren Kierkegaard, the philosopher. I'd taken Sparx because of how closely it connected to my real name, and Kierk had made a similar choice.

Trying to look Kierk in the face was like staring at the sun, but I extended my hand to him just the same. His hand enclosed mine, and I mentally scolded the tingles in my arm.

I managed to recover as everyone took their seats. I opened my notebook, pen ready.

Jeannette started the meeting. "First of all, everything we discuss here is off the record. We understand the carnival's commitment to privacy."

"Thank you," Soren said. But I knew I couldn't call him anything other than Kierk.

"But it's a hot topic right now. We want a story that will give everyone in the area a clear vision of Carnivalesque."

"We hit capacity every weekend. We don't need publicity," Kierk said.

"That may be true," Jeannette said, "but you also have had two recent safety incidents."

I glanced at Kierk. His lips were pursed and his eyes dark. I hadn't known about any safety concerns. Except—the first night I'd met Kierk, Harvey had called him down from the platform at the parade to go deal with something in the King's Court. I wondered if it had anything to do with that.

"They were addressed immediately. Nobody was harmed. We have systems in place to keep everyone safe."

"I understand that, but do parents? Do other teens? Every businessperson knows that rumors can send even the strongest enterprise down a landslide."

"What are you suggesting?" Mr. Scott asked.

"We write two pieces," Liz interjected. "One will be a brief discussion of safety plans for the carnival—without giving away anything crucial, of course. The piece will honor journalistic integrity. I must make clear it will not be a puff piece for you to control as you see fit. However, it will be honest, and if Jeannette is right—which she usually is—you have all the appropriate procedures in place."

"And the second piece?" Mr. Scott asked.

Liz nodded. "Will be written by Mackenzie from the angle of someone who attends the carnival."

"And what's the angle on that one?" Kierk said.

Liz and Jeannette looked at me. I took a deep breath.

"Self-discovery is of the utmost importance in the carnival," I said, addressing the response I'd practiced with my dad to Mr. Scott. "My recommendation would be to invite a photographer to the carnival in the middle of the week when no patrons are there. Giving a sense of the ambiance from some of the exhibits—when they are empty—would be appropriate. We could focus on more than the experiential aspects, too. The article will include the philosophical foundation of the carnival to give even those who regularly attend a deeper appreciation."

Mr. Scott surveyed me with an intensity that hinted he might finally be taking me seriously. "And if I don't agree?"

"Then, I'll write my observations—a personal essay of sorts that includes my perceptions of the carnival."

Kierk blanched, probably wondering what another personal essay about a carnival where I'd spent ninety percent of my time with him might look like—how it might violate his privacy. Again.

"We'll consider it," Mr. Scott said and stood, signaling the meeting's end. He shook hands with everyone in the room, but Kierk did not. He slipped past his father and waited in the hallway, not giving me another glance.

FORTY-FOUR

MY PHONE and I became best friends—always together. But Mr. Scott didn't call.

FLEDGLING REPORTER NAIVE TO THINK CARNIVALESQUE FEATURE COULD BE HER BIG BREAK!

He still didn't call.

IN BOLD MOVE, MACKENZIE DAVIS AVOIDS CHOCOLATE MILKSHAKES, HOPING TO SUPPRESS MEMORIES OF MILKSHAKE MAN

But it didn't work.

With my deadline approaching, I sorted through every note I'd made about Carnivalesque: my time there, my research, the philosophy, the rumors, the popularity. I could piece together an article from it all, no doubt, but it wouldn't have nearly the same effect without the access Mr. Scott could give me. Or official comment from him or someone high within the organization. Someone like Kierk.

I attempted roughly 738 different leads and drafted half as many paragraphs, but nothing came together. I could feel Liz's disappointment through space and time. And then…

UNKNOWN NUMBER RINGS ON MACKENZIE DAVIS'S PHONE

"Hello?"

"Mackenzie Davis?"

"Yes…"

"This is Trevor. I'm Mr. Scott's assistant."

My heart beat faster. Somehow, the details Trevor spoke found their way to the piece of paper in front of me. I'd be interviewing Mr. Scott at the carnival tomorrow. Finally.

I scrambled with Liz to schedule a photographer and relished the memo the assistant sent with directions to the carnival. Actual directions, not to a puzzle pick up or even the trolley transport. To the front entrance. Technically, I would be parking in the bay in the back with all the floats and town cars, but I wasn't about to be picky. The tingles behind my belly button returned as they did when I thought of Kierk. I wondered if this feeling would ever go away.

Even as I questioned whether I wanted it to.

———

I arrived at the carnival lot to Mr. Scott already waiting for me. "Miss Davis," he called. "You're right on time."

He and the younger man next to him were both masked. I knew it wasn't Kierk because of the noted absence of tingles in my stomach.

I'd worn the mask Dinah had made for me—bold, green, strong—just what I needed.

"This is my assistant, Trevor. You spoke on the phone yesterday."

"Yes," I said. "Nice to meet you."

"Trevor is his Carnivalesque name, just so you know. Although we're essentially alone here, it's best if you call me by my carnival name, too. It's Shade."

"Shade?" I said a little surprised. No philosopher name for the philosophy professor turned business mogul. "Why Shade?"

Revealing a shyness that did not suit him, he shrugged. "I like to avoid the spotlight. Which is why I agreed to the interview on the condition of anonymity."

The request had been a tough one for Liz. As a rule, newspapers avoided anonymous sources for too many reasons to count, she'd said. But sometimes the value of the information outweighed those reasons. And sometimes the content was more important than who'd provided it.

"Absolutely," I said. "My editor agreed with your terms. And you're good with the recording?"

"To be used only to ensure accuracy."

"Understood." I hit Record on my phone and moved on to the next question. "But if I may ask, why all the secrecy? Public records will show who purchased this property. Eventually, someone will trace this back to you, right? Why not use this opportunity to come out of the shadows, so to speak?"

"It's not about me, it's about the committee and the people who come here. Everyone has an equal role. For a place that aims to subvert power, it would be inappropriate for me to publicly assume that position. Your questions are good ones, and someday someone might suspect me. But I'm hoping that day isn't today."

Nobody would learn his identity from me.

"What shall we call you?" Mr. Scott asked.

"Sparx" had always been at the carnival for a story, so it wouldn't be outlandish to take the name today, but somewhere along the way, Sparx had become someone else, someone I probably wouldn't see again. "Mackenzie is fine."

He nodded as if agreeing with the weighted decision. "Miss Davis it is, then."

We chatted about the weather and the impending snowstorm until the photographer, Zoe, pulled into the lot a couple minutes later. Inside, we headed through a pedestrian door next to the massive opening the parade floats used. An eerie quiet greeted us. Sunlight filtered in through the windows and dropped patches of light onto the clean, yet worn, floor. The rock wall above us looked lonely, and so did the single parade float—a swan—in the center of the room. It all felt like a billboard announcing times had changed.

"So, first question," I said, flipping through my notebook to the list I'd rewritten four times. "How has your vision changed for the carnival since it opened?"

"My vision for the carnival is irrelevant. I inherited some money and land near here and started Carnivalesque to offer young adults a place to explore their identity and experiences they might not have had otherwise. At the heart of our philosophical experience is the self, but in contemporary culture, we deny the self too often…"

Was Kierk denying himself by refusing to be with me even though he'd said he loved me? Could his father point that out to him in a philosophical language he understood?

"Miss Davis?"

"Huh? Right."

He smiled knowingly. "I teach young adults daily. I've developed a refined skill of recognizing that glazed-eyes look."

"I bet you have."

"Good thing you have the recording, then." He winked.

I sighed, knowing there was only one way to overcome being distracted. "By any chance, will Kierk be joining us today?"

"I'm afraid he's securing equipment for a new exhibit."

"Oh."

"Miss Davis, I won't lie to you. He doesn't support my decision to grant this interview. He's very…disappointed about the situation."

In other words, very disappointed with me. Fine. He had every right to be, not that I could think about that and get through this without crumbling.

"The initial investment—this property, the exhibits, the payroll—wasn't it a major risk?" I asked.

"It's logical to think that way, and while the carnival is absolutely a lucrative business, creatively, we treat it much differently."

"How so?"

"Our mission wasn't necessarily to make money, although we have made some. We create opportunities and worlds for young adults to enjoy life and explore their identities."

"Do you think the carnival has succeeded with those goals?"

Zoe took photos of the solitary parade float in perpetual limbo as we exited the massive factory building.

"The task is a fluid thing, which is why I instilled the committee. They develop and alter the exhibits based on their vision. As a result, they explore their own identities and passions, manage projects, collaborate with other teens, and so much more to bring the exhibits to fruition. I like to think of it as a low-stakes version of *The Apprentice*, except everyone gets to be the apprentice. We recently expanded, and I'm proud to say two hundred young adults serve in various aspects on the committee."

"Wow." That was a lot of people getting the chance to work in a field they loved and gain real-world experience because of the carnival.

"Exactly. And still hundreds more work on the exhibits. We partner with high schools and universities across the region. Students from construction and carpentry programs built most of our floats. Graphic arts students designed our logo, posters, escape room documents, and so on. Interior design majors collaborated with architecture and art history students to authenticate the King's Court and Milkshake Ballroom."

"And all of these people are paid?"

"Of course," he said as if offended. "In some way or another. The high school programs might receive financial support for future projects. College students might earn internship credit. They all receive free passes to the carnival as well."

"I'd like to talk to some of them for the story, if possible."

"You know how we feel about privacy."

"I do. Maybe you can offer them the option of contacting me directly? I can publish their carnival name, not their real name, but it would be a chance to highlight the practical job training the carnival provides."

"Trevor, can you take care of that?"

"Yes, sir."

I smiled at the small victory. "And the committee? Are they paid?"

"A stipend for serving on the committee and an hourly wage when they work in the carnival."

"With so many people involved, how did you maintain secrecy?"

He smiled. "Confidentiality agreements, buy-in from the staff about the importance of anonymity, and—I won't lie—

the occasional fear tactic. We expected teens to respond well to the experiences here, but we could have never predicted the instant popularity. That worked to our advantage because everyone wanted to be here. And they believed if they violated the tenets of the carnival, they'd be denied entry. Popularity is a powerful tool."

TEEN REPORTER PERFECT EXAMPLE OF CARNIVALESQUE DENYING ENTRY

Trevor led us through the hallways in the factory building to the Starlight Café. The quiet beauty of it struck me. The glow of the twinkle lights wasn't as strong without the night sky above. Every chair sat in perfect position, awaiting customers.

One sniff of the air revealed no scent of beignets. Good thing readers couldn't smell the place from the photos, or they would have been disappointed. I'd have to fill in that detail through my words.

We continued through the carnival—me asking Shade questions about funding, vision, safety, the future; Zoe snapping more photos than she could ever use; and Trevor jotting in a notebook as if he were the one writing the article. My mind wavered from being focused on the interview to daydreaming about places where Kierk and I had spent time. My heart expected to see him behind the milkshake counter in the ballroom. But the blenders sat silent.

"You've spent significant time here, have you not?" Mr. Scott asked.

"I have."

He nodded. Zoe called to Trevor to ask a question about the lighting, and he hustled off to adjust it, leaving Mr. Scott and me alone. "And have you learned anything new about yourself?"

"I'm sure I have," I admitted.

He grinned, a mature variation of Kierk's grin. I looked away. "Care to share *what* you learned?"

"I'm not sure I've figured it out yet. I hope writing the article helps me with that."

"Writing does have a tendency to do just that."

"Yes, it does," I said. "Speaking of the article, is there anything else you'd like to see covered? I can't make any promises, but if there's anything we haven't discussed that you think is important…"

He gestured to a couch and invited me to sit. For a few minutes I thought he wouldn't answer, but he finally said, "I want you to tell *our* truth about Carnivalesque that we've discussed today, but I also want to hear your truth."

My truth had already found its way to the pages of a newspaper article, one that was obviously so poorly written that Kierk had misunderstood my intention entirely. Not that he would have felt any less betrayed if my message had been clearer. He knew I loved him…and it didn't change anything.

"My goal is to be objective, sir. I'm not sure my truth has a place here."

"Forgive me, Miss Davis, but no writing is truly objective. You asked the question, so I will say that hearing your truth helps me see how successful we've been at what we're trying to do. If I'm being honest, this is a selfish request and one of the reasons I agreed to the article."

The seconds ticked away too quickly. The interview ended. Everyone shook hands. I looked around, mentally saying goodbye to a place I'd fallen in love with as much as I'd fallen for one of its creators.

That moment alone told me the carnival was a bigger success than Mr. Scott could have ever predicted.

FORTY-FIVE

THAT EVENING, my fingers moved across the keyboard with such rhythm and grace that my typing teacher from middle school would have collapsed into her swivel chair with pride. After the tour with Mr. Scott, I had so much to say—how the carnival had come to be, the original intention and the current vision driven by committee members from across the region, the emotions of experiencing the exhibits, the willingness to think big and bold in ways that kept costs down and offered real-world educational opportunities to young people.

The first draft of my article came together without a single mention of anything Kierk and I had shared or done —except for the beignets. The beignets were imperative. I included a cuisine section, which detailed the various high school and college culinary programs that had contributed to the carnival food. King's Court alone had hosted the culinary staffs of six different schools since the carnival had opened.

Carnivalesque was the ultimate internship program, which I noted in another section of the article featuring interviews from young adults Trevor had connected me to. After saving the article in, like, four different clouds, I curled up in bed with a mask Mr. Scott had insisted I keep as a souvenir and allowed myself to finally daydream about his son.

———

As Liz had promised, the article ran in *The Herald*'s Sunday edition. I ran down the stairs in my PJs to retrieve it from the paper carrier's hands. I found the article above the fold on the local page, marveling at my *words* in print, but while there were many well-written lines, I spotted a few weak transitions or instances of repetitive word choice. How had I not caught those things before? How had I not written a perfect article for my big debut?

Because it's your debut.

The Herald had published an entire section for young adults with my story as the feature. The feature! Of the Features section!

The paper sat next to me through breakfast. I chewed my fingernails from across the room when my father read it. I cried a little when he hugged me and whispered, "I'm proud of you, Macky."

I froze that moment in my head, vowing to remember it always. Whenever doubt threatened me or my writing, I'd unwrap the memory and let it wash over me.

"Thanks, Dad."

I watched TV with the article on my lap. I actually paid attention to my phone and social networks. *The Herald* shared the article widely. So did I. And so did my dad.

On Monday, I accepted compliments from Mrs. Graham, the staff, and random classmates. Even Lola.

"Great job, Mac," she said.

I waited for a backhanded version of the compliment or a declaration that she would have done better, but none came. "Thanks, Lola."

"I felt like I was back at Carnivalesque. I felt the magic of the world. I wondered what spending real time there might teach me about my own identity, which is crazy because I'd thought my identity was pretty solid."

"Definitely," I said.

"You found the story behind the story—multiple stories, actually. You should be proud."

Lola smiled and walked away, leaving me to wonder if her identity had shifted after all. Or maybe she could finally see in me what she'd always expected was there. Stories didn't matter just because. They mattered because good writers made them matter.

It was a lesson I didn't think Lola would let me forget.

Friends and strangers complimented me and asked if I could get them inside the carnival.

I couldn't even get myself inside.

Colin texted. *Good writing, Mac. How does it feel to be the first and only reporter in the region to have scored the Carnivalesque story?*

I read the text a few times, imaging him in his dorm, smiling with the kind of pride he'd showed when he had been *The Muse* editor. Beyond that, not a single emotion for Colin sparked. My emotions were otherwise occupied.

Although the attention felt good, of all the texts, posts, and messages, none had been from the person I'd wanted to read the article the most.

———

Mrs. Graham sent a note to meet me in her office after school. I collected my coat and books, slammed my locker, and hustled up the stairs. Still high on the compliments, attention, and fruition of a nearly lifelong dream, I bounced into her room with the swagger of a very happy Tigger. My springs went limp when I turned the corner to see Mr. Scott in her office.

"Miss Davis," he said with a smile. "Good to see you again."

"Hi, Mr. Scott."

"I read your article," he said.

I had to remind myself that I didn't need his approval. I'd written the story I'd believed in, and I was proud of my work. Still, the words on the tip of his tongue already mattered more than I could explain.

"I was surprised by your amount of research. Have you been reading philosophy?"

"Yes, sir," I said. "Quite a bit, actually." *Don't think of Kierk,* I told myself. *Don't do it.* But "myself" didn't listen.

"I could tell," he said. "That's why I'm here to offer you a job."

I looked at Mrs. Graham. She only smiled.

"What kind of job?"

"I'd like you to join the committee as the public relations representative for the carnival."

Public relations? I'd never given any thought to public relations. I knew reporters tended to go into PR eventually, but I wanted to write the truth about the world, not spin it for…well, take your pick of reasons.

"I'm not sure I'd be the best choice," I said.

"You know the carnival better than most current committee members. You respect its intentions, you've researched the background and history, and you're clearly a good writer."

By then I'd seen so many sides of Mr. Scott that I could barely register his complimentary nature. "I appreciate the offer, but the carnival has been adamantly against public relations and marketing before. What has changed?"

He sighed. "Look, Miss Davis. I took a chance on you because despite what happened, I trust my son's judgment. He had reason to trust you, and it might sound crazy but I believe in some ways that trust was warranted. I believed you'd write about the carnival in a way that was fair."

The Muse staff had largely believed my good work and rewards from the year before had been due to my dating the editor. That he'd given me the best stories. That he'd helped me write them. That he'd edited them to utter perfection.

It'd been lies, of course.

And now, my big break—the article that'd slept on the pillow next to me the night before—came my way because of yet another guy.

"Thank you, I appreciate that," I said. But I couldn't help myself. "What does your son think of the offer?"

"He doesn't know."

"Oh."

"Miss Davis, I'm within my rights to hire whomever I like." He smiled. "Without asking my son."

"Of course." I returned his smile. "Then I also expect you're within your rights to negotiate such an offer as well."

He laughed. I saw an undeniable resemblance between him and his son, which tore my heart into a few more shreds.

"What did you have in mind?"

FORTY-SIX

FRIDAY NIGHT, Harvey met me at the back access point to the carnival. My stomach warned me not to even think about drinking milkshakes or eating beignets. My head warned me to turn around. My heart was strangely quiet.

The floats waited patiently for the upcoming parade. Part of my negotiation with Mr. Scott was access to the carnival and Harvey's phone number. Harvey's plan had been for me to board the summer wedding float, which was making its final appearances this weekend. He would then drag Kierk onto the float to act as my summer prince. We'd recreate that parade magic from months before. We'd reconnect, and he'd forgive me.

It was a ridiculous plan.

"Let's get you into a costume," Harvey said.

"I can't do this."

"Listen, Sparx, I like you. Despite what you did to my boy, he was happy with you. Now he's miserable. I thought bringing you here would change that."

"I want to change that," I said. "But not like this. I won't corner Kierk at the top of a parade float where he can't escape. I won't force him into talking to me."

"I see your point. Hard to grovel when you're still screwing up."

"Exactly."

He crossed his arms. "Got another plan?"

"I need your help to pull it off."

―――――

With the parade about to begin, the Milkshake Ballroom reminded me of what the place had looked like when Mr. Scott had given me the tour. Practically empty. I unloaded the ingredients from my shopping bags and mixed up the first shake. My heart raced at a pace comparable to the blades of the blender.

The ballroom cleared out even more for the parade. I blended the second shake.

In my peripheral vision, someone walked down the stairs toward the bar. I turned away, not ready to face him.

"Excuse me?" he said. "Do you work here?"

I coaxed myself to around. "Hi."

His eyes widened behind his mask and his perfect mouth dropped open. "Sparx?"

"Hi," I said again.

"How did you get in here?"

"Harvey."

"Well, he's fired." He marched to the computer behind the bar and tapped his band.

I didn't tell him his father had offered me a job and I could be here any time I wanted—if I accepted. I had no intention of accepting, though, if Kierk didn't want me around.

"Please don't call security—I want to talk to you."

His fingers paused above the touch screen. He wore the same mask from the night I'd met him. His messy hair swooped and curled over the mask's edges. He looked as good as ever.

"I'm so sorry," I said.

"Are you?"

"Of course."

"You say that as if it's obvious, but it's not to me. How many days did we hang out together? How many times did I tell you I wasn't the game-playing type? How many times did you lie to my face to use me for a newspaper article that wasn't that good, by the way."

"You're right. Completely."

He crossed his arms.

"Not about the quality of the wri— Oh, forget it," I said. "I didn't mean to hurt you." The heaviness in the air multiplied, threatening to suffocate us both. "Can I dull the pain with a concoction of sugar?"

He scowled at me.

"Kierk, I came here looking for a story and with a twisted view of what the carnival was all about. At first, yes, you were the perfect source. You had unlimited access, and you knew so much and…you shared it with me."

"Because I trusted you."

"And you had every reason to."

"That makes no sense."

"Did you read my article in *The Herald*?"

"No."

"If you had, you'd see how much I love this place and what it stands for. I told the truth about the mission, the philosophy, the reality, and the relationships that people develop here."

"But you had no right to tell that story."

"I didn't include a single word you said to me—or

anything we did together, for that matter. I used only information and quotes from the official interview and tour with your father and my own research."

"Don't say that," he said, looking around as if someone might actually be there, let alone listening.

"What?"

"Don't call him my father. People here don't know."

"Absolutely. I can keep a secret."

He tried to slice me in half with his eyes.

"Of course, you already knew that." My joke fell flat.

Before I'd come to the carnival to grovel, I'd anticipated a tough sell, but I'd also walked in not willing to take no for an answer.

Some guy, clearly lost, called to us from the end of the bar. "Can I get a shake, man?"

"Bar's closed," Kierk called without taking his eyes off me.

I slid the guy one of the banana butterscotch shakes I'd mixed up for Kierk. "On the house."

"There's one thing I don't get," Kierk said.

"What's that?"

"Lola published your story for school without your permission, but you still went ahead with *The Herald* story."

I shrugged. "I guess I figured at that point, why not? I'd already lost you, and I believed in the story I wanted to tell."

"And it was a good opportunity."

"Kierk…"

"Wasn't it?"

It was the opportunity I'd worked all these years for—and the one I would have given up for him if it would had made a difference.

But I had to be honest. "Yes, it was."

He nodded at me as if that settled it.

"Just like managing the carnival is a good opportunity

for you. And designing King's Court is a good opportunity for architecture students. And the food in the carnival creates an opportunity for culinary students." He looked away. "You live in a world that creates opportunities for people like me, yet you want me to give up my own?"

"That's not fair," he said.

"Maybe, maybe not. But it's also not fair to give up on us without even reading what I wrote or trying to understand why I wrote it."

The determined look on his face told me my words had little, if any, effect.

"Fine. I only have one more thing to say."

He managed to make eye contact.

"The people closest to me were shocked I'd give up my writing, my chance at making editor and the summer program I'd worked for forever." I swallowed and urged myself to have the guts to finish the speech I'd practiced. "I decided there would be other chances. There wouldn't be another you."

Kierk swallowed hard, but he dropped his gaze to the floor, no longer able to look at me.

"I was able to reshape my beliefs, but by the looks of it, you're not able to reshape yours."

The voice of a security guard caught me by surprise. "Everything okay here, sir?"

I wiped away a tear threatening to sneak out from under the mask Dinah had made me.

"No, actually. Can you escort Sparx from the building, please?"

"Kierk." I reached for him, but he stepped backward.

The milkshake drinker from earlier appeared as if out of nowhere. "What flavor is this?"

I picked up one of the other milkshake glasses I'd driz-zled with butterscotch sauce and chunks of bananas and pushed it in front of Kierk. "Butterscotch banana," I said, and then I let the security guard lead me away.

I took one last look at Kierk over my shoulder. This couldn't be it. This couldn't be the last time I saw his face. That expression wouldn't be the one he left me with.

But he'd left me no choice. He wanted me to go.

So, I went.

In my car, I leaned over the steering wheel and cried until I was empty. My fingers fumbled for the satin ties of my mask. When it fell from my face, I tossed it over my shoulder into the back seat. I wouldn't be needing it anymore.

FORTY-SEVEN

FIVE MONTHS LATER

"I'M HAVING the best time, Dad! This morning, I read a story draft about the new river walk on the North Side and gave comments to the writer for revision. I don't know if she'll use any of them, but it was still pretty cool."

My dad's laugh sounded in my earbuds as I walked down Forbes Avenue in Oakland toward the Cathedral of Learning, where I spent my afternoon breaks from *The Herald*'s summer program. I'd review my notes from the day, brainstorm story ideas, and do anything I could to make every moment of the amazing experience last.

"That's wonderful, Macky," Dad said. I could practically hear him smiling. "You're like a regular college girl down there. Don't grow up on me too quickly."

"Dad, I'm a senior. It's about time that I start thinking about college."

"You mean Northwestern?"

In the five months since I'd last seen Kierk, my dad had been there for me, with food, laughter, encouragement.

Anything I'd needed. We'd spent more time climbing together, even taking up outdoor climbing with a Pittsburgh club. Northwestern had always been my dream, but the reality of leaving my dad to move five hundred miles away to Chicago terrified me.

"Go, Cats," I said, hoping to lighten the mood.

Not enthusiastic enough to be convincing, Dad repeated, "Go, Cats."

We said our goodbyes, and I slipped through the rotating doors of the Cathedral. Despite the summer heat, the building was cool. The dim interior also contrasted with the bright sun outside. I took a deep breath. Every visit reminded me of Kierk, but in a good way. Time had mended some of the fissures enough that I could think more about the good times we'd shared and less about the pain of it all ending.

Feeling nostalgic, I took the stairs to the third floor, finding the Austrian Nationality Room with ease. I'd visited a few times since being there with Kierk, yet the room's beauty still struck me. It rivaled the grandeur of the carnival, and I wondered if that was why Kierk had liked it so much.

In the small space, I remembered Kierk and me together on the table, his arms around me as I'd looked out the window toward the museum across Forbes Avenue. How he'd discussed the artistry of the ceiling and the chandelier with reverence like he hadn't been reading from the information sheet by the door. I leaned on the back of one of the chairs until the weak feeling that sometimes surfaced when my thoughts of Kierk went too deep passed.

The Herald's summer program met every expectation I'd ever had. I'd learned so much, and since I'd be the editor of *The Muse* the following year, I'd earned a seat in the special editor training that would follow the regular two-week program. Still, a tiny voice at the back of my mind reminded me too often of the price I'd had to pay to get here.

I shook the thought away. Time to review those notes and make it all matter.

On the way out the door, I crashed into a solid someone.

"Oh," I said. "Excuse me."

"No," he said. "It was my fault."

Recognition hit me. His familiar eyes. His undeniable scar.

We stood awkwardly, not sure if we should shake hands, hug, or throw something at each other.

"It's so good to see you," I finally said. "What are you doing here?"

He glanced over my shoulder at the Nationality Room behind me. "I'm taking a few summer classes. Trying to get back into working on my degree."

"That's great. Congratulations."

"Thanks. What about you?"

I cringed. Sensitive subject. "I'm down here for a couple weeks. For *The Herald*'s summer program for young journalists."

His smile was genuine. "Wow. That's impressive."

I nodded, and we watched each other, unsure if the polite, even friendly catching up had run its course. Or if there was more to say.

"How are things at the carnival?" I asked.

"Great. A lot of new exhibits for the summer."

"Still busy?"

"Incredibly. Although…I haven't seen you there at all."

"Well, given everything, I figured…you know. It's your space. I didn't want to intrude."

"It's hardly my space."

Was he encouraging me to come back to the carnival? Was he suggesting I'd be welcome? After my last visit, I'd rejected his father's job offer, convinced Kierk and I had needed a clean break. He didn't want me around, and I didn't want to be in the carnival without him.

"I read your article," he finally said.

"You did?"

"You were right. Your representation of the carnival was brilliant. You discussed the philosophy so relevantly. People were talking about it for weeks afterward."

It was the exact praise I had needed to hear. "Wow. Thanks."

"Kind of made me realize that not all press is bad press."

"I'm not sure that's how the saying goes."

We laughed before falling again into silence. This was getting awkward.

"I should go," I finally said.

"Right. Yeah. Me, too. I have class."

"Great."

He nodded. "Yep."

"Well, have a great class."

"Yeah. Definitely."

I snuck one last glance at him. How strange to see his whole face up close. No mask, no mystery, just a raw, beautiful Kierk.

"Take care," I whispered.

But before I could walk away, Kierk stepped in front of me. "You told me you didn't believe anything real could happen between two people in the carnival."

His statement felt like an invitation to be honest, to break free from our polite chatter, to be real.

I shifted my bag on my shoulder. "I was wrong."

Kierk's smile of encouragement awakened every feeling I'd ever had for him, no matter how deeply I'd buried it and how much baggage I'd piled on top. My head warned my heart of the danger in flirting with him—a guy who still had my heart after the past five months. This moment felt like an opportunity—much like the one I'd seized at *The Herald*. I wasn't about to waste it.

"I guess you won the bet." I held his gaze.

His smile widened. "Did I now?"

"Everything that was real five months ago is still overwhelmingly real."

His smirk uninhibited by a mask rivaled the difference between a night light and staring directly at the sun. "This might be something we can agree on," he said.

The fluttering of my heart silenced any warnings my head emitted. "What prize did you have in mind if you won?"

He smiled, an air of shyness swimming across his usually confident expression.

"What?" I prodded.

He moved closer, brushing his fingertips through my hair. He smelled of chocolate and sugar, as he usually did. My milkshake man. I closed my eyes and welcomed the scent. He tipped my face upward and whispered against my lips, "I wanted this."

Kierk's kiss was strong. Confident. Utterly delicious. Someone down the hall let out a little whoop, and we broke apart in laughter.

Kierk leaned his forehead against mine. "I've missed you."

"I missed you, too."

"I'm sorry I sent you away when you came to the carnival to apologize."

"I'm sorry I lied to you for so long."

He nodded. "I needed time to see what was important, but then too much time had passed, and I thought…well, it was over."

"Me, too." But my heart never quite accepted it. "I can't believe I ran into you."

He smirked. "Um...about that... I might have seen you here the last few days. I didn't have the guts to talk to you until I saw you come in here. I thought maybe if you were feeling nostalgic..."

"Aren't you sneaky."

"Are you mad?" he asked.

I kissed him again, relishing the opportunity to bury my fingers in his hair.

Kierk's phone beeped, and he pressed against his pocket to silence it. "I hate to go, but I really do have class."

"Likely story," I teased. "You know, phones—"

"Interrupt real-world experiences." He laughed. "I've heard that before."

I shrugged. "It's true."

His phone beeped again. "Will you come to the carnival this weekend?"

The Herald staff had packed the weekend with socials and workshops. "I can't. The program lasts for another two weeks, and the schedule's pretty tight."

It was awful to admit, but the sweetness of his disappointment launched me to the clouds.

"But I can meet you here tomorrow at the same time. Or after your class, we could grab dinner."

"Like a date?"

I smiled. "Definitely like a date."

EPILOGUE

WHILE I HAD BEEN at *The Herald*'s summer program, Dinah had spent her summer studying drawing and painting at an overnight camp offered through the Museum of Art. The Friday night we returned, we binged on pasta and tales of our adventures. Despite Dinah's insecurities about being so new to artistic aspirations, she practically glowed when she spoke about the new drawing techniques she'd learned and the college professors she'd met, and if I hadn't known already, without a doubt, Dinah Zimmerman had been meant to quit journalism and be an artist. She even brought me a glittery painting of a carnival mask for my room.

"It's gorgeous," I said. "Thank you!"

"My pleasure. So…how are things going with Kierk?" She'd responded with all capital letters and a shameful display of exclamation points when I'd texted her about bumping into him at the Cathedral. And of all our dates that had followed.

I leaned my head against the couch and sighed.

"That amazing, huh?"

"It's perfect. Truly perfect." Especially given the fact

that my article, the power of *my* writing had brought us back together. "Like we should be characters in a movie or something. We completely fell for each other wearing Mardi Gras masks. Now, being out in the city, going on dates, seeing each other's faces. . . it's like we fell again but in an entirely different way. And—oh my gosh, I realize how corny I sound."

"You do. No doubt."

I twirled a bit of pasta onto my fork. "I don't even care."

"I'm really happy for you, Mac. I hate that I wasted so much time on Todd." The dreadful duo had broken up right around the time Kierk and I had split. Turned out Chanel, as feared, had been just one of many. Dinah had apologized for not believing me, but I got it. Sometimes, it was easier to put off facing the truth. My best friend and I had both learned nobody could hide from the truth forever.

"Don't think of it as a waste but, instead, a learning experience."

"To avoid cheaters and losers? I definitely got that."

"I'm sorry, D."

She shrugged. "I'll get through it. In fact, I have an idea."

"Uh-oh."

"My parents read your article, and they trust your opinion on the carnival..."

I could barely hear the rest of her sentence over my squeal. "Are you saying what I think you're saying?"

She smiled coyly. "Don't you think it's time for your best friend to meet your dreamy boyfriend?"

I couldn't think of anything more perfect.

———

I snuck up on Kierk in the Milkshake Ballroom as he was clearing glasses from a table. When I was sure he wouldn't drop one of them, I wrapped my arms around his waist and hugged him from behind.

"What the—"

"Hey, boyfriend."

He turned and scooped me off the ground. "I wasn't expecting you."

I kissed him—a privilege I had no intention of giving up. Ever. "I want you to meet someone. This is my best friend, Dinah."

"Cool carnival name," Kierk said, shaking her hand.

"Actually, that's my real name," she said.

Kierk glanced at me.

"She'll go by her carnival name for everyone else," I whispered. "But you're different."

Dinah looked him over. "Yep. I see why you've swept her off her feet."

"Speaking of that." I looped my arm in Kierk's and led him to the bar. "We need your expert services."

"Two milkshakes coming right up," he said. "Would you like to try our signature butterscotch banana? It's a new carnival favorite."

"It isn't!" My recipe was the hit of the Milkshake Bar?

"Our current bestseller by a long shot!"

"I love it, but I wasn't talking about those services." I pointed to my best friend who deserved so much better than her slimy ex. "Dinah's looking for a man. Someone who's worthy of her. I seem to recall you having a strategy for how to meet someone here and develop something real."

"It worked out well the last time," he said.

I kissed him. "Don't I know it. So can you help?"

He smiled at Dinah. "Definitely. Let's start with King's Court."

"Who's heading to King's Court?" Harvey said from behind us. "Good to see you again, Sparx. I knew you'd be back eventually. This guy over here was too smitten."

Kierk punched him in the arm.

"Have to tell the truth, man." Then as if he'd satisfied his duty to me, he turned to my best friend. "Hello, beautiful! Wanna dance?"

Kierk and I intervened. "No. No way."

But Harvey couldn't be deterred.

Dinah looked like she was ready to drink the Kool-Aid. "I'd love to."

Harvey spun her to the dance floor while I cringed and watched through an opening in my fingers. "This is not happening."

"Ah, deep down he's a good guy."

I glared at Kierk. "She broke up with her last boyfriend because he was hooking up with other girls at the carnival."

"Okay, fine," he said. "It's not happening. Although it could be cool if my best friend was dating your best friend."

"And twenty other girls?"

"I see your point," he said. "It's settled. One dance, and then we take her to King's Court. In the meantime, there's an exhibit I've been dying to show you."

I took his hand. "Lead the way."

I could see the headline now:

MACKENZIE DAVIS AND SOREN SCOTT LIVE HAPPILY EVER AFTER.

ACKNOWLEDGMENTS

How exciting to be working on a new series! When I read about Bakhtin's concept of Carnivalesque, a wave of creativity struck. We live in a time that is so exposed. We are constantly filmed. Privacy is a struggle. Like Kierk says, we need opportunities to explore our passions and identities *privately.*

I could not have brought this book - my FIFTH young adult novel - to life without the help of so many people. Thank you to everyone who read any version of this book over the years, including: Kathleen S. Allen, Hetal Avanee, Jeff Boarts, Jennifer Camiccia, Tara Creel, Annette Dashofy, Kimberly Gabriel, Tracy Gold, Gwynne Jackson, Adiba Jaigirdar, Despina Karras, Caitlin Lennon, Deborah Maroulis, Gabriela Martins, Kara McDowell, Sara Metz, Shanah Salter, Abigail G. Scheg, and Elliot Smith, Miriam Sptizer, and Mary Sutton.

Thank you to Lindsey Davis, Erin Sullivan, and Elesha Teskey for assisting with the climbing scenes! Thank you to my writing friends—the best friends—in PennWriters, the Mary Roberts Rinehart Chapter of Sisters in Crime, and Pitchwars 2016 class! Thank you to the team at Wise Wolf Books, especially Kristin Yahner, Rachel Del Grosso, and Mandi Andrejka for their editing expertise and the design team for the most gorgeous cover!

Readers, thank you! I hope you enjoy the intrigue of the story. Make yourself a milkshake, throw on a Mardi Gras mask, and start turning the pages.

To my family and friends, thank you for the encouragement and the inspiration. I have so many good people around me. Because of you, I can be my true self. All my love...

A LOOK AT BOOK TWO: BEHIND THE MASK

From the author of *Above the Fold* comes a charming romance in this dreamy contemporary novel.

Budding artist Dinah Zimmerman is recovering from a relationship with the boy next door who happens to be hounding her to get back together. When she visits the famous Carnivalesque one night, she meets Harvey—a smooth talker who asks her to dance. But their dance is interrupted when several of his exes bathe him in milkshakes and douse him with water balloons.

Dinah has little interest in dating yet another bad boy. Nonetheless, her plans are derailed when Harvey offers her exactly what she needs—space from her ex. Wanting to "fake date" Dinah to convince everyone he can be a serious, one-woman guy, Harvey offers to be Dinah's buffer so that she can focus on her art. He even sweetens the deal by offering her a chance to paint exhibits at the carnival.

As the two work to sell their ruse, Dinah begins to confuse their fake relationship with reality, and when Harvey's ex—the one who got away—comes back into his life, Dinah has to risk telling Harvey the truth…or letting him go.

AVAILABLE NOW

ABOUT THE AUTHOR

 Tamara Girardi writes books for children and teens. Her debut young adult novel, *Gridiron Girl*, tells the story of Julia Medina who quits the volleyball team to compete against her boyfriend for the starting quarterback position. Three additional sports novels in the Iron Valley Vikings series followed in 2022. *Above the Fold* is the first book in Tamara's second series, all about teens exploring their dreams and their true selves through exhibits at a popular, mardi-gras-esque hotspot called Carnivalesque. Also an academic, Tamara is a college English professor. She lives in a suburb of Pittsburgh, Pennsylvania with her husband and four adorably rambunctious children.

www.ingramcontent.com/pod-product-compliance
Lightning Source LLC
Chambersburg PA
CBHW052024240626
47153CB00006B/1938